# Memory Gap

## Version 1.03

by

## Alexander Francis

# Memory Gap
# by
# Alexander Francis

# Table of Contents

Introducing the second and third Mick Grundy Thrillers

The shaking returned, and the shadow man stood there with

his hands describing small arcs in the night air. The shadows from the fence played across his face as he fought his body's urge to faint. In the distance, a peacock's cry hung in the night air. There was a subtle motion from the other side of the fence, and a woman's silhouette appeared framed by yellow light cast from tall poles standing guard in the parking lot.

"What are we supposed to do now?" Ahmed asked not too

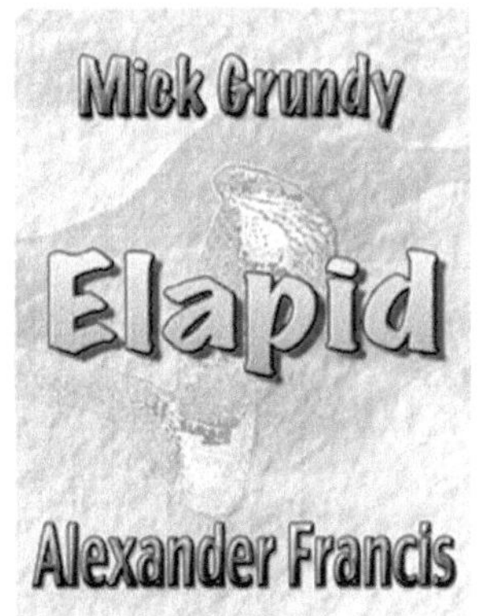


quietly, continuing to play nervously with the safety on his rifle.

"Plainly, we are about to die. We have executed a plan doomed to fail from its inception. Mick Grundy will kill us, and we have only ourselves to blame. We came looking for him only to find his shadow, and now we have run out of options."

*Read Excerpts from other novels by Alexander Francis*
*At afnovels.com*

*Are We A Band Yet?....Beware the Exit....The Green Scarf*
*Revenge of Jesus....Geminknot....Anthology of Childhood*
*Schemers and Dreamers.....Memory Gap*

# Chapter 1

## *Reunion*

Her car door closed softly, even shyly, clicking shut as she stood looking over the car roof toward the coffee shop across the street. A glare from the plate glass window prevented her from seeing if he was there yet. She had purposefully delayed leaving her apartment so that she would arrive later than him, a tactic designed to demonstrate dominance, independence, especially so since Jeff was the one asking for the meeting.

Gale stood there for an awkward moment, looking around by force of habit but seeing nothing, her mind actually elsewhere, until she realized that her hesitancy would also show weakness, assuming that Jeff could see her. In some ways, she longed for a reunion such as this one but, at the same time, dreaded a return to their former relationship. She had adamantly refused to admit to herself that she still had a pull of desire toward Jeff. It was there, though, an attraction, both emotional and sexual, hovering just below her conscious thoughts. He was the one who had ended things between them just over eight months ago. Since then, she had caught only occasional glimpses of him on campus, his long strides and flowing hair so representative of the impatience and assertiveness of the man.

# Chapter 1

Once, briefly, they had locked eyes in passing, hers blank but his sending a message of mixed emotion. No words were spoken and neither one hesitated, a clear signal that the relationship was truly over. Now this. *Whatever could he want,* she wondered. More than likely, she reasoned, he wanted to test the water to see if things had changed. Gale would have told him if he had asked...*nothing has changed, it's still hopeless, and you should move on.* He didn't ask, though, and she was glad, because she didn't really want to move on. At least a fragment of her mind didn't.

A break in traffic allowed her to stroll, unhurriedly, across the street, watching her enlarging image reflected in the glass window. Her multicolored scarf fluttered and floated over her shoulders, briefly placing itself in the position of wings seemingly sprouting from her back. The street was still littered from the detritus of winter, which crunched under the stiff sole of her high heels. A slight wind carried a chill from lingering spots of snow, yet unmelted, but she had chosen to dress fashionably instead of warmly, and the puffing wind raised a chill across her unprotected back.

She pulled the door toward her, and the aroma of fresh coffee and bakery goods enveloped her, enticing her inside. As usual, there was a line waiting to place an order for some unique concoction and combination of a coffee beverage. Several pairs of eyes poured over her, assessing her station in life as well as her proclivities, her age, and, in the case of some, her availability. Gale ignored them, casting around for Jeff in a visual search of the corners of the irregular room. His eyes met hers, and he gave a tiny wave with his fingertips. There were two large paper cups on the small table, one obviously meant for her. Jeff would remember her preferences, she knew, and his offering was meant to soften her, at least a little. For a moment, she considered getting in queue just to establish her free spirit, but the line was too long, the statement too large. She picked her way between the tables, her eyes searching his face as she moved toward him.

"Hi." His greeting was expressed flatly, without flavor or emotional connection. Gale pulled out the metal chair, looking away from his eyes.

"What's this?" She nodded at the cup in front of her.

"Your favorite. At least what used to be your favorite. A plain latte, no sugar, no flavoring, using two percent. Does that still work?"

"Sure, thanks." She sat down, putting her forearms on the marble and fixing his gaze. "Want me for something?"

Jeff resisted answering her. He could have gone on for half an hour on what he wanted her for. Looking across the table, he was flooded with all the emotions she always brought up in him. Right away, he caught the scent of her perfume, the same one that unfailingly aroused every male impulse he possessed. Other than dream about her nearly every night, they hadn't been this close in months. He had tried to move on but couldn't. This woman was the one he wanted, every bit of her, and none other would ever connect, emotionally, so completely.

Jeff fought with himself to hold back any trace of emotion and cleared his throat to control a choking sensation, to remove any hint of pleading in his voice. After a moment, he felt ready to respond to her, while his eyes searched her face for any similar feeling. Her face was blank, her big eyes looked robotically into his, giving nothing away.

"How have you been?" he started.

"Me? The same. Same studies, same apartment, same coffee. You?"

"Good. We started a new project recently. Kind of thought you would be interested." She didn't answer or move. At least she didn't refuse to hear about it. Jeff thought it over before telling her the details. She would assume that it was an excuse for getting together, not realizing the real reason.

"You ever heard of Dr. McLally?" he asked.

"The name seems to echo a bit, but I really don't know anything. Should I?"

"He's here, recently arrived from Ireland. It was in the papers."

Gale sat expectantly waiting for how this news was connected to her. An explanation was in order, and Jeff struggled to put his careful thoughts into words. Gale, sitting across from him, was a presence different than he had imagined, more powerful, her mind penetrating into his, scrambling his well-rehearsed plan.

"It's good to see you again," Jeff said instead. "I've missed you," he added. He hoped for a slight crack in her protective casing, any sliver of light emitting past her wall. Instead, she just sat there silently, causing further chaos in his brain. He nodded, the realization hitting him that she was still impossible to decipher. *No, nothing had changed.*

"And?" she urged.

"And, we are going to be doing some interesting research together. He is going to be the principal advisor for my doctorate." Again, Gale unblinkingly waited for him to get to the point, if there was a point. Although she gave no outward sign, she *was* looking at him, remembering how much she had been attracted to him. Jeff had a way of holding his head low and looking up at her with his brown eyes, striking some sort of harmonic chord inside of her. Her eyes flowed over his strong shoulders and upward to his head of dark, unkempt but masculine hair. Yes, she found him attractive, very attractive, and there had been no other man in her life over the past several months. If there was ever a man she wanted to be around, this was the one.

"You *are* going to tell me why you invited me to meet with you, aren't you?" she asked, still looking into his eyes without emotion.

"Well, this is awkward, Gale. I don't want to say even the slightest thing to upset you. I have thought about this at least a thousand times, but having you look into my face like you are doing makes my train of thought evaporate."

"What am I going to do...walk away?" she asked, smiling. It was true, he had nothing to lose; she was not his any longer, so it didn't matter what infraction he might stumble into. He couldn't make it any worse so he might as well tell her.

"This is about something we never discussed. At least, you wouldn't discuss it with me, so what I have is conjecture, you understand." Jeff took a big sip of coffee to bolster his confidence, quickly continuing before the opportunity evaporated. "It's about you, and, I think, a moment in your past that causes you problems. A moment, or an event, that only you know about," he stopped and looked at her for permission to continue. She sat unmoving, her coffee untouched, her eyes fixed on his.

"Continue," she said softly.

"I've had eight months and two days to think this over. About us, I mean. I was an ass about it then. I made mistakes. You know that, but now I know that as well. Thinking about it, I was focused on me when I should have been focused on you. I began to see things differently after we were apart. Then, just as now, your physical presence does something to me, you see. Or perhaps you can't. I don't really know. It was your reaction to my touching you. It made me angry...frustrated...and I said the wrong things. Afterwards, I realized that it wasn't about me at all. You were reacting to a previous trauma of some sort. Does this make any sense?" he asked, looking up at her in that special way.

"I've heard this before, you know. Old news. Do you have some connection with your research and me that you want to get out?" Her face betrayed no emotion, if there was any in her after all.

"Forgive me, Gale. Please forgive me. It does, I believe, but I don't know what you will think about it."

"Jeff!" she exclaimed. "Just out with it." Her mind was racing with memories. She recalled the event with Jeff all too well, but it was just another thing that she didn't want to think about.

"All right. My research will involve memories. Where they are stored in our brain, how they are stored and…this is the key part…how they can be changed."

"So?"

"I'm going to ask you straight out, Gale. Is there a traumatic event in your life that you repress?"

"There are a lot of things I no longer think about. Isn't that true with all people?"

"You didn't really answer me, Gale."

"Is there any reason that you would ask me that?"

"Of course, my dear. I want to walk beside you, hear your voice, feel your hand in mine again. I want to help solve whatever problem is between us."

"I don't like being groped, Jeff. You took liberties not given to you. That is not changeable."

"As I recall, I only briefly, lightly and innocently, I feel, laid my hand on your hip. That's all. Was that enough to revolt you?"

"Do you recall my hand on your hip, Jeff? No, you don't. Because I went out with you doesn't change my view that my body is my own, not yours. Do you see that?"

"I do. Really, I do. But, your reaction was still pathologic, Gale. Admit it."

She abruptly stood to leave, slinging her purse over her shoulder. "Thanks for the meeting. It's cleared up nothing for me, and I'm sure not much for you either. Congratulations on your research, and I hope that it makes you famous some day. But if I want to be psychoanalyzed, I'll visit a physician, not a grad student in a coffee shop. Anything else?"

Jeff spread his hands out on the table top, palms down, and shook his head. "I was afraid of this. I've managed to make things worse, haven't I? Please, Gale, sit back down, and let's talk some more. We have feelings for each other, and we are both good people. Surely, we can just talk?"

"Jeff, supposing that I did have some dark secret, as you imagine. Do you think I could describe it to you over coffee with thirty people within earshot?"

"Of course not, Gale. I just wanted to see if I was on the right track. It was a desperate move, I know, but at least you can trust my sincerity."

"My private life and past will stay that way. I realize if you got close with me again, the groping and expectations would start over anew, and we would end the same way. Move on, Jeff. The campus is full of energetic women who would love to see to your needs. I am not one of them."

"At least go to one of Dr. McLally's lectures. It might change the way you think," Jeff nearly pleaded as she was moving away. Her back receded from him and out the door, her coffee still untouched. He watched as she crossed the street, her long cinnamon hair swinging behind her in its rhythmically seductive way.

# Chapter 2

# *Moments of Doubt*

Gale reached for the valve and shut the shower off after a long soak. She stood there in the stall for a moment, still gathering her thoughts, then opened the shower door.

"Will you be much longer, dear? I really have to get moving or be late," Sibyl called through the door. It had been a long shower, and Gale hurriedly toweled off and opened the door a crack.

"I'm sorry, Sibyl," she said. "I just lost track of time. You can use it now, and I'll dry my hair afterwards." She wrapped the towel around her and stepped past the impatient Sibyl.

"Gee, I knew something was up this morning. You didn't sing a note. Something wrong?" Sibyl said through the closed door.

Gale hesitated. "No, just a lot on my mind," she lied.

The toilet flushed and Sibyl emerged, puffing her hair. "You never told me how it went with Jeff. That the prob?"

"He wants me back. I'm not sure about it, that's all."

"From what I can tell, you've not managed to find another to replace him. You even have rejected the ones I've sent your way. Ever think that you *need* to get back with Jeff, if even for your own reasons?"

"Stay out of it, Sibyl. It's more complicated than you know."

"I worry about you, girl. Something is out of balance with you. I'll be back at four, we could have a talk?"

"No, we won't have a talk, but thanks anyway."

Sibyl shrugged, tossed the comb on a table and reached for her tattered backpack. "Later then. Have a good one," she said as she closed the door behind her.

Gale glanced at the wall clock. Her first class was in forty minutes, and she still hadn't eaten. The walk over there would take at least twenty. She had to hurry and started rushing about, her mind still processing Jeff's words. In the middle of the night, she had looked up the lecture schedule for Dr. McLally. There was a lecture scheduled this afternoon, not too far away. It was possible, she just had to decide, that's all. If Jeff were there, it would be awkward for her. She debated the possibility as she fried an egg. The lecture was more of an introduction to McLally's theories for undergrads taking physiology. A doctoral candidate would not likely be there, she reasoned. Unless Jeff wanted to see if she attended. It didn't take long to decide. She would not go, it would give Jeff too much satisfaction to see her there.

Just before opening the door to leave, Gale put her eye to the peephole and studied the hall. The device had an especially wide angle to view anyone lurking, even those pressed up against the wall. Nope, it was clear. Gale opened the door, quickly looked around, and listened before venturing into the empty hallway. The building was older and cheaply constructed. Any footsteps were easily detected through the thin door. Their apartment was on the second floor, and the staircase had only one landing, the exterior door leading directly to the parking lot. She hurried down the creaking staircase and, with relief, exited the building. Each day was the same, unless she left with Sibyl. Nervously, she glanced around, looking for other students walking in groups toward the University complex. There were few evident and none in groups. At least it was broad daylight, and she quickly headed toward the spires in the distance, using brisk, long strides. They hovered just above the trees, a mixture of brick and concrete pretending to be stone but still awe-inspiring, timeless in some vague way. Occasionally, she glanced behind her and was constantly alert for new noises. It had been this way for so long that she didn't even think about her strange routine. It was part of who she was. At last, she caught up with a small, mixed-sex group and fell in behind them, slowing her pace to match. Her tension diminished, and she could think about the day's schedule. The first class was an elective, an easy one, requiring little study. Actually, the class was enjoyable, and she looked forward to listening instead of taking notes, while the older professor droned on about the ancient Roman poets. She always learned something new there. Useless though, at least for now in her life. There was only one additional semester of classes before she completed the requirements for her Master of Music degree. The future after college loomed out there as an insolvable riddle, like driving in an indistinct fog toward something just out of focus. She sighed, trying not to solve a problem which required more factors in its equation than she had. One step at a time.

As she walked along, thinking randomly, she wondered again what she actually wanted in life. Some of her friends were clear about their desires. Money mostly, and then the right mate, the right job in the right town. Some of her girlfriends would do pretty much anything for a guy who seemed to be headed toward success. Gale shuddered. *Not that, not me.* At the same time, she dimly was aware what she was missing. A lot, judging by their comments, the small bits of their exploits they were all too willing to share. Part of her wished that she could do the same, at least to see what it was like. But she couldn't. Her brain quickly shut down that line of thinking. It would not allow her to think along those paths. Yes, there were experiences and memories in there acting like a cancer, occupying a part of her mind that was off-limits. Every time she felt herself recalled to that area, even by a thought or a sensation, it was quickly blocked. She knew better than to try to recall even a fragment of it. That had been done by a psychiatrist once, in an attempt to allow her to cope. It was a mistake, a bad one, which resulted in a lost year of school. No, that memory and everything connected to it was off-limits to even get a whiff of. Of course, Jeff was right. Bull's-eye. Good for him, but it didn't change the impossibility of dealing with it. By experience, she knew that the right method was avoidance of anything triggering a recall. That also included someone touching her in nearly every place except her hands. She didn't want to go for treatment, for discussion with a friend, or with the opposite sex. Especially that. It was impossible if she wanted to keep her sanity. Later. There was enough time in her life to deal with it later. For now, she had to keep a balance and make it through school. The future was going to have to take care of itself.

After her last class, an impulse made Gale glance at her watch. Yes, she had time to make the McLally lecture. It was just in the adjacent building, the old lecture hall complex dating from a distant previous century. The need to attend had been building subconsciously all day, and now her brain had come alive with insistence about hearing what the man had to say. It had nothing to do with Jeff...doing his bidding, that is. She needed to go and learn how her brain worked and how to fix what is forbidding her from having a full and normal life.

The lecture was to be given in the antique Pearson Amphitheater. It was constructed back in the twenties, and though it lacked comfortable seating, it did provide good acoustics coupled with an elevated and hemispheric area for attendees, much like the ancient Greek designs. The lecturer entered via doors on either side of the stage, the backdrop being a very large blackboard with sliding panels. The room was slowly filling. Gale was glad she had positioned herself in the upper rows, from where she could see both the attendees and the lecture. Jeff was not present as far as she could tell. Given the age distribution of the audience, Gale assumed that McLally was able to generate interest across campus.

Just as the second hand crossed the twelve, the door on the left side swung open and Dr. McLally entered, walking rapidly to the podium. He wore a dark, European tailored suit, was redheaded and slightly portly, and, from her distant seat, appeared to have abundant freckles. His bushy eyebrows, also red, hung and moved like independent living creatures. He put his papers on the desk, his hands on his hips and slowly surveyed the room as the last of the students found a seat.

"My name is Gregory McLally. I have recently arrived from Europe, and I am delighted to be invited here to do research and to teach. You need to know my educational background and how I am qualified to teach. I obtained my M.D. degree in Ireland and then entered a residency program in Neurology in Edinburgh. That didn't totally fulfill me, and I stayed on and took a Pathology Fellowship with an emphasis on diseases of the CNS. Before I had the chance to settle down and actually use my training, I was offered a position in London to do research and eventually was awarded a PhD in Neurophysiology. From there, I came to the States to do research on memory. Where I go from here is a question, isn't it?"

There were headshakes and laughs rumbling from the appreciative audience. He was very good, Gale admitted. He already had the students in his grasp, and he hadn't even started.

McLally methodically looked over the students, appearing to gaze into their souls, before beginning. "It's really all about memory, isn't it? I mean, that's why each of you are here. It's no good to teach you anything if you don't remember it. Right?" Heads nodded again. "So, today, we are going to cover the storage of memory. At least we are going to touch on it. After all, that's what the research is all about. We don't really know much about it, and what we do know comes from careful observation of patients with injuries, tumors and following surgery and how that relates to their brain function, including memory. It's research which is basic and goes way back in time. The other method is to test volunteers, such as you college students, with memory storage and retrieval tests. Terribly boring to take and to give such testing, but it has yielded a vast amount of information. Another method is the one I am taking, using tools such as positron emission tomography or PET scan, and its new brother, SPECT scan. We also have access to a fMRI over at the hospital. And there are new tools we are just beginning to explore, such as the Microbubble-enhanced Focused Ultrasound, which is also becoming a surgical technique. Dare I mention the latest darling of research? It is a microwave-based beam of my own design, able to focus down to the molecular level." He stopped and again looked at the faces in the room, checking if there were any who appeared lost.

"Now to basics. Being physiology students, you have studied the basic neuron and already know the many different types of cells. You should know that neurons in the central nervous system have a vast array of connections with other neurons. Each connection is called a synapse. There are other connections as well, but for now I will keep it simple. Memory is the pattern of connections between neurons...the pattern of connections, I emphasize. That is a memory. It is formed at the time of the event to be remembered, and things will either strengthen the pattern or repress the pattern. Suppose you are a musician. You play a piece of music given to you, and you need to play it right and will need to remember it. At first, you make mistakes, but at last, you play it well. You have to play it many times to get it just right, and you will need to play it rather constantly to keep it up. Think about it. Your brain is expected to learn the mechanical, muscular patterns, the emotional patterns, the sequence of notes and many other things. In addition, you make mistakes during learning which have to be repressed. Once the process is learned or memorized, it goes into long-term storage, and you will be able to access it forever. Each time you bring up the memory to use it, the memory gets more established, also altered at times. You may decide that the way you played was archaic and will choose to replace the memory with a better one.

Several examples of memory storage are applicable here. The memory you create from cramming just before a test will not be retained for long. You already know that, right? The memory has to be reinforced to be retained. Right now, you are probably thinking about using memory for a written exam, but I am thinking about real world events. Ever been mugged? I have. It's a memory that you don't want, and it involves several different systems, such as the emotional aspect, the physical one...the beating you took...the police interview later, questions from friends, the visual memory of the event. And many more. The point is that this memory is triggered by several different body systems which are stored in several different locations. Your memory is reinforced after the event and remembered for life, even if you don't want to remember it. A tip here for your studies is to convert your information to visual, mechanical and auditory. You read it, you write it, and you speak it. In addition, you have your roommate quiz you on it. Then you will recall it later in life and remember that I was correct."

Gale was impressed. This guy did know his stuff, and whether she liked it or not, he had nearly zeroed in on her problem, describing it more or less accurately...except the horrible parts. She glanced around the big room and saw that the students were busily taking notes but were't engaging in conversation or looking around. McLally had them right where he wanted them.

"Now to specifics for a moment. I am aware that this is an undergraduate class, but knowledge is knowledge, and some things cannot be simplified. Here we come to disagreement about where memory is stored. There are two principle schools of thought. One, the older one, says that memory is stored in the hippocampus area of the brain...a central location, but links to that specific memory are found in a broader area of the cortex. In other words, you can access the central data storage by activating one of the links. It makes a lot of sense, this theory. I can recall a memory by the odor of a perfume or perhaps a chemical smell, or I can recall a memory based on a tune or a taste or a touch. Then the memory returns to me, and I can recall the entire event. Same with you, I'm sure.

"Therefore," he started, looking around to be sure the audience was attentive. "Memory may be considered in three phases. The first is the event which is encoded into the neurons of the brain, the second is storage of the memory, the third is the retrieval process back into consciousness. So, how, as scientists...we in this room all are, are we not?...do we investigate this complicated system?" Heads were swiveling to see if anyone had a clue as to the process, then turned back to the professor at center stage.

"A few years ago, it was discovered that radioactive water will produce detectable and specific CNS radiation after intravenous injection of a primate. The isotope chosen has a brief half-life of no more than ten minutes in the body. After ingestion, the radiation source may be detected by our PET scanner and is concentrated in brain tissue in areas which have an increase in blood supply. The theory is that brain activity, thinking or processing areas, will result in increased blood supply. Therefore, testing of the brain during scanning will show active areas specific to task. The focus of the instrument is limited to roughly twenty millimeters of brain matter which is also averaged over one minute or more. The test is reproducible, results vary, but it does show something. What is questionable. Simply put, the test is crude but does further our understanding of brain function. Are there any questions so far?" He stepped from behind the dais and put his hands in his jacket pockets. Several hands shot up at the same time, causing him to smile. He pointed to one of the closer students and signaled with an up motion that she should stand.

"Professor, you mentioned that there are two theories of memory storage. Can you describe the other?" The woman was a statuesque blonde, and she aroused several male murmurs of appreciation in the audience. She glanced around quickly in a defiant manner, then resumed looking at McLally.

"Looking at you, my dear, makes me forget your question," he quipped, creating a small wave of suppressed laughter. "Seriously, though, I will attempt to answer. We first have to separate short-term memory from long-term memory. That being obvious at first glance, we then make the assumption that, under certain circumstances, short-term memory items are converted and stored for later retrieval. A theory of neural networks has emerged, and under most modern interpretations, we now feel that the hippocampus does not store memory but facilitates its retrieval and, in fact, is essential to memory retrieval. Frankly, this particular discussion is trending to a scope beyond this introductory talk. If any of you are really interested, come see me about post-graduate studies."

The blonde resumed her seat and whisper-mimed, "Thank you," to McLally, who blew her a kiss and winked, to more laugher.

"A few points worth making," he said loudly, suppressing the attention being directed at the blonde student and bringing the focus back to the front. "Want to have a memory quickly imbedded and permanently stored in your brain? Then it would be one which involves both a strong emotional memory combined with a complex memory with input from all of the senses at once. A romance in the backseat, a beating from a gang, war. This memory will be recalled the rest of your life by many things even remotely similar. That implies association of the specific memory with everyday occurrences. Now one last item and then on to your post quiz." A murmur of concern from the audience swelled amid the sound of shuffling of papers. "Now don't get excited folks. This test will demonstrate how short-term memory is converted, and if I get my way, it will become a standard of this university." On signal, the side doors opened and two teaching assistants moved up the aisles passing out exams. One of them was Jeff, who busily searched the students faces on his side of the room.

"One last item while the tests are being distributed and something you might find interesting. We have developed two experimental drugs to assist with our investigations. One is called Puszithrin and is an anesthetic agent with unusual properties. The other, for the moment, we call Ted-Zeththrinoid and is formulated to contain a rare earth isotope. Both are unique to our laboratory at this university, but you can expect to hear more, much more, about these agents in the future. That ends our discussion for today, and I hope I have piqued your interest in memory research. Good luck on the test and may we meet again." He took a small bow to enthusiastic applause and, with a last wave, disappeared by a side door.

Gale was on the opposite side of the room from Jeff and averted her face from him, sliding downward in her chair. As she glanced up, she noticed the controversial blonde student on the stage just opening the door that McLally had exited. The girl wore very tight spandex, thinly covering her curvaceous derrière, and seemed to be in a hurry. Gale looked over the questions and mentally checked them off. No need to assist her long-term memory storage. For her, the emotional impact made the memory of this lecture certain to be retained. She thought it over while pretending to study the paper but really waiting until the right moment to exit the room. Now she understood why Jeff wanted her to attend. The research, or whatever they were doing, would be applicable to her condition. The problem was that she knew better than to revisit her trauma. It could prove destabilizing just when she was able to get by. She didn't want to be reminded of an event she worked so hard to forget. Still, was there a chance to finally rid herself of this curse of memory? She decided that more information was necessary to make a decision, but for now, she would go on with her life and let the matter drop.

24

# Chapter 3

## *Reminders*

"Say, are you going to call that guy or what?" Sibyl asked. This time she had irritation in her voice.

"You mean Jeff?" Gale answered, knowing that would irritate Sibyl even more.

"Of course I mean Jeff! I'm getting tired of talking to him. I feel like a State Department spokesperson lying to cover up something. Why are you afraid to speak with him for God's sake?"

"It's hard to explain. Don't worry, he'll give up soon. We went through this when we broke up." Sibyl responded by slamming her bedroom door, and Gale could hear the muttering continue. There wasn't any reason to respond to Jeff. She was not going back to him, and she wasn't going to show any interest in the memory lecture, no matter what. She decided that her sanity was at stake. After all, a well-respected psychiatrist once tried to help her, and she ended up spending four months in a locked psych unit. Enough for a lifetime. It shouldn't be a crime to have mental health problems, especially when you have a reason. No, she was done with the entire bunch of fakes. All the respected textbooks say the same thing. If you can't overcome a bad experience by talking about it, the next best thing is to try and forget. Time heals all wounds, at least that's the common wisdom.

The telephone rang again, and Gale let it ring. Sibyl's door opened after the fifth ring. "I'm not answering that."

"I know," Gale said and resumed reading. Sibyl sighed, walked over and picked it up.

"Yes?....Sure, she's about four feet from me. No, she won't talk to you. It's very clear by now, isn't it? No, there's no chance. Now quit calling here, dammit, or I'll report you for harassment." Sibyl slammed the receiver down and then slammed her door shut.

Gale sighed. Perhaps that would end it for now. She began to run through what other actions Jeff might take. He could show up at the door or follow her around campus. Given that Sibyl just brought up the harassment implications, Gale didn't expect that Jeff would be that stupid. Or would he? The idea was creepy, especially so since Gale was already afraid of her own shadow. Looking out for Jeff showing up at any time could make her system of stability shaky. She decided to call him and deal with it directly.

"Hi," she said after he picked up her call.

"Well, this is a surprise!" Jeff beamed over the line.

"No, Jeff, don't get up about it. I'm calling to tell you that I don't want you to bother me again. Don't call, don't follow me, don't anything. Is that clear?"

"You went to the lecture. I saw you. Didn't it seem interesting?

"I told you, Jeff, to stop analyzing me. Enough. Can I make it any plainer?"

"I love you, Gale."

That stopped her. It was unexpected. Blunt and out of the blue. It took a long moment of silence before she responded.

"You hardly know me, Jeff. I don't believe you. There are a lot of issues with me that you know nothing about, some would be hard to overcome."

"I don't care. Nothing you could possibly tell me would change my mind. Nothing. I love you."

"I'm sorry for you then, Jeff. There is no way I can get involved with you. Don't you understand that I want to be left alone? If you really loved me, you would understand."

"You need me. I want to help you. Believe me or not, it's true. After we broke up, my feelings became crystal clear to me. I've had a lot of time to try and forget you, but I can't. There are no demands I would make on you. All I want is to be close, to be there for you. Even if I never touch you again, just being able to see you is enough." His voice cracked with the emotion, and he trailed off. Gale stood there holding on to the phone, picturing Jeff on the other end, and finding the right words to tell him so he would understand it was impossible. To do that, she would have to open up wounds so deep that it would set her back. Over the years, she had learned what to allow herself to think. It was a mistake to ever start seeing Jeff in the first place. He was just so attentive and happy, it felt good to be around him. At least at first. Then as he became more comfortable with her, the physical contact started. He never groped her or made any indecent suggestions, but his arm around her shoulder, then her waist, became more common. It choked her, made her feel captured. She fought the negative feelings and hid her revulsion, but at the dance, he let his hand slip to her buttocks. That was the moment she feared. It was a switch turning on and something she couldn't fight. A profound fear grabbed her, and she pulled away from him. She remembered looking at his surprised, then angry, face through tears, blurring his image. It was over after that, and he had accepted her decision poorly.

"No, Jeff. It won't work. Please, let's part friends. No more pushing me. Promise?"

"I promise. But, Gale, I want to tell you this last thing. I am here for you if ever you need me. Just let me know, and I would cross the desert for you. There isn't anything I wouldn't do for you. Remember that?"

"Thanks. I'll remember. Goodbye, Jeff."

When she finished, Sibyl opened her door and just stared at her. "You gotta be crazy to give that one up. If I wasn't involved, I'd have a go at him."

"Be my guest, Sibyl. Go for it."

The morning sunshine came through the partially closed blinds providing enough light in the small kitchen to be able to make breakfast without the dismal overhead fluorescent light. Spring was arriving, if ever so slowly. Gale had just finished the coffee and put two cups on the small table when Sibyl came in scratching her uncombed hair.

"You look awful," Gale correctly stated. "Sleep poorly? Hope it had nothing to do with me."

Sibyl looked at her from under her unruly hair as if there was something she had to say.

"Partly you. Yes." Her statement made Gale put her paper down and look intently at her.

"And you are going to explain that, aren't you?"

"You'll just get mad at me."

"We've been living together for...what? Three years...I've been angry before and so have you. We always get past it. Shoot."

Sibyl sat down and poured herself a cup of coffee and held it up to her nose as her eyes rolled around the room. "OK, you asked. In the middle of the night, I decided to take you up on your offer. I called him." Gale's eyes went up a notch, but she remained quiet.

"And...well, all he wanted to talk about was you. Here I was throwing myself at him in the middle of the night. Most guys would offer to meet me and have a fling. Not Jeff. His every thought is about you. I felt deflated. Also, embarrassed to tell you about it."

"He told me that he loved me over the phone last night. Guess you discovered that he meant it."

"Let me tell you, he does mean it. I never felt so unappealing. Gale, honey, you are nuts to let that one go. He's off the wall over you. I mean, you could treat him like dirt, insist that he spend all his dough on you, and he would still follow you around like a puppy."

Lost in thought, Gale didn't answer or comment. She slowly sipped her coffee and looked at the rising sun through the window.

"There's something else, Gale."

"What?"

"He told me everything. If what he says is true, and I think it is, you need some help. Now I understand all your quirks better. Something happened to you once, didn't it? Something really bad. I'm your best friend, likely your only friend, Gale. Let's talk. Can we?"

"I'm only going to say this once, Sibyl. I know you are my friend, and if I could talk about my life, I would talk to you. I can't. I can't even think about it. It's hard for a normal person to accept that, but I am damaged goods, and I may be walking and talking like the rest of you, but I'm really a zombie inside. There is no possible way that I'm going to talk about any of it to you or Jeff or the President of the University or even the Pope. You've got to leave me be about this or risk me falling apart. For my sake, let me alone about it."

The tears started flowing down Sibyl's cheek, and she got up and came around, flinging her arms around Gale, sobbing into her shoulder. Gale patted her on the back and hugged back. She noticed that there was no fear, no revulsion, from this contact. It was a male who triggered her reflexes, not the act of contact itself. Was she gay? This was the first time she had considered that subject. No, clearly she wasn't. There was no, absolutely no, attraction to Sibyl in that way. The sensation of hugging was more like having a close sister. Gale was, at the moment, asexual. She realized for the first time that she had no thoughts about sex. It was repressed as well. What a fine mess she was. Half a person at best. An automaton who went to class, ate, studied and slept.

That was her entire life. It was nothing, meaning nothing, and would lead to nothing. *Suicide. Was that a way out? Was that the only way out?*

"You mean a lot to me, Gale," Sibyl said, slowly parting, her eyes continuing to gush a steady stream of tears. "I won't do anything that would harm you. You know that. I'm sorry now that I tried to steal Jeff."

"I was partly thinking of Jeff when I suggested that you have a go at him. At least you wouldn't have a problem if he touched your hip." The statement brought a smile to Sibyl, and she pushed away her tears and sat down.

"Yes, that boy missed a lot last night. He'll never know, poor thing." They both started to laugh, excessively so. Gale pounded the table and nearly slid off the chair. They laughed so much that they started coughing. Gale looked at the clock and pointed.

"Holy shit!" exclaimed Sibyl. "I've got to get outta here, quick. Can you get the dishes? I'll owe you one." She rushed out to the bathroom and closed the door.

Gale poured another coffee. She decided to miss her first class. Today she was going to try and cope by feeling happy. The warmer air and the longer days would help. That and the fact that her schedule was light and the classes mostly easy. Only a few more months to go. She had to lighten up and try to enjoy the time. Pity that she and Sibyl were destined to break up. It had been a good friendship.

## Chapter 4

# *Out Of The Darkness*

Evening light in the early spring is a precious thing. Often, in the northern hemisphere, the lingering evening light is mauve or purple tending toward the blue of the coming higher intensity sun as it moves from the south. Birds are the first to notice the change, and if a natural creature can be happy about a change in seasons, it's birds more than any other. Gale stepped out of the Hamilton building and onto the sidewalk where the street lights were just going on and scattered bird calls were heard in the distance. Most of the cars passing already had their headlights lit, and the student crowd had diminished as most were already home. It couldn't be helped, this lab counted toward her credits, and her project had taken longer on this particular day. She glanced at her wrist. Already nearly six. She didn't remember Sibyl's schedule today. Could be that she was gone on a date, and the apartment would be dark and empty. The thought made Gale shudder, and she picked up her pace. It was only two miles to their apartment, but the coming darkness made it seem longer. She contemplated stopping for supper, then remembered she would have to walk home in full darkness. Pity that the parking situation prevented her from driving. Most days, the two miles goes by without too much notice. Even helps keep her slim. Her day had been fine, so far, and her happiness plan was a good one. The streets ahead were residential and darker, and her anxiety grew as she approached. Positive thinking is a good plan, but it doesn't light the sky for you. A woman walking alone in any city takes a chance, Gale knew, but in a college town, there is usually so much activity that the risk is reduced. That is when students are present, but at the moment, none were in view. Gale felt her pulse rise, and she pushed even harder. She remembered the advice to change your routine to foil people who may track your movements. Fine. But a change would significantly lengthen the trip. She was near panic when at last she turned on the last street and could see the irregular shape of their apartment building. Almost there. She got out her keys and hurried to the door off the parking lot. She noticed that the light in the hall was out again. As she fumbled with the lock in near panic, she felt a presence behind her, then heard the footsteps.

"Miss?" a deep voice beckoned. She didn't turn and look, instead, opened the door. "Miss Randolph, Gale Randolph, isn't that you?" he asked, closing the distance. Gale was in full flight mode and started to tremble, her key ring shaking itself with little jingles, her key seemingly becoming welded inside the lock. A man's hand softly enveloped her wrist.

"Don't be frightened, Miss Randolph. We are the police. We just want to talk with you. Sorry to come up on you like that."

Gale turned toward his voice and saw that he was a middle-aged black man with a kindly, sympathetic face. He was holding up a badge, as was the other man. She started to sag as the lights dimmed and felt a strong arm holding her up.

"There, there Gale. We are very sorry we frightened you. Don't worry now, you are safe with us. Let me help you upstairs so you can lie down before you faint completely. She was unable to resist, and in a dim fog, she felt them nearly lift her off her feet as they ascended the stairs. She must have lost consciousness, because someone was putting a cool glass in her hand, and she felt a wet cloth on her forehead.

"Welcome back, Gale," he said softly. Now sit up and try to drink some of that water." She weakly did as he asked and started to feel better, more clear. She looked again at the man, then the other one just over his shoulder.

"Who are you? What do you want with me?"

"We just wanted to talk, that's all. You chose to faint instead. You are in your apartment, in your own bed, safe and sound. How do you feel?"

"Better," she said and sat up too soon. Her head spun again, and she felt sweaty, sagging back down against the pillow.

"I can hear you," Gale said. "So talk, I'm listening."

"I am Detective Peters, and this is Detective Johnson. I'm from your hometown, and he is local. We are working on your case. There are some new developments we need to go over with you."

"Detective, all that happened long ago. I don't want to talk about it with anyone, even you. If you know what happened, you will understand."

"We do understand, my dear. But we want to prosecute the bad boys. See them punished. I know you want the same."

"No, Detective. All I want is to forget all about it. I can't think about it even for an instant without severe problems. They can all go free if it means I can never remember anything again."

"It doesn't work that way, ma'am," the other man said.

"Look, Gale, we are here to help you. You are the only one who knows what happened and who did it. You were so traumatized at the time you were found that you never gave a full interview. Surely after so long, your head has cleared, and you can remember some details for us."

"No, no, no. I don't want to go there again. Don't you see that it will nearly kill me to remember? Have some pity, please," she sputtered, then started to tear, then weep, her face in her hands. She sagged into the pillow and curled into a ball. Detective Peters patted her shoulder softly and looked at his partner who was shaking his head. Peters nodded that he agreed and stood up.

"Again, Gale, if I may call you that, I am deeply sorry that you are so upset. I'll be in town for several days yet. We will both leave our cards on the table. If you sleep on it and want to talk, please call. I will visit you again in a couple of days, and this time, I won't sneak up on you." Gale didn't respond, and the two men quietly let themselves out, locking the door behind them.

After reaching the parking lot, they stopped and looked back up at her apartment, taking time to each light up a cigarette. Peters shook his head at the shoddy mouse holes the University allowed their students to rent for exorbitant fees. Not altogether different than public housing units, just more accepted by their temporary occupants.

"That went badly, didn't it?" Johnson observed.

"Poor kid. Tell you this, I hope they resist arrest when we catch them. I have four slugs with their names already on them."

"You need her testimony first, Peters. Don't go shooting anyone in this town. I'll do that for you."

Peters grunted with a little laugh. "At least make sure I'm there, won't you?"

"Count on it. Know what I hate about being a cop?" Johnson asked, blowing a smoke cloud for emphasis.

"Sure, but you can tell me anyway," Peters replied.

"When you are a cop, you have to obey the law."

"That's the truth. Now, I'll tell you what I like about being a cop. DNA," Peters said.

"Amen."


"Did you get anything to eat last night?" Sibyl asked softly as Gale sat down. Gale shook her head. Sibyl sighed. "Found the two cards on the table when I came in. Were they in here?" Gale nodded slowly.

"Wow, no wonder you were in that state. Anything I should know? Are you in some hot water?"

"No, dear. It's old stuff. My problem has returned and is wearing a suit and carrying a badge. I couldn't talk to them. Fainted. They put me in bed and left. One told me he would be back. Don't know when."

"So you have to face it again anyway. What rotten luck. Why were they here?"

"Don't know, don't want to know. I want to run way away but can't."

"You should call Jeff. You need him."

Gale shook her head again. "That will make it worse. I'd have to tell him."

"We are close, you and I. You can tell me anything, you know, and I'll stick by you."

Gale patted her shoulder. "I know. Not now though."

"I'm walking you to class this morning, and I won't take no for an answer. From now until you get back on your feet, I'm sticking to you like glue."

"I'd like that if it's not too much trouble," Gale said, her eyes moist.

"It's what you would do. Friends don't grow on trees."

## Chapter 5

# *Plan B*

This time Detective Peters was waiting in the hall for her after class. She stopped short when she saw him, allowing the students to flow around her like little streams around an immobile rock. He gave a polite smile and a brief wave and started toward her. The smile seemed sincere, even friendly, and he approached in a non-threatening way. More like an old friend, one she had known since childhood.

"Hello again, Miss Randolph. I can tell that you remember. See, I told you that I wouldn't sneak up on you this time." He lightly touched her arm. "Got a second?" he asked softly.

"Can you walk with me toward my next class?" Gale asked.

"Anything you want. Are you recovered from the shock we gave you on Tuesday night?"

"More or less. I don't really want to see you again and hear anything from my past. This is clear?"

"And I would rather be home with my two sons and my wife. That's life. We do what we must."

They slowed their pace and looked each other over. Gale had a sensation that she could trust Detective Peters, likely because of the non-aggressive and respectful approach he had taken.

"What do you know about me, Detective?"

"I've got a pretty clear picture. There's always things that only you know, and that is one of the reasons I'm here.

"What's the other?"

"That's for later, Gale. Right now, I want you to sit down with me in a quiet place and go over what you remember. Maybe look at a few pictures."

"Mug shots?"

"Yes."

"Detective, you don't know how I've worked to not think of any of that. I can't take it. It's not fair."

"Nothing about this has been fair, Gale. You are the victim, and nothing can change that. The men who...." Peters stopped and looked toward her for reaction, changing his mind on his choice of words. "Look, Gale, I can't really appreciate things from your point of view, even though I am trying. There are reasons I'm here at this moment and reasons I have to put you through the mental ordeal again. You are going to have to trust me. We are going to talk in private, and I won't record anything you say to me. I am on your side, completely and totally. There is no ugliness or depravity that I haven't heard before, and none of that will change my opinion of you. I am respectful of the way you have made it back into society, and I have, at least, a glimmer of what effort it must have taken."

Gale was silent as they walked into another building and proceeded up the stairs. Occasionally, there were glances at the couple, seemingly so mismatched by age and attire.

"This is where my next class meets. I have, at most, five minutes before it starts. Can you wait?" Gale asked.

"I will wait for you and be in the hall when the class is over." He glanced around in vain for any seating, then at his watch. "It's going to be close to dinner time when you get out. Could I ask you to go with me to a quiet place to eat and perhaps talk there?"

"Do I have to?"

"No, Gale. You don't have to do anything. I hope, that's all." Without answering, she shrugged and headed into class.

Detective Peters was there, just as he promised, stationed against the wall, his shoulder supporting his weight, and his suit jacket open just enough to expose the handle of his black pistol. He nodded and smiled, falling in with her, matching her stride.

"Got any suggestions?" he asked.

"If we must, there is a small Italian place about two blocks from here. That all right?"

"Are there private booths?"

"Of course."

"Perfect."

They walked together as a couple, without talking, silently approaching the little restaurant. Once there, Peters held the door for her, and they came into a small private atmosphere, narrow, old, but clean. They selected a booth in the far corner, sitting across from each other with a small candle between.

After ordering, Peters looked at her for a long time before speaking, carefully choosing his timing and his words. "Gale, might I ask if there is anyone in your life?"

"Like a man?"

"Anyone. I know that your family is gone, and you had no siblings. I just wonder what's going on."

"Other than my roommate, there is no one, Detective. I've had difficulty forming relationships."

"You mean with men."

"Yes, with men."

"Surely there are those who have tried?"

"Yes, one in particular. I had problems with him also."

"Are you still in therapy?"

"No longer. Didn't work anyway. Why all the questions?"

"I guess to determine if you have a support network of any kind. You don't seem to."

"No."

"You want us to catch those men, don't you?"

"I no longer care. I just want to get by and not go backwards. You don't get that, I understand, but I've become aware that I am fragile and liable to fracture. Before you start asking me to recall any events or remember any faces, I want you to realize what you are asking. Anyway, I remember that you have DNA. There isn't anything else you need for a conviction, is there?"

Peters cleared his throat. "No doubt that DNA is nearly the perfect evidence and will lead to an easy trial for the DA. But...if you have the DNA and no face, no name to go on, it will take years to finally stumble on the person."

"And apparently you have."

"We have a match…a recent occurrence led to your case being resurrected. The name was false, and no photograph was taken. I have a strong suspicion of a particular fellow, but I need something more to compel him to surrender a DNA sample. Your help identifying his face would be enough. Once I get him, I'll get the others. It's only a question of time."

"If you get him, please kill him so that I won't have to face him and the others in court. Could you do that for me?"

"Frankly, that's not my job to act as executioner without trial. However, if he resists arrest…it's entirely possible."

"I thought about all this through my last class. It's all I thought about. I should have just skipped the class. It's too hard. I can't do it, Detective. I simply can't. Please understand."

Peters sat back, silent for a long time, his eyes glistening in the dim candlelight, the emotion of the moment coming to the surface. "I respect that, Gale. I'm sorry, of course, but the last thing I want to do is cause you any additional harm. The thing is more complicated than you realize. Right now, this individual isn't aware that he is under suspicion. Probably he has forgotten all about Gale Randolph. I don't want to wake him up unless I can take him out of circulation for good. Does that seem clear?"

"Thank you, Detective. Can't you just get some item that he has touched?"

"Perhaps. I'm sure he will take off for parts unknown if he senses any dogs on his trail. I'd rather act from a position of strength. Right out of the blue, before he can react."

"Seeing his face, or any of them again, will make me relive that whole episode. I won't do it, Detective. I'd rather die first because to recall any of it would make that happen."

"Even if I could do what you suggested, when it came time for trial, the DA would insist that you go to court to testify."

"I'd rather they go free."

Peters reached across and softly patted her hand. "Gale, you need someone to look after you. You can't deal with this alone."

"So far, I've been doing it, Detective. I'm all I have, so there are no options for me."

"Seems to me there are two problems you have." Gale raised her eyebrows, her mind racing ahead to understand his implications. "You have a memory which is coloring your life. That part you know. The other is that the criminals who attacked you are still at large. What they did to you they may have already done to others. What if they come looking for you before you can testify?"

"That was another city, another life. There is no way for them to have tracked me here. Besides, you have their DNA, don't you?"

"Yes...but, again, I have no faces to connect. You are the key. I know this, and they might also."

Tears started down her cheeks, slowly at first, then a stream. She stared ahead, at nothing in particular, a vacant look, a statue with tears, and eyes that refused to look inward, trapped by the past and the present.

"Gale, you are going to make me cry also. Do you want to be seen with a sissy police detective wiping his nose?"

Gale snorted, coming back to awareness suddenly, then realizing the humor Peters was trying to interject. She smiled and patted his hand. "Sorry about that. Now you see my weakness, don't you?"

"I do. There isn't a part of me that doesn't want to fix this thing for you."

They finished the meal in silence, occasional glances across the table replaced conversation, but slowly a bond developed between them, an unspoken one, a bond that was unique and rare.

"Allow me to drive you home?" Peters asked.

Gale glanced at the dark beyond the glass, mentally considering the distance yet to walk. "It would help if it's no trouble."


Peters held the car door open and patiently waited until she emerged. He didn't offer his hand for assistance, by now aware that she wanted to avoid unnecessary contact. They walked together to her entrance off the parking lot. He looked up and saw that her apartment light was on.

"Yes, that means that my roommate is there. I'll be all right now, Detective. Thanks for the meal and the ride home." She stood awkwardly as if waiting for something. "Will you be in town much longer?" she finally asked.

"I have some more to do first. Not long though. I have a family and other assignments waiting for me."

"There is something about you that inspires trust. I want you to know that."

"Thank you, Gale. I want you to trust me, but you need more than a temporary friend."

She took a last look at his face and then disappeared inside. Peters waited until he saw what he expected. Her face at the glass looking down at him. He gave a little wave and headed back to his car.

# Chapter 6

## *Just Procedure*

She moved toward him from across the square, her hair tied up and back, her long neck glowing in the morning sun. As usual, she walked with impatience, not style. Nevertheless, her feminine grace was evident as she moved along lightly, effortlessly, her down hand slightly flexed at the wrist. It wasn't the first time Jeff had waited for her to pass. He knew her schedule right down to the minute, and his heart ached each time he caught sight of her. Always careful not to be observed, in case she would feel threatened, he stayed in the shadows of a small alley until she passed, then intended, as usual, to fall into step well behind her until she disappeared into one of the university buildings.

This time something had changed. A sensation came over him that he wasn't alone, just before a force clutched at his shoulder, spinning him around and slamming his back into the stone wall. The face before his was a large black one, an angry face, the experienced face of a man who was pointing a gun at him.

"Face the wall, sucker!" the man said with a growl. His big hand again effortlessly spun Jeff around while his feet were kicked apart. He was quickly patted down, the hand avoiding no possible hiding place for a weapon.

"What do you want? Who are you?" Jeff asked with a high-pitched voice. The big hand turned him around again, then grasped his throat, pushing him to his toes.

"I get to ask the questions. Got that?" a deep voice replied. "And the question is: why are you following that girl?"

"What girl?" Jeff foolishly asked. The big gun appeared again and was pushed into his neck under his chin. "Okay!" Jeff sputtered, and the gun eased off. A policeman's badge was thrust into his face.

"Police, huh? So what did I do?" Jeff asked assertively.

"Kid, you better tell me what I want to know, or I'll break your arm and put you under arrest. Now answer my question."

"If you are referring to Gale...she is...or at least was, my girl. I'm keeping an eye on her. Is that a crime?"

"Sure. We call it stalking. She told me that you two broke up. That means that you don't have a right to keep an eye on her. Give me your ID." Jeff reluctantly pulled out his wallet and handed it over.

"What is your name?" Jeff asked, trying to get his confidence back. The other man ignored him and, instead, was pulling out his papers, inspecting each item carefully.

"Where were you born?" the policeman asked.

"Right here...in this town," Jeff answered. The other man was busy taking pictures of the wallet contents with his phone, occasionally glancing at Jeff in a threatening manner.

"Ever work or live in Rockford?"

"Never."

The wallet was roughly tossed back to Jeff, striking him in the stomach then bouncing to the pavement.

"I am Detective Peters. Let me give you some advice, boy. Don't stalk that woman. You hear me?"

"Look, Detective. I love that girl. There is more going on than you know. I'm just watching out for her. It's not possible that I would harm her."

"No, kid. There is more going on than you know. If she said to stay away, then that is what you must do. If I catch you lurking around again like this, you are going to see bars. Could that get any clearer?"

"Seems to me that we are on the same side, Detective. We both want to protect Gale. Isn't that right? Besides, I don't understand why you are here. How about telling me what's going on."

"Police take information. We don't give out any. I can't discuss police procedure with you."

"There's something in her past. I've figured that out. What exactly, I don't know, but it's bad. Seeing you makes me realize that it's not over. You might as well break my arm and arrest me right now, because I can't let this go. She needs me, we both know that, even if she doesn't."

Peters relaxed and looked at Jeff with more sympathy. The kid was right. After Peters left for home, Gale still needed to be watched, especially since the principal suspect had moved to the same city.

"All I can tell you is that there was a crime, and Gale was the victim. Arrests have not been made, and we are still working on the case."

"That's not very helpful. Is there some local person that you believe is still a threat to her?"

Peters stroked his chin, glaring at Jeff while considering a response. "Yes, but that is all I can tell you. In this country, a person is innocent until proven guilty. I can't give you a suspect list."

"So it isn't over." Jeff concluded.

"No."

"Can I have your card in case we need to communicate?" Jeff asked. Peters nodded and offered one, assuming a less threatening stance.

"She can't bring herself to discuss any of it, you know," Peters offered. "I can't find out what she still remembers."

"I gathered that myself. She can't bear to even have me touch her. It caused problems for us, because I didn't understand at the time why. Now I do...sort of anyway."

"What do you do here, Andrews? You still in college?"

"I'm a grad student. Memory research, perhaps a PhD out of it someday."

"Does that mean you are trying to recall memories?"

"Actually, the reverse. We are studying how memory is formed and stored. Then we are going to see if it can be changed."

"You mean, erased?" Peters asked, a quizzical look on his face.

"Possibly. Lots to do before we can attempt that, though."

"Good for Gale if you can. Bad for me."

"I understand, Detective. If you can catch him without using her, it would be better."

"True, but the conviction of them, that is if I can bring them down, will require her memory."

"Them?"

"Four. At least that's what we think."

Jeff whistled softly. Much worse than he had imagined. Poor Gale. He shook his head, the image of Gale being molested was more than he could bear.

"Good for you, kid. You care. Yes, you should be involved, but you can't legally stalk her. If you want to help, you have to make up with her and get her permission."

"No way. I've begged her. It's no use."

"Find a way." Peters gave Jeff a thumbs up just before turning and ambling away, slowly disappearing into the crowd.

52

# Chapter 7

# *The Greasy Wrench*

A spanner wrench hit the concrete, ringing a couple of times before coming to rest six feet from its user. In the near distance, a brief grating noise preceded the onset of irregular thunder from a big bore motorcycle motor coming to life, partially drowning out loud cursing as the wrench was retrieved. The man returned and bent over the partially assembled motorcycle frame, studying the carcass as if performing a medical autopsy. He looked up through the open double door where a shadow had crossed the beam of sunlight. A blockish figure dressed in the regulation denim vest and jeans was looking his way. The man's hair hung over his back and chest, not too differently than the yellowed images of Christ still hanging in his mother's living room. Except that Christ had cleaner hair.

"Want something?" Merchant asked, dropping the wrench and standing erect. It was always hard to tell if Merchant was friend or foe. His demeanor was nearly the same on all occasions, likely indicating that he saw the entire world in a continuous stream of confrontation. The shadow made no move, just standing there and looking in as if carved out of some filthy stone. Merchant wiped some of the grease from his hands and dropped the rag as he moved toward the light, while trying to see the man's face more clearly.

"What say, Merchant?" the shadow called, still frozen in the beam of light from behind him.

"Chuck? That you, bubba?" Merchant said, shielding his eyes.

"Back from the dead. Yeah, it's me. Things look the same from here," Chuck replied.

"Damn! Thought you were on a tour. You back?"

"I was running with a pack on the coast. Got told to leave. Crossed some fellows."

"Well, then!" Merchant said as they embraced briefly. "Want to work?"

"Need to. Got some?"

"For a brother? Sure. Remember how to toss a piston or two?" His laugh was coughing and rough. He slapped Chuck on the back hard enough to displace him from the spot. "Come on in, bro. Toss a beer, maybe two," Merchant offered, as he led the way back into the cluttered garage toward a makeshift table in the rear.

About two blocks away, Detective Peters was sitting alone in his unmarked police car watching with interest toward the motorcycle garage and the comings and goings of its occupants. The sign above the garage...a converted filling station...had been hand-painted by someone without any knowledge or skill and was hung in the same manner...slightly off kilter. On the cracked concrete stood a row of irregular motorcycles, all leaning on the same left side and all facing, more or less, the same direction.

There was some regularity about the place, though. The resident workforce and customers all looked the same. Dirty, white, large and hairy. Plus they wore nearly identical outfits, ranging only from a choice of leather to blue denim. Peters knew enough to stay far away from their attention, even given that he was a police officer and carried a large automatic. Pity that his suspect couldn't be a lawyer or accountant. Someone clean, at least partially intelligent, instead of what was crawling around in that den of thieves. Peters had discussed this site with the local cop he had been assigned to...Detective Ron Johnson. Johnson had warned him not to approach without backup or probable cause, and if he did, he was warned to be prepared to defend himself with lethal force.

It was his third day of observation, and he had selected differing sites each day to avoid detection. He was looking for a pattern, who was there, and how the hierarchy worked. Clearly, it was a shifting, temporary, gang headquarters of an outlaw motorcycle gang. One which would pull stakes and disappear in a cloud of oily smoke if they saw any undue interest, as they had done frequently in the past. A new headquarters could be set up nearly anyplace and overnight the black and chrome bikes would assemble, indicating occupation by a small army of dedicated thugs. After a brief time, the local police would become aware of an increase in crime. First, stolen vehicles, then break-ins, muggings and beatings, followed by an influx of drugs. They worked by intimidation, and complaints or witnesses were rare and fleeting. It made the cops feel impotent and frustrated. The source of crime was obvious, but following the law to the letter was difficult and imperfect. Peters amused himself with the thought of how the big communist states would have handled the matter. Machine guns and dogs. Kill them all. Amusing to think of, but Peters knew that this solution led to worse things. American law was certainly imperfect but was the only rational solution after all.

Without binoculars, it was hard to separate gang members one from the other. After all, they dressed nearly the same, rode nearly identical machines and moved around in groups who were more like copies than individuals. Gathering a piece of evidence like DNA was impossible without an arrest. To infiltrate this group, you would have to actually be one of them.

The sample had come from Maryland, one of the few states which acquire DNA on arrest. It had been a result of a bust of a biker gang like the one down the street. Because of some error or oversight, photographs were not immediately taken. Out on bond, they all had evaporated to parts unknown. Prolonged gang rape, as had happened to Gale, was common with this particular bunch. The girls were so traumatized that few of them were willing to testify afterwards. That is, those who came through intact.

Peters had a suspicion that the suspect would return to this area, and likely, there he was standing in front of the garage, embracing his clone, all two hundred and fifty pounds of fat, muscle and denim of him. What the police needed was a raid and convictions. That was the only way in this state of obtaining a legally admissible DNA sample. The criminal would have to be convicted of a felony first, or at least accused of it. Fat chance. On top of that hurdle, he had no name, no face, no proof, other than someone's DNA had matched. One of this bunch was the perp, perhaps all of them were. The newcomer had ridden in on a bike with Maryland plates, so he was at the top of the list.

"Took awhile to find you. You don't exactly give out ads, you know. Been here long?" Chuck asked over his beer.

"Bout a month. We were over across town until the heat got turned up," Merchant answered.

"No cops?"

"Yeah. They sniff around sometimes. Nothing to worry about just now."

"I rode around this area before coming in, you know," Chuck said knowingly.

"And?"

"Well, you have at least one watching the place right now. Cop for sure. Big black dude in a suit."

Merchant stroked his beard with his greasy hand, lost in thought. "Where is he?"

"Down the street in his car. Dark blue, unmarked. Can't miss it. What do you plan to do?"

"Better that I go down there and have a look myself. At least let him know that I know."

Peters almost missed the sound of the bike closing in from behind. He turned just as the machine came to rest beside his car. The extended fork of the chopper made the entire machine nearly as long as the patrol car. Its rider stared at him, eye to eye, without a word. Not that words would be understood above the raspy idle of the motorcycle. Peters stared back, while slowly withdrawing his weapon, his action hidden by the car door. Suddenly, the chopper revved and shot forward, the message sent and delivered. Peters had been spotted.

Peters watched as the motorcycle got smaller, its rider hunched forward to reach the bars, giving his back a beetle-like appearance. The bike swung in a big arc, reflective of its extended turning radius, onto the pavement of the garage. The rider slung off and stood looking back at Peters in an obvious gesture of threat. Time to go. Peters started the car and did a slow U turn, heading away from the gang headquarters. Nothing more to be accomplished there, he realized. Now what?

# Chapter 8

# *Intrigued*

Exactly to the second, the door swung open, and Dr. McLally made his entrance. He was dressed in a white lab coat, his name embossed on a small brass plate above the pencil pocket. A protruding crimson silk tie was carefully knotted using a full Windsor. He nodded to the room and proceeded to pace the floor in front of the speaker's podium, looking at his feet, lost in thought before starting. Suddenly, he stopped and looked up at the audience.

"This is the meat of the issue, the foundation of my research, and I am privileged to outline it for you. I will assume that most, if not all of you, attended my preliminary lecture." He paused to look for nods, which most of the them returned. "Good. Then I won't need to recapitulate, and we may go forward. I'll start with a plea. For money. Research money. There is never enough, because the latest equipment is....pricey, in want of a better term. And volunteers. We are rapidly approaching that threshold of our research. After all, rabbits are cheap and don't complain, but their memory is their own, and they don't tell us about what they think." The audience laughed softly, not sure if he meant his comment to amuse.

"Be warned, however, before you sign the form, that there are complications to anything, including drinking a glass of tap water. We don't even know what the risks are, because the research is so new. We are breaking new ground, much is yet to be learned." He paused again and began pacing as the audience looked among themselves.

"The tools available for noninvasive brain function research are limited and, possibly, crude. As I previously mentioned, they are the following." He went to the blackboard and started writing in large cursive letters.

"The first is our old friend, the MRI. Most of you have likely had fun being in the noisy tube for several minutes, wondering if the thing was going to hurt you. Very clear images. Very good for diagnosis of some types of pathology. Not good at seeing where memory is stored or where the brain is active. To do that, the fMRI was developed. A functional image study using blood flow is somewhat the same method as the PET scan, but without the radiation. Here, a difficulty is the major problem of baseline activity. It has to be measured first so that any changes during testing can be detected. I can tell you that the results are not firm and continue to be controversial. Difficult and expensive also. Plus there is a fear among some that repeated strong magnetic forces may cause neoplasia…brain cancer to you."

McLally paused and turned to face the assembly. "Second is the PET scan that I mentioned last time. Excellent tool but not very focused, and the signal is averaged over a time period making any fleeting memory or thought too brief to record. Plus, the sample size is massive compared to the neural nets we are looking for. We now have the second generation called SPECT. Throw in computerized tomography, and you have it. Better, but still coarse. By the way, if you ever indulge in pot...and I know really smart people such as are here wouldn't do that...you should see the SPECT scans of chronic users." There was a nervous laugh from some in the audience, but McLally wasn't laughing, and he looked right at them in a disapproving way.

"There are other methods used for research, and some of them may someday show promise. One is application of surface electrodes to the subject's head while in a magnetic-proof room and overlaying the results with MRI data. That method is not used at this university. Far too expensive."

"I have something entirely new and unique to present to you. Let me simplify this method but also tell you that I am unable to give out all details before it is fully patented. It involves use of a rare isotope which is activated by a primary radiation source just before application into the subject's blood stream. The mixture is taken up specifically by nerve cells, and the isotope releases radioactive particles at exactly thirteen minutes, seven seconds, thirty-one milliseconds from the moment of excitation. There is only one release for each injection. It is specific, high-resolution, and repeatable. Voila! The perfect tool. The small amount of radiation is negligible and, we believe, harmless. I have tried it on myself, and here I am, still able to give this lecture!" The audience broke out in scattered applause at first, but it spread, becoming a thunderous den of clapping. McLally proudly walked back and forth basking in it, soaking in the acclaim.

"Now, yet another exciting discovery. A real breakthrough. We can sedate the subject with an agent which allows him or her to visit any place in memory. From my own experience, I can tell you that it's like being there again. Meanwhile, we inject the marker and take the picture. What is returned is the exact location of that memory. It is repeatable every single time. When I am the subject, I always go to a particularly fond and keen memory of being in the backseat with my first lover." The audience roared its approval as McLally grinned back at them, raising his hands in an Italian shrug.

"What's the point?" he asked and waited. The audience was too intimated to reply. Each person mulled it over. What practical use could be applicable after knowing where a specific memory resided? Gale didn't have to consider the question for very long. She knew exactly what should be done with a memory location that wasn't wanted. Erase it. Permanently.

"Our next step will be to attempt to remove a memory. You can always obtain new memories, but this might be a step toward removing one that is unwanted, even harmful."

Gale didn't need to listen any longer. Jeff was right. McLally was working on something that might really save her life. She sat back in her chair, this time looking at McLally as a man, not just a foreign-born scientist. Was he full of it or really on to something? And did he have enough ethics, enough character, to be trusted to perform a mind-altering treatment? She couldn't decide. There was just not enough information to form a conclusion. Jeff might know more...if she wanted to go that route again. After McLally gave his last bow, she noticed something that she hadn't seen previously. There were four...no, five...women on the first row, as close to the stage as they could manage. All were young and attractive, at least in an exaggerated way. The way they were applauding wasn't just approval of McLally's intellectual ability or his mastery of the stage. It was pure lust, and the most interesting part is that they all seemed to know each other. Gale remained seated as the room slowly emptied and saw what she knew she was going to see. One of the women followed him behind the stage, just as before. Only, it was a different woman than last time.

# Memory Gap *by Alexander Francis*

# Chapter 9

## *"Him Again"*

When Gale opened the door, she saw that Sibyl had her back turned and was engaged in earnest conversation with the telephone. The paper sack of food in Gale's left arm rustled as she closed the door, making Sibyl turn her head toward the noise. Gale made eye contact with her, at least with one eye, and discerned a furtiveness about her glance that made Gale pause, deciding to listen. Something was in the air.

"Gotta go. Yes, we'll talk some more later. Bye." She hung up and turned toward Gale, a smile of insincere welcome on her face. "Brought some food I see. Great, two more days of non-starvation. What did you get?"

"Who was that on the phone, Sibyl? And level with me cause I can always tell when you are lying."

"A friend."

"Jeff, I'll bet. It'd be easier if you just tell me so that I won't have to drag it out of you or wonder about it."

"Jeff."

"Him again. What's he want, and who called whom?"

"He called."

"I'm waiting, Sibyl."

"You already know that it was about you. Always you. Hell, I'd jump into bed with him if he gave the slightest interest but no such luck." She sighed and sat down, her legs spread apart in a less than feminine carelessness.

"Let me guess. He wants me back, and he's not above using you to achieve his goal."

"Not so fast, Miss Sherlock. He didn't mention that specifically. He wants me to interrogate you about what you think regarding Dr. McLally's lecture. Who is he, anyway?"

Gale crossed into the small kitchen and began to unload the groceries, obviously finished with the conversation.

"You heard my question, didn't you?" Sibyl persisted from the adjoining room.

"He is Jeff's boss. They are doing memory research, and I went to two of his lectures."

"Can I relay what you thought about them?"

"It's complicated. Anyway, it's only research. They don't know anything yet. It's all scientific gobbledygook at the moment."

"Jeff said that they are going to erase memories. He thinks you need that."

"He doesn't know the first thing about my memories, or about me. It's low that he would try to go through you. Be careful, Sibyl, that he doesn't cause problems between us. Remember whose side you are on." There was a soft footfall of Sibyl's bare feet against the vinyl floor. She leaned into the kitchen and waited until Gale turned.

"Your side, dear. I'm always on your side. But I think the guy is harmless and well-meaning. Don't be so...hard. What if he is right?"

He was right, Gale knew, or at least was on the right track. There wasn't going to be a yes answer from her on this subject. Could Jeff be thinking of her strictly as an interesting research subject instead of someone he sincerely wished to protect, as he claimed? Surely Jeff would not want to experiment on someone he cared about without the process being perfected first. Gale shrugged. She was handling it for now and wasn't about to rock the boat and fall into the unknown. A known is better than an unknown any time. Her mind wandered to something Detective Peters said. There were two problems, but he didn't clarify the second. There was something threatening out there, or Peters wouldn't be in town. Her mind refused to go any further into that dark corridor. There were too many fearsome doors which could open.

"So what if he's right? Don't tell him anything but to stay away from me. If there is a change, I'll be the first to let him know."

Sibyl exhaled an exaggerated sigh, and Gale could hear her fall back onto the couch.

It was a nice setup, Peters noted. Expensive gear and the observation platform were well-chosen. The large monitor showed the darkened gas station in better lighting and definition than would be seen with the unaided eye. They were upstairs from a run-down florist shop, one that faintly reeked of weed...hash or M as the locals would say. The downstairs proprietor had the scraggly goatee and the dirty white undershirt so typical of the type. Johnson had given eye signals indicating that that issue was not their concern at the moment...to let it go. Peters had.

Across the street, the rumble of the big twin motors came and went in irregular patterns, and the sound always alerted them to observe the monitor. The lens was small, nearly invisibly mounted outside the window, aiming up the street toward the biker headquarters located at right angles to the room.

"So, what exactly are we supposed to see?" Peters asked again, frustrated at his captivity in the sleazy room above an illegal drug dispensary.

"Be glad that they allocated some money and personnel. I guess we are looking at the overall operation trying to understand just exactly what is happening. We already surmise that almost every action they take over there is illegal. All we have to do is see one in person, and you'll get your raid and your DNA. It's what you wanted, isn't it?" Johnson said.

"By personnel, you mean you?"

"Me. Something wrong with that?"

"I'm sorry, Johnson. No, you are fine. I even sort of like you. I just want to shoot a couple of them and get it over with."

"Not good at stakeouts, are you?"

"In my foolish youth, I was a Green Beret. At least we got to shoot people on occasion."

"You might yet get your chance. Why don't you polish your bullets while we wait. It'll give you something to do."

There was a new noise coming from the street. A mixture of broken glass, motorcycle motors, laughing and pounding. Peters joined Johnson at the window, and they looked down at the street together. At the far end of the narrow street, just discernible in the dim street light, were two motorcycles, topped by riders, blocking entrance to the street. The same was happening at the other end, the closer end. Two hundred feet up and across from the stakeout room were two more bikes stopped nearly in the center of the street, both riderless, the missing riders engaged in the process of destruction of a parked car using small sledgehammers. The auto glass was already spread out on the street, reflecting the dim available light. Both men stopped and looked up at the room occupied by the two policemen, obviously aware that they were looking back. Just as quickly as it happened, all six bikes roared away and disappeared around the corner.

"Yours?" Johnson asked.

"Yeah, mine, or at least the Department's. One of them saw it the other day. It didn't look like much to me just sitting there in shadows. I'm surprised."

"Tough bunch. That calls it for me. They know about us. Might as well pack up," Johnson said.

"It was from that goofball downstairs. I'd bet money on it," Peters mumbled.

"Probably. Well, he's on my list for it. He can kiss the daylight goodbye. I'll bring a squad down here and teach him a lesson in a couple of days."

# Chapter 10

# *Inevitable*

"How long?" Peters asked sharply, knowing the answer would delay his exit from this crime-ridden city. The car had to be fixed, because it was not drivable as is.

"Got to order the glass. Two...three days. In a hurry?" the man-boy in the blue jumpsuit asked sarcastically. Peters wanted to hit him, strike out in anger at something tangible. This grease monkey may be the one.

"Police business. You wouldn't understand."

"Oh, sure. I do the cop cars all the time. Part of the team you might say," he smiled, showing his bad front teeth. Peters fixated on them as if contemplating how many he could knock or kick out on the first try.

"You have my number, get with it then," Peters said and turned his back and moved away before he did something or said something that was inappropriate. He was just frustrated, angry at the world at the moment. Cooperation from this police department had been scant and now was at the nothing stage. They just didn't have any more time or money to spend on Peters' pet project. The way they looked at it, the motorcycle gang would sooner or later be taken in for one of their various crimes.

Problem solved. Peters wasn't asked to go home, but he could tell that they all thought along those lines. With department permission, he had rented a car commercially but with strict instructions to see that it wasn't damaged. His issue car would likely be junked as soon as he returned home. Too much body damage, thanks to the repeated sledge hammer blows. At least they didn't harm its drivability, just its glass and sheet metal.

The loaner car was a compact. Not fast or tough and not tuned for heavy pursuit use, just drivable. He rolled down the window and started it, listening to the clicking four cylinder motor doing its best. Peters shook his head. The modern world was slipping in its standards. Everywhere and everything was made of crap, cheap crap. He pushed the pedal and waited for the car to creep up in speed suitable to his needs. He drove, not thinking about where he was headed, just driving, his mind wandering just as the car was doing. Since yesterday, he was on his own again. Johnson was reassigned to a recent murder case unconnected with Peters. No more stakeout, and anyway, the bad boys had him pegged in that neighborhood. The girl, Gale Randolph, was currently unable to cooperate and positively had no intention of revisiting the crime in her mind. Not that he could blame her. In a way, she was lucky, because some of the girls molested by the same group had faired far worse, and Peters suspected that some had been murdered and disposed of, yet to be found or identified. Alike pattern of crimes had been reported around the country, perpetrated by similar outlaw groups. People who don't obey laws sometimes have an advantage over the police who must follow the rules. *Damn the law*, Peters thought and gripped the wheel harder.

In his rearview mirror, a glint caught his eye, bringing him back to the present. Two motorcycles with lots of chrome were threading through the cars behind. As they grew larger in his view, he could see the extended forks and narrow front tires. Choppers. A raspy coughing noise preceded the bikes, settling into an even throb as they fell in behind him. He opened his jacket and made sure his pistol could be withdrawn easily as he watched the bikers from all three mirrors. No doubt that his car was the one they were looking for, because they closed within three feet of his rear bumper. Both men were wearing long beards which flapped over their shoulders, exposing a toothy grimace. Frequently, they revved their motors, announcing that they were there, in case Peters had missed the visual clues.

Peters smiled. Fortune had brought them to him, instead of the other way. They could have no idea that this well-dressed gentleman they pursued was in reality more ruthless than any gang member. The military had nurtured him, honed his skills and encouraged his willingness to kill. And he had, first in the service of his country, then in the service of his police department. Twenty-five, up close and in person. Two more wouldn't matter a bit, especially if they gave him any reason, however so slight. Knife, pistol, or with bare hands, he was expert at all levels, but he didn't want any witnesses if he could help it.

It always delayed dismissal of the internal investigation set in motion by a killing. Looking around, he saw what he wanted: a narrow street turning north toward the warehouse district and the railroad yards. As he expected, the bikes dutifully followed him, likely both men thinking the same thing from their point of view. A quiet place to do mayhem.

Peters laughed out loud. It was too easy. Lambs to the slaughter. After brutalizing his car, they had made themselves clearly the aggressors. And following a detective, pursuing him into a run-down area, clearly with the idea of harm or murder, they had sealed off any criticism of what was about to happen to them. Peters turned again, the motorcycles close enough to be tied to his car. The alley led to more and more derelict buildings, abandoned cars and idled boxcars. The perfect spot. He slowed, watching the bikes for any sudden move around him. As far as they were concerned, Peters had led himself into an ideal trap with no assistance possible, and they were grinning at what was about to happen to him.

All three machines stopped at the same moment, continuing to idle, prepared to leap into action as needed. Peters opened his door a crack and both bikes shut down, the silence overwhelming. The thickset bikers swung off and pulled up their trousers, an unbreakable and necessary habit. By silent agreement, they each veered off to opposite sides, flanking the car, which was still running. From their point of view, the black man in the front seat just sat there waiting for something, his thick neck appearing even more massive inside the somewhat undersized car. His car door opened fully and Peters leaned out, looking backward. There was something in his yellowed eye, something dreadful emitting from him that stopped Merchant dead in his boots. This man wanted an encounter. He was unafraid, even joyful about it. The menace in his eyes was penetrating, and in an instant, Merchant lost his nerve. This wasn't going to go as planned. This man was going to kill both of them. They had been trapped by overconfidence and by believing that their attire, their tattoos and their history would terrify anyone. Not this time, Merchant suddenly knew. He started backing up, reaching defensively for his large knife, carried between his shoulder blades. Chuck was surprised when he saw Merchant crouched and retreating, knife in hand, the reason obscure because he was on the other side of the car. As he watched, the big black man emerged, catlike, predatory. The eyes fell on Chuck, and he understood, immediately feeling alone, helpless, as if being tossed unprepared into the enclosure of the grizzly at the zoo. Merchant sprinted for his motorcycle, and Peters disappeared back into his car. Just as Merchant stepped on the kick-starter, Peters' car shot backwards into Chuck's bike, tossing it aside like a toy. Merchant took off, scattering road debris which coalesced into a rooster tail behind his spinning tire as the bike crazily wobbled headlong toward a narrow alley. The car continued back until even with Chuck, when he saw the big bore handgun leveled at his face, too late to reach for the automatic tucked into his pants. It was the last image of his life, and his body was flung backward into the dirt, creating an expanding dark pool of blood near his mangled face and head. Although Chuck couldn't hear it, the car door opened and feet crunched over the fractured pavement toward him. A clean swab soaked up a generous sample of blood, and the feet crunched unhurriedly away, back toward the idling car.

"So you weren't kidding about shooting someone?" Johnson asked, his face serious.

"Had no choice. They had me cornered," Peters admitted.

"More than one then?"

"Two. I chased the other one, but my car couldn't keep up with his motorcycle. Plus, he was scared."

"I don't doubt that one bit," Johnson said gravely. "What did you do afterward? I mean, it took six hours for you to report in."

"I parked in front of the garage, waiting for him to return."

"He didn't, I'm guessing, because there would be another stiff."

"Sure would," Peters acknowledged.

"Chances are that those guys are long gone now. Parts unknown. You'll never track that one down," Johnson warned.

"Don't bet on it, Johnson. I got a good look at him. According to your files, his name is Merchant, among others. Pity you don't have DNA on him. If his matches any in my case file, and I'll bet that it will, we would be able to quickly round them up."

"My experience with that type is that they won't ever implicate one of their 'bros.' If they did, they would be executed by the group. You can't break one of them."

"I can."

"Not legally."

"No."

# Chapter 10

# Chapter 11

# *Losing Peters*

A harsh buzz sounded, and Gale jumped before realizing that it was the door. She looked around hesitantly, hoping Sibyl would also hear it.

"Want me to get that, dear?" she asked, rounding the corner while wrapping her wet hair. She paused at the window and looked down. "It's a black guy, all dressed up, and he's looking at me."

"That's Detective Peters. You can let him in." Without a word, Sibyl pushed the button and returned to the bathroom and started her hair dryer.

There came a soft knock on the door, which Gale opened after the second one. "Hi," she said.

"Good morning, Gale. May I have a word?" He smiled at her and stood waiting for permission to enter.

"Come in, please. Want a coffee or anything?" she asked.

"Coffee, if it's not a bother."

Gale returned quickly with two cups and sat down across from him and waited, expecting to hear another plea to look at faces.

"I've come to say goodbye for now," he said and watched her face fall a little.

"I don't know what to say. Having you out there someplace gave me a lot of comfort. Either you got your man or you've given up. Which is it?"

"Got one. The only one I had evidence on. There isn't anything else to go on. I've been ordered to return home, both by my wife and my Captain."

"Please don't tell me that I have got to testify."

"No, you don't need to worry about that." Gale sat and looked back at him trying to discern his meaning, her mind spinning with the limited possibilities.

"You killed him?"

"Resisting arrest. It happens."

"You didn't do that for me, did you?"

"Just police work. Don't feel badly about it."

"Trust me, I don't."

Peters looked at her, slowly sipping his coffee, and was silent.

"There's something else. I can feel it. Are you sure you want to tell me this thing?"

"I met Jeff."

"Oh."

"I treated him fairly harshly until I was sure who he was. Seems to be dedicated to you. Said that he loves you. I believed him."

"I've heard it."

"He stalks you, you see. Probably, Jeff is refining his technique, since I warned him not to do it. I never expected that he would quit, but neither did I approve of it. I told him to get your permission. Thought you should know."

Gale started to tear, but she kept her head high and continued to look directly at him. The sight unnerved Peters, and he searched his brain for something appropriate to say. "Want to talk, Gale?" was all he could think to say. He wanted to press her to his chest and pat her back, but he understood that would be off limits.

"I don't know what to do. He can't touch me, I've already told him that. He'll never understand why, and he's bound to do it again as soon as I relax."

"No, I don't think he will. We didn't discuss any details of your history, you understand, but he does have a inkling of your problem. In my opinion, he will respect your wishes totally. In fact, if you want him to jump off a high building, just tell him and stand back."

"You really think so?"

"I'm sure of it."

Gale continued to look off in the distance, thinking of what she should do, blinking occasionally and silent. There was an uncomfortable pause. Her eyes came back into focus, and she looked at him again.

"Any more of them out there?"

"Truly, Gale, I don't know. I would feel better if I knew you have some protection, but I don't want to force you into a relationship that you don't want."

"When are you leaving, Detective?"

"Soon as I finish this cup of coffee, and we say goodbye."

Gale stood up when he finished the last sip, and they met in the center of the room. Suddenly, she extended her arms and wrapped them around his chest, looking up at his face. "I never heard your first name, though you call me Gale."

"Gregory. Gregory Daniel Peters."

"Thank you, Gregory, for everything," she said, again starting to tear.

"And thank *you*, Gale, for trusting me." He resisted the impulse to envelop her, though he suspected she would have permitted it. "I think you are going to be all right now. Time will heal you."

Peters turned around in the parking lot before entering his car, and they exchanged waves. After turning onto the street, he took out his handkerchief and wiped his eyes.


"I could hear most of it. Getting back with Jeff now?" Sibyl beamed, her even white teeth showing. She put down the hairbrush and waited for an answer. Gale at first ignored her, because she didn't know the answer...yet.

"It's possible. I have to think on it first," she finally said.

"Good God, girl! How much incentive do you need? Truly, if you wait too long one of us hungry gals will get him. Then you'll be sorry."

For the first time in a long time, Gale smiled, looking toward Sibyl, but really through and around her, seeing Jeff instead, his bushy hair curled past his collar, his brown eyes fixed on her face. Yes, she would contact him, or rather surprise him by discovering his shadowy presence, lurking behind her. She wasn't aware that Jeff was stalking, or at the least, following without permission, but she wasn't surprised either. At least the man has persistence, she thought, smiling again to herself.

"I saw the smile," Sibyl said. "Now I know you are going to get back together, and I don't know whether I should be happy or sad. This way I'll never have a chance at him." She shrugged, thinking of her own many pursuers. They were a dime a dozen to her. All the same and all wanting the same thing. With Gale, it was different. Love. Sibyl wished she knew what that was really like.

Only a block to the lecture halls and Gale had kept alert for any sign of Jeff without seeming to actually look around. It was harder with Sibyl, who was oblivious to her surroundings and chattered about nothing nearly the entire two miles. They were about to go separate ways, and they stopped for a moment, looking at each other.

"What time and where?" Sibyl asked.

"Love you, gal," Gale said. "I hate that you put yourself out for me like this. Really, I can manage on my own."

"No, you can't. Just tell me where and when you will be, and I'll be there."

"Four. Right about here."

"I'll be here at four then. Have a good one. If you want to know, Jeff is just over there right now, looking at us." She pointed with her finger close to her chest without looking in that direction. Gale turned and looked, seeing a quick movement disappearing behind a tall Roman pillar.

"Sure it's him?" Gale asked hesitantly.

"I know when a boy is looking at me. Girl radar never fails. It's him."

"Thanks. You have a good day yourself," Gale said and watched her walk away, blending invisibly into the rushing crowd. She continued to look in the direction of the column and then saw his eye looking back. She waved him to come to her, and he stepped out into the sunlight, looking sheepish.

"Come here, Jeff." She waved him forward.

"Hi. Caught me. I know what you must think, but I just can't help myself. So don't be sore about it."

"I'm not. You might as well come out of your hiding places and walk with me." She smiled at him, something he had not seen in eight months, ten days and seven minutes.

"You mean it, Gale?"

She took his arm, pulling him toward the lecture hall. "Want to walk me to my class?"

"Anywhere. Thank you, Gale. Can I meet you later and walk you home?"

"Sibyl already has agreed to do that, so you needn't bother....unless you insist, that is."

"I insist. Thank you, Gale. This makes my day, my whole life. What brought about this sudden change?"

"Detective Peters. He said that I should trust you again. If he's wrong, I'm sure he would like to know about it."

"No! I had a taste of that one. I'll be good, I promise." His wild look made Gale laugh. Peters was a good man to know, for sure.

At four, they were waiting on Gale, right in the spot she had indicated, both looking right and left, expecting her at any moment. They spotted her at the same instant as soon as she emerged through the bronze doors. She wore a smile and gave a wave, swinging her small pack freely in the other hand.

"I haven't see her look like that in a long time," Sibyl observed. "She just radiates joy, doesn't she?" She glanced at Jeff who had glistening eyes but didn't answer. His attention was on the young woman walking toward him, a vision that he had given up ever seeing again.

"You two! Both waiting on little me. I must be special," Gale said looking back and forth between them.

"Don't let it go to your head, dearie. You still have to do your share of cleaning the john," Sibyl said dryly. Jeff offered his arm, and Gale took it, her smile striking him like some planetary force. They started walking with Gale in the middle, her arms intertwined with each of them.

"So my friends, what's the plan for tonight? Are we all going together, and do I have to get my own boyfriend?" Sibyl asked, looking mostly at Jeff.

"I think I just want to go home tonight, if it's all right with you two," Gale said.

"Well, I could go get some food. Could I do that?" Jeff asked.

"Take it slow, Jeff," Sibyl warned. He swallowed hard, realizing that Sibyl was correct.

"Thanks, Jeff, but we'll do that another time," Gale said. Jeff nodded that he understood. Gale decided to talk about another subject, "How's your research going?"

"Oh, that. By the way, thanks for attending both memory lectures. To answer your question, it's really just starting. We are using lab animals for the present. It's interesting."

"What are you doing to the poor animals?" Sibyl interjected.

"Not much. Don't worry, none have been or will be harmed. I wouldn't stand for it either."

"I've heard that before. They always end up on some dissecting table. Call that no harm?" Sibyl continued. Jeff exchanged glances with Gale. With Sibyl interjecting at each comment, they were going to pay a price for her company.

Sibyl caught the look, quickly saying, "I'll walk ahead and let you two guys talk. You have a lot built up, I'm sure." No one objected, and she moved ahead by about twenty feet. They watched as the movement of her buttocks seemed exaggerated, even remarkable.

"Is she doing that on purpose?" Jeff asked, trying hard not to look.

"You know, I'm not sure. I haven't ever walked behind her like this, but I don't remember it being that obvious."

"I hope it isn't meant for me," Jeff added. Gale laughed, first covering her mouth with her hand so as to not let Sibyl hear. The conversation and the sight of Sibyl blocked out any other street sounds for them, until the coughing rumble of two approaching motorcycles entered their consciousness. There was something about the sound that made Gale stop walking. She didn't turn toward the noise but just stopped, her eyes unfocused, blank, as if she was lost in the dark or in fog.

"Gale, are you..." Jeff blurted, but before he could finish, the two bikes slowed, both riders watching Sibyl intently from the rear. The riders looked back and forth between Jeff and Sibyl obviously trying to determine if there was any connection. Jeff felt Gale slump, his arm suddenly holding more of her weight.

"Sibyl!" he shouted. "I need some help." She instantly turned and started back, just in time, as Gale's legs started giving way. The two bikers very slowly pulled away but continued to glance backward. After what seemed like a long moment, the bikes emitted a simultaneous roar, both disappearing into the distance. Sibyl looked up to watch them leave and then back at Gale, whose head was slumping forward as she continued to sag toward the pavement. Jeff reached down and scooped her up, holding her head so that it was close to his shoulder.

"God!" Sibyl exclaimed. "What brought that on?"

"I'm not sure, but it seemed to have something to do with the sound of those motorcycles. They were watching you, Sibyl, and I have little doubt that something would have happened if I hadn't been here with you both."

"No kidding. What do you think would have happened?" She asked intently, her brow wrinkling as she leaned forward to hear his secret.

"Didn't you get a look at them? You could almost smell them from where we stood. Anything, Sibyl. With that type, anything. Don't you read the papers?"

"Actually, no. You mean...abduction?...something like that?"

"Given what we just witnessed, probably what happened to this little treasure," he said, looking down at Gale's sleeping face. No wonder Detective Peters was rough toward him when they met, he thought.

"I heard Peters say he killed someone, a suspect, before he left," Sibyl whispered coarsely, still leaning forward.

"So he's who did it!" Jeff exclaimed. "It was in the papers. The man was shot in the face. There was a photo of his crunched motorcycle along with the story. They didn't identify the cop. So it was Peters!"

"It's making more sense all the time, isn't it?" Sibyl said, nodding toward Gale, as they walked toward the apartment.

"Unfortunately, yes. Poor Gale," he murmured. "However will we fix you again?" She started to stir, and they stopped walking. As she came to, her eyes fluttering, Jeff carefully let her feet start taking more of her weight. He wanted his hands off of her when she regained her composure.

"What happened?" Gale asked, wiping at her eyes with the back of one hand.

"You fainted, dear. That's all," Sibyl answered, looking at Jeff's face, telling him with her eyes not to add details.

Gale looked around, her hand on Sibyl's shoulder for support. "I thought I heard something," she remarked vacantly, looking around and seeing Jeff close.

"You carried me, didn't you?"

"Now really, Gale, the poor man couldn't let you hit the pavement, could he?" Sibyl asked.

"Yes, Gale. For a short while. Hope you don't mind," Jeff said.

"No, Jeff. Thanks."

"Only another block, Gale. Think you can walk there?" Sibyl asked.

"Sure. I'm all right now."

Jeff patiently walked with the two girls, their conversation scant, up to the rear entrance. "May I be here to walk with you tomorrow, ladies?"

"I would like that," Gale answered.

"Me too!" Sibyl echoed with enthusiasm.

Jeff waited in the parking lot until Sibyl gave him an OK with her fingers through the upstairs window. On the way back to the University, he mulled the episode over in his mind. It could have gone very badly if he hadn't chanced to be with them this evening, he believed, then resolving that he would always be close from now on, come hell or high water.

# Chapter 11

# Chapter 12

# *Dream*

She was walking, the darkness descending, inch by inch, like a cover slowly being drawn about the world, leaving her more and more alone. Ahead, the moist sidewalk, its corners chipped from long use, reflected small points of light from somewhere above, dimly marking the path into the night. It was early fall, cooling, smells of fresh wind, leaves, burning meat on the grill, but no voices, no other people. There was something about this particular night, the gradual onset of fear, the apprehensive air, a loathsome perception of loneliness, that made her not want to look behind, only ahead, going toward someplace unknown. Just perceptible was the rumble, familiar, coalescing into a larger sound, one that grew in power, like the gathering of a distant thunderstorm over the horizon or a piston-driven warplane just out of view but heading toward her. She wanted to walk faster, but her legs wouldn't respond, the lower half of her seemingly disconnected, leadened. She couldn't feel her feet, just the sensation of heaviness spreading up, an immobility trapping her, flight impossible as the noise grew louder, coming her way but behind her where its source was unseen. The voices...gruff, male, sneering, conspiring, behind her, coming along with the thunder. She couldn't turn and look, only go forward, stiffly, her body not running as commanded by her will, only slowly, clumsily, mechanically forward, the sidewalk turning into a hill, the path disappearing, replaced by a trail, narrowing, uphill into still more darkness. Then the hands on her buttocks....

Gale was sitting up in bed, her eyes wild, shrieking in the night, hands grasping at the bed covers, the vision slowly receding as she became aware of her reality, but her screaming continued, a force unleashed, unrestrained, the only outlet for her fear, her profound fear.

Sibyl was there, her arms around Gale's shoulders, shaking her, her soothing calm voice, her touch warm. Gale stopped screaming, the fear energy spent as she sagged backward toward the bed.

"Gale, dear, you are safe. It's Sibyl, dear, please lie down. You've had a nightmare, dear. Are you back to me yet?" Gale nodded, placing her hands in front of her face, dreading a return to the vision she had just had, the trembling just starting in earnest. Sibyl covered her with the blanket, pressing it around her neck as she continued her calming words.

"You are safe, Gale. It was just a nightmare, that's all. I'll stay right here with you until you feel better. Want to tell me about it?" Gale shook her head violently no. She didn't want to talk about it or remember. Not that. Never that. It had been a long time since one of those. Now they would be back, each time she drifted off they would be back, chasing her, catching her. The full memory just there, just about to be relived unless she awakened, saving herself in the only way possible. The fear of sleep returning abruptly to her, the dread of closing her eyes intense, unrelenting.

"Move over, Gale, I'm going to be with you tonight. We'll curl up together, and I'll put my arm over your shoulder and protect you. Nothing in the world will happen to you; I won't let it." Gale rolled over and faced the wall on her side, and she could feel the bed sag toward her back as Sibyl got in beside her and inched into full body contact, her arm resting lightly on Gale's shoulder, her hand patting in a comforting way. "There, there, Gale. Doesn't that feel safe and warm? You can go back to sleep now, dear, I'm right here." It was good to feel her presence, her heat and her smooth female voice. So different than the dream she didn't want to remember but which kept trying to return, now digging at the corners of her mind ready to peek back in as soon as her defenses sagged into sleep. No, she would fight back, not allowing her unconscious to resume control. She must not allow it back again. The rest of the dream wanting to get back in, the dreaded part, the hair, the smell, the pain, right behind the pillow's edge, ready to pull her back, the hands on her butt, the big arms, the throaty laughs. She jerked awake, flailing with her arms, a wail emerging from her dream mouth with no sound, no release, arms still pulling at her clothing, falling, blackness hiding ugliness, her only release the shriek of terror.

"Gale, wake up. Wake up. It's Sibyl, Gale. You are to wake up right now. Can you hear me? Stop yelling, Gale, I'm right here beside you. Nothing bad is happening. Gale?"

Her eyes looked at the dark out-of-focus wall, the vision receding but not the sensation of the hands. She pushed upright, the urge to run coming to her, but where to run, to whom, from where?

"Don't do that, Gale. Lie back down now. Come on, Gale. I'm right here beside you. Talk to me, Gale, let me know that you are back."

Gale didn't answer but turned over and buried her face into Sibyl's neck. She was still trembling but was finally fully awake. "Thanks for being here for me. I don't know what I would do without you," she whispered between her hesitant gasps.

"You should talk out what the demon dream was. It makes it seem less threatening in the daylight. Often mine seem silly when I tell someone."

"I can't. It was not a dream but a memory. I've been fighting it, but now it's back. Every time I sleep, it will be back."

"Is there anything I can do?" Sibyl asked.

"I don't want you to know what happened to me. It's not right that something so foul...." she trailed off without finishing. Sibyl got the idea. It was not only the re-creation of the memory but the humiliation, the pain, the horror of the event that Gale didn't want to inflict on her best friend. She held on to Gale as her own tears started to flow. Gale was trying to protect her while she only thought she was protecting Gale. Something had to be done but what? Then she remembered a fragment she heard about Jeff's research. He had mentioned memory, but Sibyl hadn't let him finish, instead only going on about the abuse of laboratory animals. Could his research create a tool able to help poor Gale? It would be the first item on her agenda for tomorrow.

95

# Chapter 12

# Chapter 13

# *Character Analysis*

When they opened the door, he was there, as promised, anxious to get a look at Gale's face, and as soon as he did, her distress struck him, the change coming just overnight. Gale was pale, drawn, tense, and something about her spoke to her physical weakness as well. She avoided eye contact with him, trying to hide the ordeal of the night.

"Gale? Are you sick?" he asked.

"No, Jeff. I'm fine. Just a poor night's sleep," she responded. From behind, Sibyl's face showed otherwise. Something had changed. Sibyl shook her head to discourage him from pursuing his concerns at the moment, and he took her message.

"Had breakfast, girls?"

"Yeah, somewhat. You?" Sibyl answered.

"Not yet. I was hoping...."

"Sure we will. Especially if you are buying!" Sibyl said, speaking for both of them. Gale didn't look at either of them and continued moving robotically forward. They started walking together but without touching as they had done the previous night. Jeff let the women walk in front of him so that he could watch for any clues to Gale's change in attitude.

"Hungry, Gale?" he asked over her shoulder.

"No, but I'll have some coffee, thanks. Don't you have to be someplace?"

"At this level, I often get to choose when and where I go. Time is less relevant."

Gale stopped abruptly and turned to face Jeff, her eyes searching before she spoke. "Jeff...what exactly happened last evening while we were walking?"

"You fainted, and I carried you for a couple of blocks. Then you recovered. Nothing else."

"Why did I faint?"

He hesitated to disclose his theory, reminding himself that she didn't want to remember anything connected with her horrible event. "I think it was a sound you heard that started it."

"What sound?" Her face was questioning, blank, innocent. She really didn't remember, or perhaps didn't want to.

"Well, if a sound really was that powerful...you shouldn't even discuss it, should you?"

"What sound?" she repeated, still holding his eyes. He was trapped. An answer was inescapable.

"Two motorcycles came by just before it started...I assume that was the triggering stimulus."

Gale turned around and resumed walking. Sibyl glanced over her shoulder at him, one shoulder rising in a shrug.

The coffee shop was nearly full, but they managed to extract three chairs to surround a very small table. Jeff appointed himself to be the one who stood in line, leaving the women seated, holding the table until he returned with the coffee and pastry.

"Are you going to discuss this with Jeff?" Sibyl asked in a whisper.

"I can't. You know that."

"You realize that all this business came to light again with Detective Peters becoming involved. It made you think about it once more. Know what I think?"

"No, Sibyl, and don't tell me please. I don't want to mind meld with anyone right now. It's all I can do to drag myself to class and try to get through the day."

Jeff finally made it back to the table with a tray of food and beverages, when placed occupied the entire small top. "Busy this morning!" he remarked, speaking directly to Gale.

"Say, are the rumors about McLally true? I mean, the gossip is all over campus. You should know if anyone does," Sibyl asked.

"You mean that he is brilliant, dedicated and liable to win a Nobel?" Jeff answered, already defensive because he understood what she was really asking about.

"You know that he has a harem of sorts. He can't get enough of having women around him. That one."

"I've seen a lot of girls come and go. He's popular. Sort of has a magnetic personality."

"From what I hear, they aren't just *around*."

Jeff nodded without answering. Sure, the rumors were true, and there was a lot the rumor mill didn't even know. Jeff wished he didn't know either. His future was tied to the man, after all. McLally was a genius...inspiring...and an insatiable womanizer. There was a steady stream of them in the lab, sometimes...no, even often...interfering with their research. Jeff frequently thought that McLally should have become a gynecologist instead of a neurologist. Given the number of women he saw, he practically was one. Pity.

"My question is, Jeff, do you think that he can do real, valid research with all the distractions?" Sibyl asked, coming to the real point of her questions, her eyes never leaving his face.

"He seems to be energized by it. Something in him requires it. But he remains focused on his research, and I think he is on to something big."

"And how do *you* handle being around all those available, horny women, Jeff?" Sibyl smiled at her question, watching Gale's face, her eyebrows up a notch, a slight color returning to her face.

Jeff sat back, looking over both of them before answering. His answer was an easy, clear one. "I am in love, totally, completely. No other woman could tempt me. All of them just pass me by like I'm a fly on the wall, because they can tell." His answer made Gale smile, in spite of her depression. She glanced at Sibyl's beaming face, her eyes telling Sibyl thanks for her question.

They accompanied Gale to her first class with instructions to meet in a certain place at mid-morning and waited together while she limply entered with the other students.

"She have a hard night?" Jeff asked, still watching the door in case she came back out.

"Nightmares. Bad ones. I don't think she slept for more than five minutes. Up screaming three times."

"Wow. Were you able to get any sleep yourself?"

"Don't worry about Sibyl. I can take care of myself. Now what about McLally? Can your research help Gale or not?"

"It's too early to tell. We haven't begun any human experimentation. It will take approval by the Board of Trustees and the Medical School before we can start that."

"Answer my question, Jeff."

"I think so, but I don't know so. There's a difference. We are talking about a real person and one whom I love. I have to be sure."

"If there is enough time, much more of last night and she'll end up back in the locked ward."

"She was committed?"

"Yes, for a period of months. I accidentally saw the discharge papers. She didn't tell me anything."

"Horrible. I didn't...."

"We now know a lot, Jeff, if we put the pieces together. She was attacked by several men. It was very bad for her, and she ended up in the Psych ward. She didn't...couldn't...even give a deposition to the cops. Detective Peters killed one of them, a motorcycle creep. The sound of motorcycles coming up behind her triggered her relapse. Clearly, it was a motorcycle gang who attacked her, and some, or all of them, are around here. It's even possible that two of them rode by last night."

Jeff was lost in a flood of thought. "If she didn't have that memory any longer, she would be better off for it. It wouldn't change what happened, but she wouldn't remember it or be incapacitated by it. Since she can't bring herself to testify, it wouldn't matter that she remember. It's likely that the offenders' DNA is on file."

"It is. I overheard Peters say that they had it."

"I'll discuss it with McLally this morning."


Jeff nodded at Ms. Peterson on the way past her desk. At least this one poor woman was spared from predation by McLally because of her age and the fact her husband was more gorilla than man. "Is he in?" Jeff asked over his shoulder.

"Yes, but I wouldn't go in there just now."

Jeff stopped. He could hear the murmur of voices and the occasional muffled moan coming from the back room where McLally usually trysted his female groupies. He sighed and looked at his watch. There were things he had to catch up on anyway, and he veered off to the right where his computer was stationed. The main laboratory room was spacious and remodeled to the exacting specifications supplied by McLally. The university had been happy to comply, anything to lure the notable and promising professor. The walls, ceiling and floor were crafted in sparkling white, the effect more like an operating theater than not. In the center of the floor was a machine of McLally's design. Part MR, part PET, part computer. A recent addition was the microwave technology units, neatly tucked away in the chassis.

Jeff began looking at the recent animal data. So far, following increasing duration of the microwave beam, all the animals appeared to be functioning normally. That round was designed to test for lethality, not memory retention changes. Animals were difficult to test for memory issues, unlike humans. At Jeff's suggestion, they had suspended sedated rabbits in a positioning device and subjected them to differing noises, determining the location of resulting neurologic activity using the injected radiation source. It was reproducible, and various sounds were causing an allied unique response in the same location, without fail. The next step will be to use the precision-focused microwave beam to lyse whatever neuron was lighting up. In theory, the animal should, for instance, lose its instinctive fear of certain sounds, such as a dog bark. It was a big step, and publication would surely generate rebuttal from other scientists who would challenge both their premise and their result. Getting to the point, an application of this science to human memory seemed far away into the future. Jeff wondered that he may have made an error in the choice of McLally and his damned memory research. If McLally only spent less time with the female body and more on research....

McLally's private door opened, and a long-limbed blonde emerged backward, blowing a kiss into the room. Her hair was rumpled, and she pulled at her clothing on the way out, ignoring Jeff, as usual. Jeff decided to wait for a moment to let the air clear, both figuratively and literally. He wanted no part of that game, even vicariously.

After a moment, McLally came out smiling, surveying the room before noticing Jeff bent over his computer. "Ah, Jeff, my boy. Tabulating results I see. Anything new from your perspective?"

"No, Dr. McLally. No surprises. Say, I need to discuss something with you, if you have the time."

McLally checked his watch and looked lost in thought. Jeff wondered if he were contemplating the next female visitor or planning for supper. "Sure, Jeff. Come into my office in a moment. I need to clean up a bit first, you understand." Jeff did understand and much preferred waiting instead of speculating. After ten minutes, Jeff strolled in, closing the door behind him. McLally sat back, putting his feet on the now orderly desk, getting comfortable and focused.

"I'll give it to you straight out, sir. It's about a woman who is very close to me, and I'm having a hard time being objective about her problem. She would be a nearly perfect subject for our testing, should the time ever come."

"Well, I'm anxious to hear about it. I assume that her problem isn't one you've generated for her?" he asked with a laugh and smile. Nodding agreeably at the possible intimacy revealed if it were true.

"Nothing like that, sir. She was attacked a couple of years ago by a group of men. She was severely traumatized mentally by the event and still has difficulty coping. I thought..."

"Well, Jeff! Already, you have described an ideal situation for testing and therapy. Ideal! Let me ask, however, is there any need, legally that is, for her to testify, identify, or participate in the criminal prosecution of these men, should they be caught, and God help me, they should be caught."

"The prosecutor would prefer that she assist, I'm told. However, she may not be stable enough to be abused by a defense attorney or even by the recall of detail itself. I'm sure that her life, her health, is endangered by her memory. She needs to forget the event."

"It's exciting to consider treating her, but you will agree, however, when I suggest that she see a psychiatrist, get some therapy, try some medication, that sort of thing, first."

"Already done. She was on a locked ward at one time. Nothing has helped. I even set off a crisis by lightly touching her hip while dancing. We broke up for eight months over that. Yesterday, she fainted at the sound of two motorcycles and had a sleepless night and nightmares. She needs help."

"I see," he said, leaning back and looking at the ceiling. "I have tried Puszithrin, the hypnotic drug of ours, several times. I can direct my memory to the exact spot I want while under the influence of the drug. What I haven't tried is the addition of the radioactive nucleotide while recalling my memory. And, of course, using the destructive beam of ours." He thought for a long time just staring at the ceiling. Jeff let him think it out without suggestion. McLally was, after all, the creator and owner of the theory he propounded so frequently, the point of their research and the reason for extravagant donations and endowments from wealthy donor alumni.

McLally finally spoke, "Yes, then, it's settled. I will be the first human lab animal. Let the testing begin. If we cook my brain, then you can go get another advisor and project. Fair enough?" He smiled with satisfaction at Jeff who was trying to take in the implications.

"Sir, your brain is more valuable than most. We...society...can't afford to lose someone like you. I don't agree that it's a good idea for you to be the first, especially since we haven't had a chance to test the whole project on animals."

"Rather your girlfriend be the first, or you?"

"Well, not her for sure."

"Are you volunteering in her place?"

"I suppose I am." He swallowed hard. He had been tricked by McLally, falling like a dove into a sticky web. Of course, McLally wasn't serious about using himself as the first test subject. Only he knew enough about his own theory to use the technique on someone. But, of course, Gale could not be the first. Only...he just didn't know enough about the results of the destructive beam. What if it resulted in great harm?

McLally smiled, satisfied that they now had a test subject. The project was what was important, not their test subjects. Whatever happened was a reportable result, and if necessary, the science would take a poor result into account and adjust accordingly. Science is the study of unknowns, after all.

"When will you be ready?" McLally asked, looking at the calendar.

"Whenever."

"Great! We'll begin tomorrow. Now you must remember some event in your life that you can be permitted to forget. Think on it tonight, and we'll see what we can do. Anything else?" McLally asked, rising to his feet and looking again at his watch.

# Chapter 13

# Chapter 14

# *First In*

They walked back to the apartment as a group again, with Gale looking slightly better and somewhat more communicative. "Did you have a good day, Gale?" Jeff asked.

"Better than I expected. You?"

"Turned out to be interesting. Tomorrow should even be better." She looked interested, intrigued, and waited for an explanation.

"Let me guess, Jeff," Sibyl cracked. "You fried a couple of animal brains today."

"I thought you would get over that childish sarcasm, Sibyl," Jeff responded sharply. Sibyl put on an exaggerated pout, bringing a laugh from the others.

"Well, then, what is going to happen tomorrow, or do we have to guess?" Sibyl came back.

"I get to see what it's like. From the other side."

"Does that mean what it sounds like?" Gale asked.

"Yes. We are going to erase a memory of mine. I just have to decide which one."

"Erase me," Sibyl suggested, grinning at him.

"Are you scared, Jeff?" Gale asked.

"I will admit being first on the moon must have created some apprehension. Sure, a bit."

"We'll worry for you, Jeff. You can relax," Sibyl offered.

"We can be there during the test if you want," Gale said.

"Not necessary. We've already used the beam on animals...our rabbits...and none have shown any detectable changes or injury. Who knows, perhaps it doesn't even work at all. We'll see tomorrow."

"Or maybe it did work. They may have forgotten their own mother. You'd never know," Sibyl quipped.

As Jeff thought it over, he realized that Sibyl could be correct. Something had to have happened. They just didn't know how to evaluate it. He knew the steps which were to be taken, having performed the procedure on several animals himself. First, of course, seeing to the equipment set-up, usually the assistant's task...that would mean that Jeff would get the equipment ready for his own treatment...then preparation of the anesthetic agent, the syringes to be used and the IV drip. Next would come testing the power source and aligning the firing heads for the burst-beam microwave. It was computer driven, but software glitches were the norm for a new process. The alignment and power settings were critical. McLally's previous research had developed the quadra-angular beam of microwaves emitted from four nearly microscopic dish devices. All had to be focused on the same spot and coordinated with MRI data of the subject. Detectors modified from a PET scan unit would identify the emitted signal from the tagged neuron, presumably the one activated by a memory, and a microwave burst would be focused on the target with a duration of only ten milliseconds. The postulation being that inadequate time would have elapsed to heat the tissue enough to cause damage to the neuron, but the synaptic junctions would be affected, at least in theory, hopefully causing a disruption in memory. Neat concept, he thought, and one, if proven, would be a gift to humanity. There was a lot of inherent risk in the endeavor and so many places that mistakes or unpredicted circumstances could compromise the result. Too much power, or elapsed time, or selection of the wrong site could lead to permanent brain injury...Jeff's own brain this time. The entire process was built on the premise that a neural network *is* the memory. The pattern of synaptic connections some sort of biological binary code storage mechanism. A theory as yet not proven by sound research.

When they arrived at the apartment, the girls turned to look at Jeff, who had been lost in thought and silent for most of the way. "Are you planning to be here tomorrow morning, Jeff?" Gale asked, hoping that he would say yes.

"I plan to be here with you both for as long as you can put up with me. But tomorrow morning I can't. I have to prepare the equipment for the test, and it takes a couple of hours to get it right. Think you could manage this one day without me?"

"Us? Sure we can. Don't you worry a bit about us. Gale has me, and I have Gale," Sibyl said.

"One question, Jeff, and I would like you to be truthful," Gale said, standing close to him. He waited, knowing in his heart what she was about to ask. "Are you doing this experiment for me, instead of me?"

"Gale, it's part of my research. Eventually, some person has to go in there. There is a long history of scientists who tried out a vaccine or potion first before expecting anyone else to take it."

"That's not an answer."

"How do I answer? If I said yes, and something happened, you would blame yourself. If I said no, then you might feel that I don't care about you." She fixed his eyes with hers, staring into his soul, seeing the answer for herself as plain as written words. Of course he was doing this for her, there was no doubt. She touched his face with her fingers, dragging them slowly away, then went into the doorway that Sibyl was holding open for her.

After the door closed, Jeff listened for their footsteps heading up the stairs. "Sleep well tonight, my darling," he said quietly.

Gale was quiet, too quiet even for Gale. "You didn't have a good day, did you?" Sibyl asked.

"I got through it, but..."

"You get lunch?"

"No. Couldn't eat."

"Poor baby! No wonder you don't feel good. Think you could down a pizza if I ordered in?"

"I'll try. No promises."

That was good enough for Sibyl, and she immediately started looking up numbers of pizzerias who delivered. She chose one and gave her order, falling into the sofa to wait.

Gunnar hated this job. Delivering pizzas for a living was bad enough but taking orders from a pimply-faced teen was over the top. If it weren't for the side benefits he wouldn't have lasted very long. It was the customers, the female ones, in this college town which kept him interested. They were sometimes polite and friendly to him and, rarely, even invited him in to perhaps share a bit of pizza and occasionally other things. It's what he lived for. Besides, he was able to earn points with Merchant and his crew when he pointed out vulnerable locations. Someday, when he had a decent chopper, perhaps they would let him in. Wear the colors. Drink and ride with real men. That's what he really wanted. They all seemed to have money, that group. Gunnar still wasn't sure where it all came from. None of them seemed to work for a living, or even needed to. They had money...and dames. That was for him.

"Another student housing delivery, Gunnar," the little stooge said to him across the counter with emphasis on the first syllable of his name. A steaming pizza was slid into its cardboard container and pushed across to him, the address written on top. "Already paid for, but no tip. That's your department," the little twerp said with a teasing smile, knowing that students were stingy with tips. Gunnar wanted to hit him, put him on notice who was bigger and meaner. But, instead, he took the box and headed toward his waiting motorcycle. After checking the address one last time, he slid the box into an insulated container strapped to the tail of the bike. He zipped up his leather jacket and pulled on his gloves before kick-starting the huffing machine to life. A couple was just walking toward their waiting car when Gunnar revved his motor, generating the glance that he sought. Respect, fear, loathing, he could see it in their faces as they stopped and watched him maneuver the machine toward the street, his feet dangling laterally for stability.

Through the peep hole, Sibyl surveyed the knocker. He was holding a pizza box up, knowing that someone was looking him over, while smiling a broken-tooth smile around the edge of the box, trying to look funny and appealing, in case the viewer was female. Sibyl took a deep breath before opening the door. They had heard the bike when it stopped down below, and the sound had sent Gale scampering for the bedroom where she remained behind the closed door.

"Can you tell me what kind of pizza you brought? I like to be sure it's what I ordered," Sibyl said, looking the delivery man in the face. The man was taller than her but scrawny and had pitted skin, visible under his scruffy beard. He tried to look past her into the room, but Sibyl knew that all he could see is their cheap second-hand couch from where he stood.

"You by yourself? Gonna eat this whole pizza by your little self?" Gunnar asked, grinning at his tactful approach.

"No, my boyfriend is hungry after football practice. He might just eat the entire thing himself. Big, you know."

Gunnar was taken back for a second but instinctively knew that her comment was a bluff, designed to keep him from guessing that one, or at the most, two young women shared this flat together. "Yeah? I'd like to meet him, being that I'm a big, big football fan myself!"

"Want a tip?" Sibyl sneered, holding the two dollars up so that he could see them. "Get lost!" she said and snatched the box before tossing him the bills, then slammed the door in his face.

Gunnar stood there for a moment, his temper rising as he glared at the peephole. He was tempted to kick the door in and slap the little bitch, show her who was really boss. But, he considered the remote possibility that there *was* a large athlete somewhere inside, ready to come rushing out and toss him down the stairs. She won this time, a temporary setback, but he would get even in the end. This place was perfect for Merchant and his crew: run down, quiet and easily accessible by the parking lot. Then she'd get what's coming to her, and also whoever else was in there with her.

# Chapter 14

# Chapter 15

## *The Beam Awaits*

Jeff took long strides, longer than usual. The early spring morning was cool but clear, a promise of a fine day ahead. The magic of dawn was evaporating as the sun peeped over the buildings east of campus, strong enough to feel good against his exposed neck and warm enough to provide the incentive for various birds to be casting about for food. He took a deep breath, trying to calm himself, the fear of being the first eating away at his usual confidence. If there was only someone objective to discuss this with, he wished to himself. Their project had not been approved by the oversight committee to proceed with human testing. Normally, it would take years and volumes of supporting paperwork to even seriously be considered for such a thing. Jeff knew that if this procedure went badly today, Dr. McLally would lose everything, might even be asked to leave the country...and the scientific community. McLally hadn't seemed worried, but of course, he was perpetually and arrogantly overconfident. Jeff realized how clear his own thought processes were this morning, while also feeling the air, the sunlight, and his strong legs propelling him to his destiny. A healthy man in his prime heading toward... To what end? Injury, brain damage? Yes, all that was possible, but so was the potential of helping Gale recover from her grievous mental wound, damage so severe that it was likely that she would never make it back to full normality without his help. He had to do this test and hope that it will work. Indeed, it *was* all for Gale, but he could never disclose that to her or anyone else.

The important question of which memory was to be blasted had not been solved. Certainly not a pleasant memory, nor a necessary one, could be selected. He needed to recall one that was both vivid and unpleasant and one that he never wanted to recall again. It wasn't as easy as one would expect. Losing something forever was a big step. He wrinkled his brow and slowed his walk while thinking. There was that business regarding his touching Gale that she so objected to. He could erase his memory of how he reacted. No...not that. He might do it again, not knowing her reaction would be the same. Suddenly, he smiled. There was one that could go and good riddance. It was the time he came home with a report card full of Fs. He got a severe whipping from his father over that one. It was a clear memory involving emotion, pain and the sight of his father's angry face. Since his father had passed away, there was nothing to lose by elimination of that particular incident.

Jeff was the first one in the lab, and he unlocked the rooms and turned on the lights. The intense white of the lab...brilliant light reflected off white marble and tile...created an illusion of purity, sterility, orderliness. It was hard to imagine evil or incompetence in such a place. Equally so, the impressive machinery sitting in the middle of the floor, a collective of objects whose value exceeded a million dollars. Jeff stopped for a moment and just looked at the massive unit. It was the best that science and society could produce up to this point. A sum total of millions of man hours of experimentation and refinement went into its production. It inspired hope but also fear of all that massive hardware which would soon be directed at his normally functioning brain.

Jeff put himself to the task of readying the room for the grand experiment, and there was much to do, the business of it replacing his reticence for the moment. When nearly complete, he returned again to adjusting the projection heads for the microwave beam, trying to convince himself that there was no doubt about their alignment or settings.

When McLally opened the door, he stopped and looked over at Jeff, who was hovering over a computer terminal. McLally gave him a big smile. "This is it, Jeff! This is the day I have been waiting for years to experience. And you? How is your attitude this fine morning?" McLally was dressed in a dapper three-piece dark wool suit, sporting a crimson bow tie. He could have stepped right out of an advertisement for a Savile Row bespoke tailor, appearing more like a British diplomat rather than a medical researcher. Jeff noticed that a burl wood cane dressed his left arm.

"I'm ready and so is the equipment. I've double-checked the settings and made some preliminary firings."

"Grand, my boy. Simply grand. And have you identified your memory, as I asked?"

"Yes, I have one which will fit your parameters. Want to hear it?"

"You don't need to tell me about it. What I want is for you to sit down and type it out. Every detail that you can recall. Spare nothing that you can remember in your description, not a single emotion or visual memory. Put down what others may have said at the time and what you said to them."

Jeff turned around and started typing. It was amazing how much came back to him. He put in dates, his age, and even how many welts the belt left on his legs. He was at it for at least half an hour before being satisfied. He got up to find McLally who greeted him wearing a crisp white lab coat. "Want a copy, Dr. McLally?"

"No. I'll test your recall sometime next week. Just send me a copy electronically. Now, are you ready for this?"

"Frankly, I'm worried about it," Jeff admitted.

"I'm sure you are going to find this a pleasant experience. Now, let me tell you what to expect. After you get the first dose of Puszithrin, I will instruct you to recall your memory. You will be amazed at how perfect your recall will be. It's like traveling back in time. You actually feel that you are there, but you will still hear me when I talk, and you will be able to talk back to me as well. You want to be at the exact spot where the memory is to be erased. It's got to be where things are going to turn unpleasant. You'll know the spot when you come to it. If you are unsure, go into the memory more deeply, then we'll administer another dose of Puszithrin, and you can start over. Does that sound simple?"

"Okay. Then what?"

"You simply tell me that you are in the location you chose to eliminate. I will administer the dose of Ted-Zeththrinoid and fire the microwave beam at the spot that lights up."

"How do we know that what lights up is the memory we want to erase?" Jeff asked.

"Oh, that! I didn't tell you the entire plan. You will receive two doses of Ted-Zeththrinoid. The first is for baseline, administered while you are resting and before memory activation by the Puszithrin. The second dose is the one which will be collected by your memory. The computer simply extracts the baseline data, leaving the singularly different one."

"But what if my mind wanders a bit? What if it's thinking about more than one subject?"

"Well, don't let that happen is my advice. Control your thinking. The computer can't tell a good memory from a bad one. It simply takes the one being processed by you, and the beam is corrected to that location. Clear now?"

"No. There are a lot of unanswered questions. Are you sure that your research is ready for this step?"

"As I recall, there was something about a girlfriend of yours. She needs this process, you said. Want her to go first?"

"No, I don't."

"Then we have to test this on someone before she comes in here. You are perfect, because you understand the entire project. No better choice could be found. Remember that we have seen no deleterious changes in animals using a far higher dose. In my opinion, there are few if any risks. The worst that could happen is that you will lose the wrong memory."

"Like my name?"

"Don't think that way. You want to have a positive attitude and be under control. Think you can do that?"

"Let's get this over with. I'm not going to ever be ready, because there aren't enough facts available to consider one way or the other."

McLally patted him assuredly on his shoulder, pointing to the gurney waiting for him.

# Chapter 16

## *The Beating*

As soon as the Puszithrin was injected, things changed. Jeff had the sensation of floating above the earth, looking down and seeing the past in all its detail. He simply had to choose where to land. He floated for a moment, enjoying the sensation of power, the feeling that he could visit any place he had ever seen, talk to any person he had ever met, information spread out beneath him like a map, but one crawling with visible detail. So much to explore, to re-experience again, to relive his youth in every detail. The sound of McLally's voice pulled at his attention for a moment, distorting his view, making images fuzzy, more indistinct.

"Go to your unwanted memory, Jeff. I know you don't want to do that right now. So many places to see. Force yourself to recall that unpleasant one you want to get rid of." His voice was smooth, commanding and persistent. Jeff remembered why he was there, where he had to go. In an instant he was standing in his home, the old one with the small oil furnace in the center of the hall. His mother was seated on the couch, her face drawn, as if something was about to happen. He had forgotten how young she was at the time. Seeing her as a young woman jogged him. There was something about the perspective of time that was out of balance. His mother was never a young attractive woman, but there she was, her clean shiny hair falling over her shoulder in a natural way, exactly as had happened, but Jeff's recognition of the meaning of life had matured. A noise startled him as his father came through the door, slamming it behind him. He was dirty from work, a hard life spent at the foundry, the means by which he supported his family, leaving him burned out, perpetually angry, unable to see how to treat his children and his wife with tenderness instead of brusqueness. Jeff saw the same images as they had happened, but his understanding was different. Although he couldn't see his brother, he sensed, or perhaps remembered, that the boy was in the back room with the door closed so that he would not have to watch what was about to happen. Jeff remembered his own room, his model airplanes, the old hand-me-down desk and his little transistor radio on the window sill. He wanted to go in and look around, but he heard his mother start speaking to his father.

"Want to know how your son is doing in school?" she asked, not looking at her husband but at Jeff. She offered a slip of paper, her arm stretched out, still fixing Jeff in her eyes. She wanted him to be punished, he could see it in her face. It wasn't only his father who administered beatings, it was both of them, just in different ways. Before he could try and defend himself, his father snatched the paper, glaring at both of them like a hawk spying his prey, his muscles already tensed. This was the moment when it would start. Should he try and stop the memory right at this spot? Was this the moment he was trying to remember, or did this one go differently? He wasn't sure, and he became wrapped up in the moment, childlike, still at the mercy of adults. Jeff knew that if he spoke, he would be talking out of place and risked a slap across the face by the back of his father's burly hand. He was silently watching events unfold just as they did, and he was powerless to intervene, just as before. It was a vortex, this memory, and it could proceed in one direction only. Part of him wanted to stay in the past, even the unpleasant past, to relive his young life, to correct his mistakes, to see his brother, to make amends where he should. Events were happening too fast to think, too sudden to stop. His father turned and stooped to Jeff's level, his red angry face only inches away when he started yelling, spittle splattering Jeff's face.

"You worthless no-good. You piece of crap. How dare you bring home a report card full of bad grades. You couldn't even tell us that your grades were falling? You eat, you sleep, and you don't work. You don't do anything, do you?" That was for starters, and Jeff knew at the time what was coming next, and he was powerless to prevent it this time, just as before. A rough hand spun him around, and in a split second, a powerful jerk pulled his pants down from behind, exposing his underwear which was also jerked violently down. He heard the belt snapping at the loops as his father pulled it off his waist, followed by a moment of silence as the belt flew through the air toward his legs and exposed buttocks, hurtling toward him with menace and anger, meant to cause pain and inflict damage. Jeff closed his eyes, squinting against the coming pain, wanting to scream but instead holding it back, trying to be a man, trying to keep some dignity, some self-worth. Not that it would matter. His father would continue until Jeff broke, and past that, into total collapse, ending with him on the floor, writhing helplessly against the slaps of the leather belt, his sense of being of value gone, pitied by no one except his younger brother who refused to watch.

"Jeff, you are past the point, aren't you?" McLally's voice said. Jeff felt his hand on his shoulder, a gentle push, reminding him that he was in a memory, not actually experiencing the event, not really returned to the past. Jeff was in control this time.

"Yes, I went too far," he heard himself answer, like his voice was coming from another place, another person.

"I'm going to give you another dose, Jeff. This time you'll know where to stop. Just tell me when. I'm going to administer the isotope at the same time. You will have just over thirteen minutes to explore. You must return to this memory when I tell you. Nod that you understand."

Jeff nodded, his legs still stinging from the belt. He felt the wooden floor against his face, the fluid from his drool and his tears lubricating the contact, making him feel that he could slither along the floor. He heard himself crying, his arm was over his face in a protective way, but his bare bottom and legs were exposed to the world of his parents.

"Get up and get out of the room," his father commanded. Jeff started to push himself off the floor, feeling limp, worthless as a dirty rag. Suddenly he was aloft again, soaring over the planet of his memories, looking down at his past life, the images flickering past endlessly under him, as he decided, godlike, which one to visit. He wanted a good memory, a cherished one, meant to erase the leg pain, the humiliation of lying on the floor.

"Two minutes left, Jeff," the voice came to him. "Get ready, go back to the memory again. You must return now."

Without wanting to, Jeff obeyed, finding himself at a slightly earlier time of the same event, his mother just opening the sealed envelope containing his grades. He had a strong suspicion that his grades were poor and didn't want her to open the envelope, wanted to snatch it from her and throw it into the furnace. She looked at him in a strange way, like she somehow knew what the paper would say but was hoping that it didn't, that she was wrong. A feeling came over him that she wanted for him to do better, that she didn't want him to be punished, but to succeed instead. He had the impulse to kiss her cheek, to tell her that he would do better from now on, that she didn't have to worry, that he would turn out good in spite of her fears, that he wouldn't become like her husband, his father, a man trying to survive in a harsh world. In an instant, he realized what he couldn't in the real past. That they loved him but were using the only methods they knew, because that was how they were raised themselves. Jeff knew that he had profited in some ways because of the beatings, but beatings weren't what made him do better in school at all. It was because he wanted to turn out differently, wanted to treat people whom he loved with tenderness instead of force. Perversely, his beatings had made him into a better man.

"Seven seconds," McLally said into his ear. "Are you ready?"

Jeff looked up at his mother who was holding the grade report, her finger just now prying at the seal, knowing in her heart what was inside. Jeff felt himself raise his finger. This was the moment. The moment before it all began again. There was a blinding flash, bright enough that he wanted to cover his eyes, turn his head away from the light. When he looked again, expecting to see his mother standing there with his grades in her hand, he only saw blackness, nothingness. He spun around in place trying to see the little house again, but it was gone. He floated as if in space or deep in a cave, absent of light, noise, the memory disappearing with no trace left, no sensation of where he was or why. Then the voice came back in his ear, the only contact in a world without reality. He was drawn to the sound, his head turning toward it without effort. McLally's face was close to his, his broad Cheshire cat smile showing his teeth. He looked past McLally into the lab, at last remembering where he was.

"Hi, pal. You're back, safe and sound. Just lie there for a moment until your head is clear. I envy you the adventure you just took, and I can't wait to hear about it," McLally said, moving away from the gurney, his words echoing off the hard walls and floor, doubling the sound of his voice. Jeff looked up, craning his neck in an effort to see behind his head. The gurney had been pulled free of the machine before he had recovered. How long had the process taken and what had happened? Jeff couldn't remember any of it but a sensation of flying above a world of some sort. A pleasant experience for sure, but was there any more to it? Many times previously, he had dreamed a complex dream during sleep but awakened to find it gone, and no amount of memory searching ever resurrected it. He knew that something had happened, but whatever did, it was gone. He sat up and stretched, feeling like he had just awakened after a long sleep.

"How long did it take?" he asked.

From somewhere unseen, McLally's voice answered, "Roughly thirty-five minutes from start to finish. Recall anything?"

"Something. But I can't describe it. Maybe a floating sensation. That's about it."

"Grand, simply grand," McLally said, his voice coming closer. He appeared in front of Jeff, his lab coat replaced by his tailored suit jacket. "You are done for today, Jeff. That's enough. Go enjoy this beautiful day while you can, and tomorrow morning we'll discuss your experience in depth. Feeling back to normal yet?"

"I think so. What happened?"

"Success, Jeff. We both had success." McLally gave him a last artificial smile then quickly left the lab, checking his watch one more time.

Jeff stood, his legs a bit wobbly at first, and made his way back to the restroom where his clothes were hanging. He tried to recall the morning's events, but the last thing he could clearly remember was the prick of the IV, then next to nothing. There was a sensation of pleasantness remaining, but Jeff didn't know why. He did recall typing out a lengthy report prior to the test, but reading it would have to wait until another day. He longed to see Gale, her face, her long fingertips, her red lips that he couldn't as yet touch or be touched by. As long as she was close, it was all he could ask for at the moment.

# Chapter 17

# *Reappraisal*

After dropping the girls off at the entrance to the lecture rooms, Jeff hurried back toward the research lab. He had spent the previous afternoon with Gale and, of course, her self-appointed chaperone, Sibyl. Actually, he was growing to like, or at least respect, Sibyl for her loyalty to Gale. The fact that both women were strikingly attractive wasn't at all hard to get used to either. Jeff was self-elected to pay all the bills when they ate together, and he did so gladly, without reservation or complaint, because it was a small price for such wonderful company. He had begun to jibe back at Sibyl in a friendly but competitive way, and he saw that his image was improving in her eyes as well.

The aftermath of the experiment was, so far, mild, resulting in a frontal headache, and, for some obscure reason, excessive thirst. By morning, the headache had relented, but he still could not recall anything that happened during the experiment. Gale and Sibyl were both anxious to learn if it had worked, and Jeff answered truthfully that he had no idea until he discussed it with Dr. McLally and read the document he had prepared before lying on the gurney. It sure didn't seem like anything was out of place or changed in him, and the thought was depressing. All the research, and his possible PhD, was in jeopardy if the experiment turned out to be a failure.

The door to the lab was open, and the lights were on. Jeff came in quietly, expecting to find an unauthorized person being where they don't belong. He could hear voices coming from McLally's private office. Standing still and holding his breath, he could just make out what was being said, or not said. It was another tryst in progress, and McLally was one of the combatants. He sighed. *This early?* he mused to himself. The man had no end point of saturation or satiation.

Jeff threw his jacket into a chair and turned on his computer. At least this would give him the chance to see what he had written. It was strange that he could remember the process but not the words or concepts. He did remember that it felt important at the time, and he recalled working diligently on it until just before the experiment started.

As he read, his jaw fell open. He started scanning the document faster and faster as he became incredulous, appalled. There was simply no way he had written this document. There were things, events and situations, recorded which had not happened. What was incredible is that the feel of the document, the words, sentiments, the places, were all correct. He became angry that he had been deceived. McLally had altered the document to prove that his experiment had worked. It was the only explanation. What a cheap trick. He was tempted to open the office door and walk in, demanding an explanation, watching the two scramble trying to cover their indecencies. Better, he would tell the administration what was happening regarding the research, even though it might cost him his degree. He stood, still leaning over the screen, rereading the words that someone had typed in.

Behind him, voices suddenly grew louder as McLally and a young woman emerged, giving each other a last embrace and lingering kiss. When McLally noticed Jeff, he looked flustered, even embarrassed, the first time Jeff had seen that response. Jeff looked again at the departing woman, his memory searching for her identity. Perhaps he had seen her before he realized.

"Well, my boy! I thought we decided that you were to take a couple of days off. Your return to work is rewarding for me to see but not necessary in the least. How are you today? Any lingering effects?" McLally said as he walked across the room, pulling on his lab coat, smiling as though he was about to pat Jeff's head affectionately like a wayward dog who had returned at last. Jeff stood erect and watched him come without comment.

"Is something the matter, Jeff? There is a strangeness about you that I haven't noticed previously."

"I read this document. Someone has altered it. I think that it is an attempt to validate your experiment at my expense." Jeff was seething in anger and trying to hold it in. He could feel a rage building.

"Let's not think that way, my boy. First, look at the date-time stamp and see when it was created and when it was altered." Jeff turned back and clicked some keys.

"It says that the creation date and the alteration date match. But that's not possible. I didn't type this document. The things in here never happened. This is going too far, Professor."

"Jeff! Don't you see! We erased a memory! This proves it works. You don't remember what you put down, because you were drawing on a memory which no longer exists. That's why you think it is a false document! It worked, Jeff!" McLally's happiness, his joy, was infectious, and Jeff felt his face flush as he sat down looking again at the words on the screen.

"Now I see that I made a mistake," McLally admitted. "I should have had you write it out longhand instead of typing it in. That way there could be no cry of foul. I never thought about what would happen when you saw it for the first time."

"It's amazing, Professor. I can't remember any of this. It's hard to believe that any of it happened, but as I think about it, I remember dimly something similar, but not the same."

"Jeff, that fits with some of the theories of memory creation. When you come across some event or information which is similar to one you had experience with, what happens? I'll explain it for you. It means that your brain compares this event to a similar previous experience, judges how it is different, and stores the information as a variable, not a completely new event. Our experimental process identifies a neuron, or perhaps more than one neuron, then we cause that neuron to lose its synaptic connections by subjecting it to a brief energy burst. That would imply that a single unit may manage similar memories, even all of them. It's a breakthrough in our understanding of memory. I couldn't be happier."

Jeff was silent, still considering the implications. If McLally was correct, then the microwave energy could alter a vast amount of information without intending to. It could imply that the brain's memory storage process is far more densely packed than anyone anticipated. Their tool was a cannon, not a scalpel.

McLally was wound up and continued talking and thinking out loud, pacing the room, occasionally with a finger pointed upward as he thought through their unexpected findings. "That fits with what we already know about learning and memory. Learning something similar is always easier, and the more a person is exposed to, the faster they can take in new information. Recall the adage about teaching an old dog. It fits! Jeff, we are really on to something!"

"But, Dr. McLally, it does bring up a concern about just how much memory will be cancelled each time our subject receives a dose of energy. We could wipe out years of learning in a scant millisecond."

"I see that your reasoning ability remains intact, Jeff. All you have lost is an unpleasant memory, one that you yourself selected, and seeing your reaction after reading your own document, it was of benefit to you to lose this episode in your life. Would you not agree?"

Jeff shrugged. It was, on the surface, true enough, but...there were many unknowns. "Yes, Doctor, I see your point, but you and I are very different. You are the opposite of cautious, which I am not."

"How so?" His question was curt, spoken slightly louder and more cryptically.

"The woman who just left, I remembered who she is," Jeff said.

"So?" McLally seemed to square off at him, his body language one of confrontation.

"So, a reasonable person, a cautious person, would not go there. The risk is very high if word were to get out."

"And I am in your hands? Is that what you are saying?"

"No. I would never do such a thing. Never. I'm thinking that if two people know a secret, that is one too many. You are only one part of the party."

"The woman scorned. It's true. I've seen that act before. Sorry I misjudged you, my boy. You and I have to stick together, you know." He made a hesitant move toward Jeff, then apparently thought better of it. "Now, are you prepared to offer our treatment to the young woman acquaintance you spoke of?"

"I have to give it some time. We should be sure that there are no late repercussions, don't you think?"

"Most assuredly, Jeff. You will want to be sure. Take your time." He seemed to want to say something more, make some additional gesture toward Jeff, perhaps buy his silence on this issue of the private liaison he had witnessed  this morning. "Jeff," he began, looking somewhat furtive this time. "I remember that you said that your female friend was bothered by a touch you inadvertently gave her."

"I placed my hand a bit too far below her waist. Her reaction was instant."

"So there is no physical contact between you two at the moment?"

"Not now or ever. She's been too traumatized for any."

"That would mean, I presume, that you are celibate at the moment?"

"True enough." He began to catch a glimmer of where McLally was headed with this line of discussion.

"Say, I've come into a wealth of that sort of thing recently. A trove of riches, you might say. Too much for any man, even me." His large eyebrows went up as the suggestion slid across the floor. Jeff saw it coming. He was about to be silenced by sex, cast-off secondhand sex, to be sure. Jeff waited for the rest. Might as well let him say it clearly.

"And, I was just wondering if a young healthy man such as yourself would be willing to take some of the pressure from me. Give me a break, as it were."

"I don't understand."

"There are several of my female fans who would benefit from seeing to your needs. It would be a relief for me to see this happen."

"Professor, I don't want to hurt your feelings, and I do think that I would rather enjoy the experience, but I must decline your offer."

"Tell me that you didn't just say no. Have you seen these gals?"

"Some, at least. Professor, I have a valid reason to reject that offer. I am in love with Gale. To consort with another woman wouldn't blend well with my conscience."

"Jeff, on the Continent, that is a rare feeling. Truly, you need to get past that old-fashioned sentiment about sex. Your feeling of love is commendable, and, trust me, you won't lose that at all by cavorting with other women. It just adds to life to have variety in your diet."

"See what I mean? We are different, Dr. McLally."

# Chapter 18

# *Relapse*

She looked worse in the morning light. Far worse. Bad enough that Sibyl was taken aback. Her first thought was to contact an Emergency Room, tell them what is going on, let them make the decisions. The night had been a bad one, and Sibyl had gotten nearly no rest either. Two nights in a row like this was taking a toll on her judgement. At least her own appetite was undiminished, even enhanced. She craved sweets of any kind, pastries, pancakes, or even candy bars. Gale, though, had not consumed any food, or even liquid, for more than two days, and it was showing. Gale looked out with sunken eyes, a glazed, blank expression on her face, and a languid, weakened movement of her limbs that indicated that she had given up, that there was no fight left in her. In the middle of the night, Sibyl started to understand why. It was that Gale was afraid to sleep, afraid of the gut-wrenching fear that returned with sleep when her brain would allow the visions to encircle her in full force. The screaming returned after only a few moments of rapid eye movement, the dream state. Gale would lurch to a sitting position, her hands trying to push something or someone away from her as her face contorted into a wretched ugliness. It was hard to watch, and Sibyl was also coming to the end of her own rope, her compassion limited by lack of rest and the repeated nature of Gale's problem. It was startlingly clear that Gale needed professional help, not just the kind understanding of a close friend. It was that or lose her, Sibyl realized. There was no return to routine for either one of them at the moment. They both were trapped in the apartment with Gale unable to go out, Sibyl unwilling to leave her alone.

Treatment might mean return to a locked psychiatry unit, a visit which could stretch out into limitless time, a trip of no return. Sibyl had heard the stories and shuddered at the thought. After checking her watch and taking a peek into Gale's room, she silently closed the door and stepped out of the apartment while tapping the number on her phone that she had committed to memory.

"Jeff! Thank God I caught you," Sibyl whispered coarsely, trying to hold back her tears.

"Sibyl? Is something wrong?"

"Sure is. You better come over here and give me a hand. Gale is sliding into trouble. We've got to do something today, or it'll be too late."

"I hoped that wouldn't happen. I'll be right there...fifteen minutes."

They stood over her bed looking down, and Gale, the sheet pulled up tightly against her neck, looked back. They could tell that she could see them, because her eyes followed their faces and eyes, but she wouldn't or couldn't talk.

"She looks very weak," Jeff observed, wanting to touch her, caress her, some physical contact, some caring gesture that would reach her, bring her some feeling of safety. He knew better than to attempt it. It could make her worse if she fought back.

"I can't even get water into her. Think you can try?"

"Gale. You must, must take in some food and water, or we will have to call in the medical people. We both are right here with you, you are safe, no one can hurt you. Can you please try for me? If you do, even just a little, I'll tell you what happened with our memory experiment on me."

She held his eyes but with no emotion from them, a doll's eyes, blank, too perfect to be real. Slowly, nearly imperceptibly, her head nodded a weak yes. Jeff repressed showing relief or emotion but nodded to Sibyl who scurried away to rattle in the kitchen, excited to at last have some help. She reappeared shortly with a glass of water, an unopened bottle of cola and a glazed donut. Jeff slowly and tenderly slid his hand and forearm behind Gale's shoulders and pulled her slowly forward while speaking softly to her. "We are going to try to get a little nourishment into you, dear. Just try for us, and I'll entertain you while you eat."

Jeff sat on the edge of the bed, his arm protectively around her shoulders and supporting her weight, leaning conspiratorially into her, his voice controlled, compassionate, loving, while plying her with little sips of liquid and small bites of confection. A little at a time, she was taking it in, robotically at first, but after awhile, her eyes looked more intelligent as she fought for return to the world. Jeff could sense when she looked at him now, she was taking him in, wanting to look in his direction, intentionally allowing his arm to be in contact with her without protest. It was the closest moment they had ever shared together, and for the first time since he had known her, he felt as if she might someday belong to him.

"Now that I have your undivided attention, I'll tell you what we've learned about memory and erasing memory. The first thing you should know is that it works, no question about it. And the process is pleasant, aside from a little lingering headache. A simple IV and suddenly you are awake, remembering nothing about it. I successfully erased an episode in my life that shouldn't have occurred but did. Except for my notes, written before the procedure, I can't remember anything about it. The first time I read my own report after the procedure, I was convinced that someone other than me had written it. After reading it again, I know I made the right decision on that one."

From behind, Sibyl interjected, "Doesn't reading it re-create the memory?"

"No. Reading a document creates a memory of reading about an incident, not the actual incident. They are not the same at all," Jeff said, not turning his eyes away from Gale's face. This was the longest time he had ever spent looking into her eyes, scanning her lips, her nose, her hair, memorizing every small detail, absorbing her into his soul. He would never hope to love anyone so completely again. She must be restored to normal at any cost.

"Can you erase mine?" Gale asked. Jeff tried not to flinch, recoil, stutter or hesitate when he answered. He was not ready in his own mind about the treatment. There were still grave doubts about it, about risks unknown and known. But there seemed to be no choice at this moment but to agree. The risks of any treatment must be weighed against non-treatment. In Gale's case, the balance was clearly heavily tipped toward treatment. The alternative was to surrender her to the old methods, a cascade of drugs, therapy and confinement. Could it be so simple that a burst of directed energy would have an immediate effect, an instant return to normal?

"Yes. I believe that it is the right thing to do. Erasing the memory of what eats at you will give you a better life."

"I wouldn't be expected to write out my..."

Jeff cut her short. "No, not that. I don't want you to go there at all. But, you have to understand that erasing the memory means that you have to recall it, however bad it is, during the procedure so that we can identify the correct spot. You have to go there again, but for the last time."

"I don't know if I can do that."

"You should know that I'll be holding your hand, exactly like now, and I'll be speaking to you, exactly like now. You'll be in control this time. You will know that it is only a memory, not a reality."

"How do you know this if you can't remember anything about your treatment?" Sibyl asked from behind.

"We discussed it afterwards. Only thing I recall about the experience was that it was pleasant. I awakened feeling good."

"There is no choice for me, is there?" Gale asked, her eyes wet with emotion.

"Sure, but this just may be the best one."


Dr. McLally answered on the third ring, his voice impatient as always. "Yes?" he spat out.

"This is Jeff. I need to talk with you, got a moment?" It was always wise to ask given that Dr. McLally could be in the presence of someone important or someone passionate. Either way, his attention would be diverted. Instead, McLally seemed to be glad to hear from him.

"Let me guess...you've changed your mind. I knew the thought of what you are missing would sink in."

"Not that, Professor. I have a sort of emergency on my hands. The young woman I am concerned with...you remember, don't you?"

"Sure. Your would-be girlfriend who is troubled. That one?"

"That one. She needs to go under the anesthesia and receive treatment. Today, if possible."

"You're absolutely sure that you don't want to have the medical people have a go at her first?"

"I'm sure and so is she. Can we do it this morning?"

"Without question. You can inform her and prepare her better than anyone. Do that and get her over here. I'll be waiting."

Sibyl was watching his face during the phone call. "Are you sure, Jeff? I know how you feel about her, but she isn't a lab animal to experiment with. You aren't going too fast, are you?"

"The situation is critical, isn't it?" he responded thoughtfully. "You are the one who called. Don't you think we should try and do something for her today?"

Sibyl took a deep breath. "I suppose so, but what do I know? This decision is yours to make."

"I'm aware of that. All I can say is that it appears to have worked on me."

Gale looked so completely helpless on the gurney, the big machine behind her was already humming in a threatening way. This was worse for Jeff than when he had submitted to treatment. Having to subject Gale to the beast was making him regret his decision. Dr. McLally had started her IV and was now typing furiously into his computer, occasionally looking over at them in a patronizing way. When he finished, Dr. McLally moved up beside the gurney and patted Gale's shoulder as a medical professional concerned about his patient.

"Now remember that once the anesthetic drug starts, you will seem to be a god, your choices infinite in returning to the past. It can be very addicting, and I know that from experience. You must do as Jeff tells you, and when he tells you to, you must go back to the place and time which so frightens you. No matter how afraid you become, remember that you can choose to leave at any time. You will not be there in reality, just in your memory. When you become stressed, we will be able to tell, and at that time you will receive another dose of anesthesia. This will allow you to regain control again. When you return to the point you wish to forget, just raise your finger like this, and we'll do the rest. Understand? Simple?"

Gale weakly nodded that she understood. But she didn't. She would be forced to return to the most profound memory of her life, one that she desperately didn't want to relive. She was not sure that she could cooperate. Jeff held her hand, occasionally squeezing it to remind her that he was there for her, but still, she could feel her pulse increasing in anticipation along with an increase in her breathing. She felt that she was about to die, that she was being tossed back into a cave of demons which would do their will on her. The last thing she remembered was Dr. McLally leaning over and administering the anesthesia.

# Chapter 19

## *Chased*

Gale banked, taking the wind on her outstretched arms and veering off at an angle to the ground, swooping in a controlled arc. Far below flickered her memories, each lighting briefly as she passed by, looking down with her head slightly cocked to one side. She was master in the sky, lord of her memories, each waited for her return, tantalizing her with pinpoints of delight, of people who were once known but long forgotten, of places, fond places, where happy moments were spent. The brief seconds of acclaim that each person so seldom attains were there also, beckoning her to stop, to relive vicariously a precious moment in time so long ago past. None could tempt her as she sought the one, the dearest one to her heart, with her eagle eye relentlessly scanning the surface.

At last, she banked, settling down, dropping out of the heavens, falling like a dart to the time she most wanted to see. At once, she was small again, standing in front of a lovely woman who stooped to push Gale's hair into place while rewarding her with a beautiful, enchanting smile of love. "There, Gale," her mother murmured, caressing Gale's face as she stood looking down with pride. "That's perfect now. Are you ready?" Her mother was elegantly dressed in white, the sheen of the satin brocade gleamingly perfect under her long, lustrous, blonde hair. Gale's eye was drawn to a glittering locket around her mother's neck. She had seen this precious object in the past but was never allowed to touch or play with it. "My mother's," she was told, "someday it will be yours." That day never came, and now Gale tried to see the detail of the piece as it swayed seductively from side to side, bringing with it a trace of her mother's perfume, a delicacy of flowers mixed with an aroma of jewelry and fashionable clothing.

"I think so," Gale could hear her own voice saying. A child's voice, higher pitched but clear. She looked up at her mother for more reassurance, realizing that she herself was also dressed in a flowing and extravagant gown, more suitable for a late teenager than a ten year old. She felt the pressure of her mother's warm hand at her back gently guiding her forward toward the brightly lit stage, in the strong light the painted guidelines worn to faintness by so many previous feet. Past the edge of the curtain, she could see a bobbing ocean of heads, waiting, waiting for her to appear. A last push by her mother propelled her forward to be captured by the attentive and expectant audience who immediately started a sustained applause. Gale glanced back at her mother who was holding her hands together, fingers intertwined, the glitter of rainbow lights from diamonds reflecting back for just Gale alone to see. Her mother formed the words, "Good luck, I love you," with her lips and her eyes, words that Gale had heard so many times before. She turned back to the audience and was partially blinded by the footlights, still perceiving shining faces, most fading out into darkness toward the back of the large hall. The conductor was looking at her, baton in the air, as the audience finally grew quiet. Gale swallowed, trying to moisten her mouth, trying to catch her breath as she looked blankly at the open air in front of her, her mind returning to the task at hand, the song she had rehearsed so many times that it was part of her.

"Gale, you must go to your bad memory. There isn't much time left," Jeff's voice came unwanted into her consciousness, breaking the trance, aborting her complete return to the living past. The scene changed abruptly, the noise of the crowd disappeared, and the long dark sidewalk appeared in front of her. Little available light was present, and she found herself walking with big strides, hurried strides, toward something, to a place waiting out there in the darkness. In the distance, a dog barked and a faint voice answered back. It was late, there were more blocks to walk, and she already felt tired. A small backpack dug into her back as she walked, finding her mind occupied by a memory of her mother. It always hurt to remember. Not that she didn't feel an intense flood of love and reverence well up, but because her mother was gone...forever. It wasn't just the loss of her wonderful mother who had always been there for her, with patience, supplying both gentle firmness and kind understanding. But also the circumstances Gale found herself in after her mother's loss. This foster home was better than most, but compared to her mother's waiting arms, not enough, not nearly enough. Something in her soul hurt when she thought of her, but she knew after shedding gallons of tears that no remorse, no longing for the past, would ever bring her back.

A light, a moving light, cast a long shadow down the sidewalk in front of her. She watched the shadow of herself walking flatly against the walkway, shimmering from side to side as the motor grew louder behind her. More than one motor, loud rough ones, the sound seeming to come at her from adjacent buildings, then the voices. "Hey! Babe!" one called from behind. Gale continued to walk, not wanting to look behind her into the blinding bright lights. There was laughing and the roar of the motorcycles diminished as they idled irregularly behind her. "I'm talking to you!" the voice shouted, followed by laugher, a guttural laughter, a vulgar, demeaning, coughing laughter. The motors drew closer, just beside the curb, the headlights now illuminating the street instead of her. "Want to party, little girl?" the man asked. Gale was frightened, she was alone and the street ahead was dimly lit with no commercial establishments to run toward. The motors stopped abruptly, replaced by sounds of rustling as several dismounted just behind her. Gale started to run, at first trying to be careful not to trip on the edges of the walkway, but then started to run with abandon, her backpack flopping from side to side on her back, slowing her progress. Behind her came the sound of running feet, the hard click of boots against the pavement, propelling large, heavy men toward her. A couple of motors started back up, moving toward her. Her pulse increased, her breathing neared maximum, and her heavy backpack started slipping off of her shoulder, interfering with her stride. The feet were right behind her, closing each second. "Wait, don't run from me. You'll be sorry," the voice said breathlessly, near enough to give her chills. Then the hands, finding her buttocks, pulling at her dress, dragging her backward. She felt her dress pull away as she started to scream, falling face forward onto the hard concrete.

"She's there," McLally said. He pointed to the screen showing her pulse and blood pressure, both doubled from her resting baseline. "Gale, listen to me, dear. We are going to let you get out of this trouble. It's just about over," he said into her ear as he pushed another dose of Puszithrin into the running IV. He stood back up watching the monitor, then smiled as her pulse rate started dropping. He nodded his satisfaction to Jeff, who was still holding her hand, his brow remained furrowed from when he had watched her writhe against her restraints, her neck veins standing out like blue ropes under her transparent skin. Her body started to relax as her pressure fell, as her memory was thankfully released.

McLally removed the syringe of Ted-Zeththrinoid from the radiation chamber and held it up to the light, tapping the cylinder with his nail to mobilize any bubbles before injection. He glanced at Jeff and nodded as he started to apply the isotope into the running IV.

"Gale, this is Jeff. You have twelve minutes. I will tell you when to return to your bad memory. You must return when I say. Nod your head that you understand."

Gale slowly nodded, tears running away from the corner of her closed eyes, the droplets glistening under the bright lights as they tracked like little rivers across her pale skin, forming a dark circle on the covers beside her head.

Her head was tilted back, her voice soaring into the air, blending with the symphonic notes from the orchestra just feet away and below her. It was a voice familiar, but yet, Gale had never heard her own voice in this way. It was an angelic but powerful voice, majestic but tender, youthful, full of promise of even better things to come. Gale sang but also listened to herself, listened to the faint gasp of the audience as they took in the singular beauty of the moment, the perfection of the young voice captivating each of them, making them yearn for more and more. Gale finished, holding the tone, shrill and high, as her breath slowly ebbed into nothing, and her voice trailed off to thunderous applause. She glanced to the side, offstage, as her mother held her hands over her mouth, her eyes reflecting the wetness of her utter joy. Gale took a deep bow while noticing that the conductor and the orchestra were applauding as well. She hurried, almost skipping, to the sidelines and took hold of her mother's hand, nearly dragging her back toward the center of the stage with her. The crowd got to their feet with the appearance of her mother who bowed graciously as she had done for so many years as prima donna of the opera. Gale and her mother locked arms, giving one more deep bow as the audience continued louder and louder, yelling acclaim and stamping their feet.

"Gale, return to your bad memory at once. There are only two minutes left. Now, Gale, you have to return now," Jeff said, close to her ear. Her face was calm, the tears had dried, and she wore a slight smile. Both men knew that Gale was involved in a pleasant memory and would not want to return to danger.

"Gale, you need to return now to the previous memory, or we won't be able to help you. Do you hear me?" McLally said forcefully while tapping her shoulder. A small frown appeared, a slight wrinkling of the forehead in horizontal lines while the eyebrows narrowed. Both men watched the pulse slowly start to rise along with her deeper breath. She stirred, attempting to move both her arms and legs as if trying to run.

"Tell us where you want to end this memory, Gale. Raise your finger, and it will be over," McLally said. They tensed, watching the timer which was rapidly approaching the radiation release moment. Seconds ticked slowly by as the PET scan started to move independently. Jeff checked the lights on the four microwave generators once again, reassuring himself that a release of energy would actually happen.

Slowly at first, then suddenly, her hand strained against the restraints as she attempted to hold her arm up, finger extended. She was panting for breath, her head starting to move back and forth. Jeff looked at McLally, concerned about her movement.

"Not to worry, Jeff, the computer will account for that motion. Time's coming up ...five ...four ...three ...two ...one.

They heard a simultaneous knock from the four machines, and the unit started spinning down. The firing was complete. Gale's arm dropped back to the bed as she sagged into sleep.

"Well, that went well, I'd predict. Better let her sleep it off, Jeff. She's had a rough day. Might take a couple of hours. We'll talk tomorrow and perhaps have her back in three or four days. Call me if anything unusual occurs. Okay?"

Jeff nodded that he understood, and together they pulled the gurney away from the unit. Jeff pulled up a chair to sit beside her for as long as it took for her to awaken.

# Chapter 20

## *Recovery*

Jeff held her hand with one hand, the other occasionally and affectionately stroking her forehead as she slept. Gale had a troublesome pale color, but her vital parameters, as displayed on the monitor, were normal. He wanted to touch her neck where he could see the pulsations of her heart traveling upward, but he restrained himself. She was as safe in his hands as she could be anywhere. His utmost wish was that she be returned to normal and be happy. Judging by her pacific face while under the Puszithrin, he was sure that there had been happiness, at least once, for her. She never told him very much about her past, her relations...even her previous friendships. Nearly nothing. All he knew is that she was a music major in grad school. A singer. He had never even heard her perform. Why he loved her was not based on shared interests or values. For his part, it was simply chemistry or even destiny.

He could see that her eyes were moving under the slits of her eyelids and that her pulse was rising slightly. She turned her head slowly toward him as if expecting that he would be there. Her eyes opened fully, looking into his face without blinking, her emotions hidden from him, as always.

"Have I been asleep?" she asked.

"For a little while, perhaps two hours. Feeling all right?"

"I've been dreaming...about my mother. Something that occurred long ago," She looked around the room, remembering where she was. "Did something happen to me?"

"We attempted to remove a bad memory. That was two hours ago. You've been asleep since."

"What memory?"

"I don't know the details, but it was bad enough that you could no longer function."

"You were here the whole time?"

"Yes."

Gale reached for him with a delicate hand, first placing it lightly on the side of his neck, then slowly slipping her fingers behind his head as she drew his face down toward hers. The kiss was full and long as well as passionate. Jeff pulled away but allowed her cheek to remain touching his as he looked into her eyes.

"Wow!" he said.

"You deserved it, and it was long overdue."

"Gale, I love you."

"Yes, you've told me more than once. I know that you do." She pushed him away, then grasped his hand to assist her to sit up. After she did, she stretched, reaching her arms in the air while arching her back. She turned her head toward him, aware that he would notice.

"That was a nice sleep and an even nicer dream. Thank you, Jeff," she said and spun around allowing her long bare legs to dangle enticingly from the gurney, She was watching him through slitted eyes, her face blank, yet inviting. "I'm hungry. Want to take me to lunch?" she asked, already knowing the answer.

Across the table from him was a woman that he didn't know at all. She had the same face and body but even they were different. The change in her was dramatic, fundamental. Her previous blank face was now alive with subtlety, a flicker of change each time a thought passed into her mind. Some of it was for him, some really her, the beautiful female emerging like a moth, spreading its lustrous and colorful wings for the first time. The way she moved her hands or head was different, seductive, compelling, and she knew it. He could see it in those deep blue eyes which held him in suspension, in disbelief and totally in her control. It was as if his independent will had been removed by her to be replaced by a robot of her design whose only desire was to be compelled to do her wishes. This wasn't just love, it was subjugation, submission, human slavery, and he wanted it that way, demanded it to continue. He couldn't take time to look at the menu, so enthralled and captivated was he by her presence. She smiled, and he felt his eyes wandering back and forth between her lips and her eyes, undecided on which was the most alluring. As if she understood, she reached across and laid her hand atop his, sending a shower of nerve fibers gratefully firing into his brain.

"You must order, Jeff. The poor waitress has been back three times!" she laughed, tossing her head back, flipping her long hair over the other shoulder then recapturing him with the magnet of her eyes.

"McLally is a damned genius," Jeff said quietly. His words bringing another smile to her face.

"What did he do to earn that remark?" she teased.

"He has created the most magical woman ever to live, that's all."

"You mean me?" she giggled, smiling more broadly. "I'm afraid that you are just seeing me for the first time, Jeff. You can thank my mother, not Dr. McLally. I do thank McLally for enabling me to have that dream about her, though."

"Tell me about your mother, your dream," Jeff asked.

"That was the most important day of my life, the most memorable, and also the worst. Seeing her alive and wondrous again was..." She broke off, her face losing its smile, her eyes fading as she looked into the past.

"Can you tell me what happened?"

"That was the night I sang at the opera. Just me on the stage. I was only ten, and my mother was standing in the shadow of the curtain about twenty feet away. It was her training and coaching and her contacts which made it possible. It was really her night, but she didn't want to take any credit. I pulled her out on the stage when I finished, and we took the applause together. What a moment it was." Gale sagged a little, reliving the moment in her mind.

"Incredible!" Jeff exclaimed. "Then how was that also the worst?"

"After the performance, they dropped me off home, then went to a celebration party. She never came back. She was murdered that night."

"Oh, no! How did that happen?"

"It was a carjacking. Both she and Sir William Greyson, the conductor, were shot by assailants. They never were arrested."

"What about your father?"

"I never had a father. Don't know anything about him."

"Mind telling me what happened to you after losing your mom?"

"There was no one to take me. I was a ward of the court and quickly assigned to various foster families. I had a small inheritance which was under management by a court-appointed attorney. The money is mostly gone now. The only reason I am in school was because of a guaranteed scholarship I won that night on the stage."

"I'm really sorry that I never heard you sing. You never told me."

"It's been rather curtailed. I think that the professors are disappointed in me. There are, occasionally, mandatory performances, but I have been passed over for the more glamorous parts. The ones that get all the attention."

"You know, I think that is all going to change from now on," Jeff said. It had to happen. This was not the same girl he knew this morning, he thought. Her personality, her appearance have exploded. "No doubt about it," he added.

"I was a bit out of it this morning," Gale admitted. "I haven't slept well recently for some reason, but I feel better now. The rest I had in your lab was good for me."

"I'll say it was." He didn't want to bring up the reason for her treatment. Perhaps she wouldn't remember the real reason. "Don't you think you should call Sibyl and tell her that you are feeling well?"

"I did call her. While I was in the restroom. I guess I forgot to tell you. She's waiting for us to come back to our apartment."

"She's a fine friend, Gale. There could be no one better."

"Except you, of course! Did you forget yourself?"

"I was hoping to be in a slightly different category." After he spoke, he saw the taunting glint in her eye and her sly smile. He didn't have to worry, not at all, not about that.

The walk back was pleasant, especially so since Gale was no longer adverse to body contact, and she made sure to demonstrate it by frequently giving him an embrace from the side. He watched her face, because he couldn't help himself, the radiance from her lighting up the world. It was the quick glances, the blank look she had worn, cast aside for an exchange of intelligence with one look. One little neuron, a few microscopic synaptic junctions and she had been born again. Pygmalion creates Galatea. Jeff felt pride, harmony and endless love, all swirling about, tying him to this perfect nymph who had been created this very day.

"Now tell me about yourself, Jeff, and don't be shy. I want to know everything, every detail, every female you ever looked at or thought about." She grinned at him with her perfect teeth, her eyes radiating her captivating soul.

"Not that there is much to tell. Compared to you, my dear, I have almost nothing to offer. I come from hardworking, honest parents who made a lot of sacrifices to send me to college. There were only a few dates I ever had, probably because I just matured late, and they all found me uninteresting. There was one, though, a dish, a real head-turner, and the most amazing thing is that she didn't even know she had that kind of appeal. The absolutely perfect woman. One who is beautiful but doesn't know it. At least until this morning. Now I'm really worried."

"You have proven yourself. There is no need to worry one little bit." She took his arm in hers and pulled him down for a brief kiss. "There. That should say something."

"My point exactly," he retorted.

In the distance and at first beyond their hearing range, there was a muffled rumble. Thunder moving in their direction. Jeff turned and stared at the street, straining at the limits of his vision, seeing no present threat. They continued to walk, chatting aimlessly, but the sound grew louder, more evident the source. A group of motorcycles was headed toward them. The sound was biting, harsh, distinctively from large two cylinder motors running un-muffled. Gale obviously heard the sound but appeared unconcerned, ignoring them as if she had heard the sound most of her life.

A quick look and Jeff could see the sparkle of several headlights, the light jumping as the motorcycles traversed the uneven pavement on their minimal shocks. Perhaps ten, even more. He eased Gale toward the far edge of the sidewalk and picked up their pace. She noticed and gave him a questioning look, glancing backward herself to understand his concern.

As he feared, the group slowed as they approached from behind, punctuated by occasional bursts of revs, the signal to be noticed. Jeff glanced over at the bunch who were looking back. It was amazing the similarity between the machines and the men. In some science fiction films, the troops are always identical, clad in white armor, alien-like visors covering their faces, if they had faces. But here, these were real men, all dressed alike, bearded alike, the same dirty rag encircling their heads. The machines were likewise identical in black and chrome. A ragtag army of sorts, but one with their ideals reversed.

"Nice dame," one called out. "Want to share?" The others laughed and revved their motors, wobbling back and forth because of the slow speed. Gale continued walking, not looking in their direction but with no hint of collapse.

"You trying to cause us trouble, buddy?" More laugher, more revs.

Jeff was looking for a place to duck into, even a nearby home, but there wasn't any hiding place close. In the distance, on the other side of the street, car lights came on, the car lurching forward quickly enough to squeal its tires. A blue light blistering from inside its grill, the light intense, blinking, just as the siren started. Thank God, a patrol car, Jeff realized.

The effect was immediate. In a roar, the motorcycles simply vanished, some forward, some to the rear, but the street cleared in seconds.

"You folks all right?" the detective asked when he rolled down his window. There were two of them in the front seat, both dressed in suits but both were large and experienced looking.

"You are a welcome sight," Jeff said. "I think the action was about to start."

"Yeah. We know about that group. That's why we were sitting there just now. From now on, you should choose a different route to wherever you are going. Stay off this road, especially when it gets dark. Next time we might not be around."

Jeff waved at them as their car slowly pulled away. That was a close call. He realized that he had started perspiring from stress. He reached out to Gale and turned her toward him.

"Are you handling that without problems?" he asked, looking for any sign of syncope or weakness. She looked perfectly fine and was smiling at him.

"Me? Sure. I had you, didn't I? I wasn't worried a bit." She smiled and tugged at his arm to go forward.

"McLally is a damned genius," Jeff repeated.

"You already said that."

# Chapter 20

# Chapter 21

# Gale Unleashed

Even Sibyl's jaw dropped after a few moments around Gale. She looked back and forth between Jeff and Gale, trying to understand what had happened. This was a different woman, one who only superficially resembled the girl who screamed in the night. Gale, the new Gale, was radiant, in control and independent. Yet, it was Gale, the same one that they both had loved, just more of her.

"Seriously, Gale, the treatment they did on you, didn't it hurt or anything?" Sibyl asked in her signature manner, half conspiratorially, half secret sharing.

"Hurt? Why not at all. I had a nice dream, and I woke up rested. And..." she said, pulling Jeff's face closer for a buss on the cheek, "I have him!"

"Well, isn't he the good luck man!" Sibyl said, sarcastically looking at Jeff, wonder, perhaps envy, on her face.

"We had a close call with a gang on motorcycles on the way over here," Jeff added. His comment caused Sibyl to inspect Gale more closely, recalling the last time. She shook her head in disbelief in the change. "A couple of cops saved us. They said to stay off that street," he continued.

"What are we supposed to do now? Fly home?" Sibyl sneered. "Can't they just arrest them?"

"Personally, I'm glad that they didn't wait until we were actually attacked," Jeff responded.

"But, Jeff, how are we going to ever get home safely again if a bunch of predators are stalking us?" Sibyl whined, her hands in the air.

"Easy. I'll be here to drive you to school every morning, and I'll drive you home every night."

"You dear boy," Gale said. "That's a real hardship on you. You sure you need to drive us for only a two mile walk?"

"I absolutely insist that I do, and I'll accept no refusals."

"I won't mind a bit. Can you take us to breakfast every morning as well?" Sibyl asked, the teasing voice inviting a rebuttal from him.

"Oh no, he won't," Gale interrupted. "The least we can do is give him breakfast here. Don't you think?"

### *Memory Research Laboratory*

Dr. McLally was finding her nearly irresistible, much to the irritation of Jeff who was trying to hold his temper. "My dear Gale, if I may presume to call you Gale?" he oozed, smiling his most alluring smile at her. "You simply look wonderful this morning, so much better than the day we met. Can you tell me what has happened since last you were here?" McLally reached out, pretending to take her pulse but wanting to have some body contact with her, to show his concerns and his interest at the same time.

Gale, glancing at Jeff's face and noticing the tension building in him, decided to have some fun at McLally's expense. Her eyes twinkled, and she cleared her throat, deciding quickly the best method. "Why, you dear, dear man! You've practically saved my life! You have transformed me completely inside and outside in a stroke of pure genius, and for that I am humbled and grateful to you. Is there any way I can show my gratitude, anything that will show you how I feel?"

Her comment was an opportunity that he couldn't pass up. She was radiantly beautiful, nearly magical, the way she sat, her back erect, her gorgeous cinnamon hair spilling over her chest on one side. But the most appealing feature was her penetrating intelligence, the intense magic of her eyes which said that she adored whoever was under their spell. No woman had ever cast a net over him as strongly as the one before him. He simply had to have her, no matter the costs.

"No! It's I who's grateful to you. It takes my breath away that I was able to serve your needs. You may rest assured that I am completely at your disposal. The fact that you were successfully restored to health by my methods makes all my years of research and hard work come to fruition. You are the shining light of my entire life, the one truth that marks the pinnacle of my endeavors. If I were to die at this very moment, I would die fulfilled and happy. And to realize that my first patient is so positively beautiful, so enchanting, so perfect, makes it all the more complete. You and I are destined to be friends, to chat endlessly about the change rendered in you, to celebrate the good times unleashed. If you want to favor me with anything at all, it would be your presence, little visits from time to time so that we might grow closer."

"Ah!" Gale sighed, taking his hand in hers. She leaned forward, bringing her face slightly closer to his, knowing that his eyes would pour over her as if she were water brought to a starving man. "I would love the chance to know you better, Dr. McLally. You are a most attractive man, for your age, that is. I hope that when Jeff reaches your point in life, that he holds it together as well as you have. You are my father figure from now on, since I never knew my real father. May I presume to feel that way about you?" She smiled sincerely, allowing her affection to spill over him. His eyes changed, imperceptibly at first, then seemed to sag as he looked away from her gaze and down at his slightly protuberant waist. A foolish old man, he realized. His time was past, over. To presume that this little flower would be sexually attracted to him was a fable of his own creation. His shoulders dropped, and he sat back feeling the weight of years for the first time. He looked at the broad shoulders and youthful face of Jeff and remembered when it was him sitting there, in the peak of health, limitless ability, the best years ahead.

"Yes, my dear Gale. I will be your devoted father, if that is what you want of me. Anything in the world that I can do for you, or Jeff, I will. Count on it." He couldn't help himself. It was the proper thing, after all. It wasn't just an admission of a lost, hopeless conquest, but a turning point. Gale, beautiful Gale, had made McLally realize his true place in life with a well-chosen word or two. He sat up straight, his head clearing with the realization of the onset of a new phase, a better one, all starting in one instant, the crest of a long steep slope had been reached, one that now descends instead of ascends, the meaning of life striking him with clarity. He was now only the caretaker for the next generation, enabling their ascension to control, relinquishing his place for theirs. It was the way it had to be, the way destiny and evolution dictates what must happen.

## Cassandra's Coffee Shop

Jeff watched her face as he poured her another cup of coffee. She was full of surprises as well as life. Her eyes flicked over the other customers, and Jeff briefly wondered if she was picking out another to dominate.

"You were surprising, to say the least. The poor man had it coming though, I must say. I never thought he would grovel like that," Jeff said. She didn't register any change in her face whatsoever, and he realized that either she didn't hear him or her mind was engaged elsewhere. "Gale? Are you still sitting here with me?" he asked and saw her focus come to his face, feeling the jolt when she looked directly at him.

"I just said what was in my heart," she said calmly. "He's on the right side of things now." She continued to look far away and inattentive.

"What are you thinking?" he asked.

"First, how my mother would be disappointed in me if she were here."

"You can't mean that. After all, you are in graduate school, in music, just as she probably wanted."

"She said I would be a star. If she were still alive, I would be."

"All right, I won't argue that point with you. What's number two?"

"I would like to see her again."

"Gale, why would you dwell on the impossible? We all would like to see our parents once more, but we have to accept what is past and go on."

"When you got McLally's treatment, did you revisit any memory?"

"Presumably, but that was the one which was erased. I have no recall of it at all. It's gone forever. Without my notes, I wouldn't have a notion of any of it."

"I visited my mother. I already told you about it, and the memory was very vivid. It was like actually being there. The entire memory came back, the sights, sounds, the smells. I even saw her breathing, saw her pendant swinging back and forth. I was there for real, standing in front of her, looking into her eyes. Her hand was warm against my back."

"Someone said that everything we experience is still retained as a memory. We just can't recall most of them voluntarily, but certain things will bring the memory back unexpectedly. It must have been a wonderful thing to again see her like that."

"Yes," she said quietly, then turned to him and put her hand over his. "I want to do that once more."

"You mean, go under the anesthesia...that?"

"Yes. I must see her again. Can't you do that for me?"

Jeff sat back and studied her face before answering. "During one of the lectures, didn't McLally admit that he has visited one of his memories repeatedly. Something to do with a sexual encounter?"

"Yes. I also remember him telling me that the drug is very addictive, " she recalled.

"Addictive not in the way of a narcotic. Addictive in that you will want to do it again and again. Just like you do."

"Can't you do this for me? Just this one more time?"

"But Gale. What is the point? You can't go back in time for real, and I also think McLally's warning about addiction should be taken. It'll never end once you start."

"I want to tell her about myself, get her approval. It would mean a lot to me."

"Think about what you just said, Gale. You are talking about a memory, not a dream. We can't even control a dream, but a memory is entirely different. It is what happened. You can't change a memory."

"While I was there, I felt that I could have said anything I wanted to her. I didn't try, because I was swept up with the moment. I'm sure I could talk to her if I have the chance."

"Well, I'm not sure that McLally would permit it. I couldn't do it without him present either. After all, he is a physician, and I am only a grad student. It would break the law, rules and common sense for me to attempt this alone. Another thing is that the drug is kept in a locked cabinet like all Schedule III drugs, and I don't have a key."

Gale thought it over and took a sip of coffee. "I'll have to ask McLally myself. He said he would do anything for me. Perhaps he will keep his word." A faint smile of satisfaction came over her face. She would have her way in this and was prepared to use any means.

"Please, Gale, don't rush into this and don't involve McLally. You handled him this morning, but he has a taste for women beyond normal. Don't give him any opening. You have experienced a metamorphosis worthy of a tale by Ovid. It's like the world will be at your feet soon. Please accept this as a gift, and let it go. No one, not even McLally, knows what will happen if you try to do what you just said."

"My mind is made up, Jeff. Is yours?" The way she put the question left no room for discussion. The matter was, in effect, settled. She would, by whatever means possible, revisit her memory.

Jeff knew that he was beaten. Acquiescence was the smarter plan. After all, what could it hurt? McLally apparently had had repeated doses, and he remained brilliant afterward.

"You win. I'll talk to him in the morning for you. Don't do this yourself without me. Promise?"

She smiled and affectionately patted his face. He was hers, entirely hers, to do with whatever she wanted, and they both knew it. "I promise."

173

# Chapter 21

# Chapter 22

# *Altering Memories*

## Memory Research Laboratory

"You're telling me that she won't take no for an answer, not listen to reason?" McLally asked with interest.

"Haven't you heard me? I was forceful about it, but that's what she wants, and she means to have her way. Do you think that it's risky or not?" Jeff said, becoming impatient at Dr. McLally's not immediately agreeing that the idea was a bad one.

"Some items you should know, my boy. As you may have heard me admit, I have taken the drug on several occasions myself and without supervision. There is a romantic partner in my past that I enjoy revisiting from time to time. She was the first, if you know what I mean, and the most intense. It is the only way I can ever have that feeling again. I never try to change anything, because it was perfect the way it was. No harm has come out of it that I'm aware of, and I don't feel compelled to do it all the time. Just once in a while."

"The other is altogether a bad piece of news. I had an assistant in London when we first developed this drug, and we lost him," McLally said solemnly.

"Lost him? Did he die or just wander off someplace? And what does that have to do with the matter anyway?"

McLally looked serious and rubbed his chin. An admission was coming. "It means that the lad took the drug for recreation and had to be confined to a mental institution. As far as I know, he's still there."

"Was it because he tried to change his memory or... was that the primary reason he became insane?"

"Truly, I don't know. We only found out after he was committed that a quantity of the drug was missing. The presumption is that he took it. The reasons only he would know."

"So it's possible that he didn't take the drug or that it had nothing to do with his illness?"

"Yes, possible. However, we should assume the obvious, that he took the drug and it caused damage to his brain."

"It's as I feared and as I told her. The whole thing is a bad idea. She should quit while she is ahead," Jeff said.

"Yes, but her idea intrigues me and brings up unknowns. It never occurred to me to try and change my memory while I was under. As I think about it, I wonder what would actually happen. It would mean erasing the memory and creating a new one in its place. When I mull it over, it's just a variation on what we are doing with the microwave energy. It might be that we were on the wrong track all along. What if we don't even need the microwave burst? What if a patient could just imagine a different outcome to an unpleasant experience?" He paused and sat down trying to paste the unknowns into a coherent theory.

"No, Doctor, it's not the same at all. The difference is a false memory over one that is gone. A lie, a memory of something that did not happen. To me, it's a very bad idea."

"I see your point, and it is a valid one. But, there is another view of it...no risk of damage because of a microwave burst placed in the wrong spot. Remember when we were treating Gale that she chose the spot herself. We couldn't tell what we were firing at. What if she had refused or wasn't able to pull herself away from a good memory? We would be responsible for erasing the wrong one."

"So. More unknowns. We know that we can erase a memory. There's me and Gale as examples of that fact. We don't know what will happen if she tries to alter one, if she can, under the drug. I wonder if she will just create a lie for herself that will be worse for her in the long run."

"Now, a question for you, my boy. Do you want to keep Gale as your girlfriend? If you do, I'd suggest that we give her what she wants."


## Memory Research Laboratory

"Please listen to me one last time, Gale," Jeff nearly begged. He leaned over the gurney, looking into her face from the head of the bed. She looked back up at him with a determined glare, her mind obviously rejecting any contrary opinion regarding her plan. Jeff could tell that his was a hopeless crusade, that his fears had been rejected by her. McLally was of no assistance, and Jeff could tell that the scientist in him wanted to find out what would happen. Gale meant no more to him that one of the rabbits from the pens.

"You cannot change the past by changing a memory, Gale. Let this idea go...can you do that?"

"I have to, Jeff. She was so real to me, and she's gone from my life. It can't possibly hurt to see her once more as she was. I can't make you understand, because your mother is still alive. All you have to do is pick up the telephone. My mother was my entire life. When I lost her, my world came crashing down on me. Is it too much to ask for only a few moments with her?"

Jeff stood up. It was of no use to argue with her, because it was emotional on her part, not logical, and if he were in her place, perhaps he would feel the same way. Besides, there was no proof of harm coming to her from this procedure. She might find what Jeff predicted was accurate after all. You simply cannot change a memory by wanting to.

"Then, visit with your mother, relive the past if you want. Just don't change anything." Her eyes were on him, and she clearly understood, but that didn't mean she agreed with him at all.

McLally was pushing the medication cart toward them, its wheels clicking over the joints in the ceramic flooring. It was time to start. Jeff took a deep breath, trying to calm his nerves and trying to think positively about this adventure. Gale was in control, it was her vision, her demands, and the risks were hers to take. Both he and McLally were only tools for her to use. He couldn't get over the change in her since her bad memory was erased. She would have never acted this way previously. Her self-confidence overwhelmed everyone she touched, bowing them to her will as she pleased. In a way, she had become the prima donna that her mother probably was. A true force of nature.

"Ready, Gale?" McLally said softly as he prepared the injection. He was smiling and happy. His star test subject was being sent on another mission, her findings advancing the cause of science.

"Ready and willing!" Gale beamed. She had no anxiety at all and was excited to see her mother once more. She held out her arm for the injection, a smile of victory on her face meant just for Jeff to see. This was going to be her day.

Hers was the joy of flight as man has always imagined it would be if he could only inhabit the body of a bird, even for a moment. Gale felt the air sweeping over her face as she glided effortless over the terrain. Only a small twist, a nearly imperceptible will to change direction accomplished what people had always sought. Gale glided under bridges, between tree limbs, soaring into the clouds, always with her eye on the ground, searching her memory cluttering the landscape, little points of light containing precious moments of the past. It was a powerful feeling to be able to determine to visit any one she chose. To, in a way, travel back in time, to see things as they were but with a perspective of ultimate knowledge of what would happen. To her, the feeling was similar to watching an old movie from the distant past where you know the plot, the actors and their personal lives, their deaths, seeing the movie in a different perspective, being able to look around at the details, already knowing what will happen. It was time to begin, and she chose, selecting the very moment she was looking for.

Josephine Randolph led the way through the crowd assembled backstage, all trying to give their best regards to both of them. Gale held her mother's hand, following her closely, at eye level with the shimmering white bow tied at the rear of her waist, something she never noticed or knew that she remembered. Various hands carefully patted her back on the way past toward the dressing rooms, all giving heartfelt praise of her singing tonight. She could feel the moist warmth of her mother's right hand and her rings which had sparkled so intensely. Gale realized for the first time that there was no wedding ring or engagement ring on her mother's other hand, the telling absence of a husband in her life. The journey seemed to take on the character of a trial, a gauntlet, and she found herself wishing for it to end. The crowd were all either old friends, familiar stage hands, or fellow performers, and Gale realized that her mother could shun none of them, nor did she desire to. It was part of the job, an inevitable result of fame.

At last, they reached the privacy of the star dressing room. Gale noticed the flake encrusted star affixed to the door on the way in. It looked worn, perhaps seedy, defiantly tacky, but nevertheless marked the most sought after door in the building. "I'm so proud of you, Gale," she said, tossing her lace shawl carelessly aside. "You were tremendous tonight! How did it feel?" she gushed. There were traces of lipstick on her teeth, and Gale felt herself wanting to wipe them away, to remove any imperfection from her mother's beautiful face.

"I was scared," Gale heard herself saying. She felt the urge to look in a mirror, to see herself as a child again.

"You were exceptional, my dear Gale. Now you understand why we had to practice for so many hours, don't you?" Gale just stood there, a child in an adult's world that she barely understood. Yes, she had sung as she was taught by experts, and the impact on the audience was powerful, but this was really her mother's voice singing through her. She was a bird, saying what she was taught, really not understanding the impact, the historical meaning of the words. She felt little pride in her achievement, only a sense of tiredness, relief that the ordeal was at last over.

A soft knock on the door came, unwelcomely, unexpected. Without waiting for permission, an older man's head appeared as the door slowly opened. He was smiling broadly at both of them, and Gale recognized the man as the conductor, the celebrated one from Europe, the one who would be murdered that very night.

"My fair young Gale Randolph!" he remarked, his hand in the air like he was still standing in front of the orchestra. "You are being celebrated tonight! What an achievement for us all, and to think that you are only a mite, a fledgling, not yet a woman, and still you have the world in your grasp. I bow to you." And he did, lowly and sincerely. He reached for her hand and kissed it noisily. Gale felt his saliva on the back of her hand and fought the urge to wipe it off using her gown. Sir William Greyson stood erect, his attention on Gale's mother, the real reason for his visit and his praise of Gale. Gale looked at each of them in turn and realized that there was more than professional praise circulating in the room. There was *amore* and a history, probably a future in the works. Sir William had breeding and cultivation all about him, it was his essence, hovering nearly like an aroma. And he was completely distinguished in appearance, a perfectly fitting tuxedo in highly finished fine wool and perfectly groomed and greying hair. In every way, he was the ideal image of a famous conductor, one sought after from every corner of the globe.

"Thank you, Bill, for all your patience. She is remarkable, is she not? After tonight, she'll be the talk of the opera world, even praised beyond anything I have achieved."

"No, I'm sure that won't happen. You have earned your reputation over many years. No fad will erase that. I'm sorry, my dear Gale, that you heard my comment, but I assure you it was meant as no rebuke. You truly were outstanding tonight, and it is my wish that you be seen by the cultured in Europe as well."

"Bill, if you will be patient, I need to change Gale's clothing. She'll be more comfortable, and then we can drop her off at my apartment before the party." Her words sent a chill into Gale. It was what happened, but what should not have happened. She, her mother and Sir William, didn't deserve that this day end the way it was going to.

"Mother, can I talk to you in private?" Gale asked. The words came from her own lips as if they had actually happened. She was standing there between two adults, looking at them differently than a child. She was taking charge, destiny was not going to rob her of her mother.

"A true star's wishes have to be obeyed," Sir William said, nodding his acceptance of her request. He pointed to the above and said, "I'll be waiting upstairs when you are ready. Take your time, my dears," then made his exit, closing the door behind him. Her mother sat down, waiting for Gale to talk and explain.

Gale stood, looking her mother level in the face, trying to choose her words carefully. "When I grow up, I won't become the singer that you hoped I would."

"Of course you will, Gale. Everything is in place for you. Tonight is only the start. I know what will happen, and it is everything you could possibly want. Why would you think like that?"

"I always wanted to know who my father was. Isn't it time that you tell me?"

"That has nothing to do with what we are discussing. He was never part of your life and will never be. He doesn't even know that you exist." Gale could see the quick painful reaction her words elicited. It was a deep pain, tightly and privately held in a fortress of her mother's mind.

"If something happened to you, I would have to be in foster care. Doesn't that make it important, don't you want me to have a place to live? Don't you think I should know who he is, that I have a right to know?" Gale was talking as an adult to her mother, the shock of hearing these concepts pour from a child's mouth took the breath from her. For a moment she was silent, stunned by Gale's questions.

"I suppose you are right but telling you won't change anything. You understand?"

"Yes. Who is he?"

"John Graymoure. He's now the principle violinist of the Los Angles Philharmonic, the concertmaster. Then, he was just a member of the orchestra, a chance encounter for us. A fling, to use the vulgar expression. He never knew. I had moved on by the time you were born, and I didn't want him in my life. Now you know what I never wanted you to know. I feel soiled, humiliated, and I'm especially sorry for you, my love."

"Thank you, Mother. Now listen carefully to me, because I know what I'm talking about, but you won't believe me." Her mother dabbed away a few tears with a lady's delicate handkerchief and sat back, now determined not to be surprised at anything her gifted child could come up with.

"You can't, simply can't, go to your party and leave me home."

"Well, my dear, you can't go to the celebration. There will be drinking and smoking there, and you would be underfoot and feel awkward. It's what we always do, don't you remember?"

"Yes, I remember. But not this time. You have to stay home with me."

"We have plans, Gale. Important people will be there."

"Don't you think that I'm entitled to something after working on those songs for more than a year? I feel that you owe me, Mother. You have to stay with me tonight. I'm counting on it."

"But, Gale. You'll be asleep, and besides, Nanny Becker will be there the entire time. It may be true that you deserve something special for tonight's performance, and Bill and I had in mind a quick trip to New York tomorrow. It was to be a surprise for you."

"Mother, if you go to the party, you will be killed. I know that this will happen. You have to believe me." Gale started spilling real tears and fell sobbing into her mother's lap. Her mother placed her hand on Gale's head and stroked her long hair, running the strands through her fingers.

"What made you come up with that idea? It's ridiculous, impossible. We are going in Bill's car and will be as safe as can be. That's not a good reason for me to stay home, Gale. I know that you want my company, and I am grateful to know that, but don't make up a story just to force me."

"Mother, please, I'm begging you," Gale sobbed, grasping her mother's satin gown and balling it into her clenched fists. Josephine Randolph was silent, while she patted her child's back. In one single night, the little thing had become a celebrity, learned of her mother's wayward life and was to be cast against her will into bed. No, it wasn't right. Gale was important too, perhaps more so than any of them. She did owe Gale. The child was so often alone because of her mother's career, and there was no father for her to depend on, thanks to a personal decision of her own. She realized that she had to start thinking differently from now forward. Gale would come first.

"All right, my darling, we will stay with you tonight. We won't go to the party and won't complain about it, and tomorrow morning we'll board the train and hello New York. Does that please you, dear?"

"Oh, yes, Mother! It's what I want. You can't leave me any longer. From now on, you and I will stay right beside each other." Gale heard her own small child's voice saying words that came from an older Gale, a wiser Gale, who had just saved her mother's life.

"I can see her eyelids fluttering. Isn't that a sign she is emerging?" Jeff asked, not taking his eyes from Gale's face.

"Soon," McLally said. "Gale. It's Dr. McLally. Are you ready to wake up? Do you hear me, Gale?" It took a moment, but Gale's head shook no. She wasn't ready, just yet. There was more for her to do.

McLally smiled at Jeff, understanding why he was anxious that Gale wake up before she could do too much damage to herself. "Might as well leave her alone for now, Jeff. She might not get another chance at this. It won't be much longer, rest assured."

Sir William Greyson knocked at the door with the tip of his walking stick. He wore a magnificent black cape with crimson lining which was gloriously exposed when he moved his arm. He stood away from the door beside Gale and her mother, politely waiting for Mrs. Becker to open it for them.

"Well, don't the three of you look handsome! Indeed!" she exclaimed, clapping her hands together. "And how did our young singer do tonight? Did she bring down the house?" Nanny Becker was always the same happy person, always willing to give another her respect and well-wishes. She was dressed up tonight, at least for her, and wore a smart black apron, trimmed with small white lace. It looked new, and Gale suspected that it had been selected for this special occasion. It was good to see her again. Gale had forgotten the portly woman who spent so much time trying to please both her and her demanding mother. She wondered what would happen to Nanny Becker when Mother died. Of course, that wasn't going to happen now. Things were different.

"Change in plans, Mrs. Becker," Josephine Randolph said as they came into the well-appointed apartment. It was on the second floor and, as Gale recalled, had an excellent view of the park across the street. The windows were not visible at the moment, because the heavy drapes had been pulled together. Gale had a strong desire to look out the window, to remember the scene that was just now dim in her memory. Sir William assisted her mother with her fur, handing it carefully to Nanny Becker, then took his cape off and neatly folded it before handing it off.

"Might we have a cocktail, at least?" Sir William suggested to Nanny.

"Well, sir, that will be my first task. One for Madam, also?"

"Yes, thank you," Josephine said and collapsed into the sofa. "And milk for the lady of the hour, the incomparable Gale Randolph," she said loudly, laughing a bewitching laugh, mostly for Bill who did notice.

"A quiet evening at home, eh?" he commented, while casting about for an ashtray.

"Don't dare light that thing in this house, Bill," Josephine scolded. "We aren't permitted to smoke around Gale. It sets a bad example."

He silently put his pipe back into his jacket and looked thoughtfully at Gale.

"My heavens, you impressed me and everyone else tonight, Gale. Outstanding, and that's no exaggeration from an old man. You will rise quickly. Perhaps too fast for your age. The thought concerns me a bit. Does it you, Josephine?"

"Constantly. But are we to hold her back? I think we must make the best of it. Her singing will open so many doors."

"Truly, it will. Also, the wrong ones."

"You will be there to guide her, Bill?"

"Indeed. If she will have me, that is. Gale, I have a serious question and request for you. May I?" Sir

William asked and waited calmly for Gale to respond. He was treating her with respect, as he had always done, never losing his even temperament even while rehearsals occasionally went badly. Gale didn't feel that she knew him, that is, really knew him. It was the formality of the man, his distinguished air, that kept him from being familiar. She didn't recall actually ever seeing him out of formal wear.

"Please," she heard herself say. To be asked in such a manner from someone so imposing was...well, enchanting.

"Gale, I would like to become your father. I am requesting that you approve of my asking your mother to be my wife. It would mean ever so much to me if you were to agree." Gale could see her mother cover her mouth with her hand. She didn't know it was coming either. She wondered if that had happened on the way to the party, or had she created the opportunity for it by changing what would happen?

"If Mother loves you, then so do I. You may ask her." Gale was delighted to have a father, any father, and Bill was certainly better equipped than most. Of course, he could ask. Such a delight, such a wonderful change from a life in the bondage of foster care.

Sir William Greyson rose to his feet and came toward Gale's mother, digging in his pocket while smiling down at her. He went to one knee and held up a large diamond ring which showered the room with color. "Josephine Randolph, will you give me the greatest triumph of my life and consent to be my wife?" It was a picture that Gale would never forget. A grand proposal of marriage right in front of her. Her mother threw herself into his arms and wrapped hers around his neck, drawing him forward for a passionate kiss. Her happy eyes looked at Gale over his shoulder, beaming her delight and her gratitude that Gale was present to see a cherished moment. Gale felt herself rushing toward them, her arms extended, her feet barely touching the carpet, then the feeling of impact, her head with their heads, all laughing, crying and happy together, a family at long last.

# Chapter 23

# *Back From The Past*

*H*er eyes opened suddenly, finding Jeff's face floating above hers. He could tell that she was conscious and thinking as her pupils swept his face, dilating and constricting as she took him in.

"Hi. How was it?" he asked.

"Simply wonderful. Thanks to you for making it possible."

"I'm glad to have you back. Frankly, I was worried. I assume you saw your mother."

"Yes, I did. It was like being there in person. I even noticed things that I believe I never saw before. A most pleasant trip."

"Feel like sitting up now?" he asked, taking hold of her hand to assist her. She sat up easily and brushed her hair back into place, while looking the place over.

"Where's McLally?"

"He had an appointment and left just moments ago. He stayed with us the entire time, making sure you were stable."

"I wanted to thank him."

"He'll be glad to hear it from you. You're supposed to return for debriefing in a couple of days."

"Great. Want to take a traveller to lunch?"

"It would be an honor and privilege. Want to invite Sibyl?"

"If you don't mind."

Sibyl watched Gale closely, listening to every word she uttered without comment. Jeff could see her intense observation and wondered what she was thinking, and if she was thinking the same thing he was.

"Can you tell us what happened, what your memory was about?" Jeff asked, anxious to get the detail out, to calm his fears that Gale had not done something that might have brought her harm.

"I visited a moment that I don't think either of you ever heard about. I repressed the memory for years, but I'm very glad I went back and saw it again. It was the night I sang at the opera to a packed house."

Jeff and Sibyl exchanged glances. They both remembered that as the night her mother was murdered. They wondered the same thing; why would Gale want to relive a horrible night?

"Did you hear yourself sing? Were you any good?" Sibyl asked convincingly.

"Not this time but I did on the previous trip. Not bad if I do say so. The audience surely thought so and so did the conductor."

"I never heard why you had such a rare opportunity. After all, not many ten-year-olds get a chance like that." Sibyl inquired.

"A couple of reasons: First, I must have been that good. Second, my mother and Sir William Greyson were in love."

"That would help," observed Jeff.

"Oh, and something new. I discovered who my real father is."

Jeff frowned. That information seemed out of place. "Let me get this straight. You never knew the man's name before?"

"No. It's a surprise to me."

"How did you find out his name?" Sibyl asked.

"I asked Mom. Actually, I forced it out of her. She said that it was from a fling, whatever that meant. It was embarrassing for her to tell me."

"Gale, was this part of your memory or something entirely new?"

"No, I remember that she told me. I must have previously forgotten about it." Her answer did nothing to quell Jeff's fears that something had changed. He began to sweat. Surely such an important piece of information as her father's name wouldn't have been forgotten. But how could she get this out of her memory unless she made it up, dreamed it up.

"Okay, Gale. What *is* your father's name?"

"John Graymoure. He was with a symphony orchestra on the West Coast. Where he is now, I don't have a clue."

"So you never heard that name before entering your memory?" Jeff persisted, while Sibyl busied herself with her smartphone.

"How long were you with your mother? I mean, what happened after the concert?"

"We went to my, actually her, dressing room, and Bill joined us there."

"Bill? You mean Sir William?" Jeff asked.

"Yes, we became closer that night."

"You told me previously that they dropped you off home. When did that happen?"

"No, you got it wrong. We all went home together. They didn't drop me off. I wouldn't let them." After he heard that, Jeff lost his color. This was as bad as he feared. Gale had managed to change her memory, overwriting what actually happened.

"Did all of you stay at your house?"

"Up until I woke up. It was the most wonderful thing I ever experienced. Bill asked my mother to marry him right there in front of me. We all hugged and cried. I'm so glad I got to be there again."

"You mean that no one was murdered? That nothing bad happened?" Jeff asked, his voice growing a bit louder.

"Murdered? What gave you that idea. No one was murdered. It was a happy time, and we were all together."

Sibyl spoke up, tapping her cell phone with her index finger. "There is a John Graymoure. He's the conductor of the Los Angeles Symphony Orchestra. He's about the right age. Says here that he has been with the orchestra for many years. Even a photo." Sibyl held up the phone and on the screen was a clear photograph of a middle-aged, but very distinguished man. He was very attractive and had light-colored, somewhat reddish hair.

"That's him?" Gale said and snatched the phone and stared at the little screen. "Think I should call him?"

"And tell him what? That you overwrote your memory and cast his name in there as your father? What do you think he would do or say?" Jeff asked.

"I don't understand your implication, Jeff. What are you talking about?" Gale said. The anger in her voice was clear. Her memory may have been altered, but it was now part of her. It was the way, in her opinion, that events had actually happened.

"Gale, can I ask you a question, please, before you get mad at us?"

"You can ask. I'm listening."

"When did your mother die?"

Gale blinked, her mind racing to find the answer but coming up blank. "I don't recall. As far as I know, she is still alive."

"Do you remember being raised by foster families?"

"Of course I do. You and I have talked a lot about it. What's your point?"

"Gale, if your mother was alive, why would you need foster parents?"

A stricken look came over her. A horror had revealed itself that she had never considered. "Those bastards!" she said with venom. "They must have run off together after that night and left me alone. How could they do that to me? Especially since they made such a show of including me, of asking my approval, of catering to me. Mother said a trip to New York was going to happen. It didn't. They dumped me." The agony returned to her face, and her tears flowed faster and faster. Jeff could hardly bear looking at her, while struggling with his own emotions.

"I don't understand any of this," Sibyl said, perplexed. "Jeff, what just happened? I want to know."

"While under the anesthesia, Gale was able to manipulate her memory to turn out better than the original. She remembers what she wanted to happen, not what actually happened. Now that new memory is the one she believes is true."

"Gale! You must remember telling me that your mother was murdered. I think it happened on the night you sang. I'm sure that's what you said." Sibyl was nearly pleading for Gale to remember the correct version.

"No, no, no. My mother was not murdered. She left me. I never knew until now. The truth was so bad that I probably repressed it and made up the story that she was murdered. That was better than being abandoned."

"Now I am confused. Jeff, what if she's right? What if she had repressed the events, and we were told the wrong story all along?" Sibyl tugged on his sleeve, trying to make her point.

"I don't know. It's confusing. Either way, it was a horrible thing to remember. I'm sorry that I let her do it. It's my fault for being weak, for feeling that I had to let her have her way or lose her. McLally was no help because he just wanted to see what would happen. He didn't care a bit that harm could happen to his patient. For him, it's all about science with no connection to people. He's a user."

"There is a way, Jeff," Sibyl said. "We can search out the facts. There are records of events like this.

We can dig around and discover the truth, and we have to do it for Gale's sake. She has to know the truth."

"I remember the events clear as a bell. What happened is what happened. I would swear that it happened just as I recall," Gale said forcefully.

"You remember me asking you not to change your dream, don't you. I elaborated on it at some length," Jeff asked.

"I do remember, Jeff, and I didn't do anything like that. I just relived what had happened."

"You wanted the memory to happen the way you described. You created it, forced it to happen. I'm sure that we will find that your dream isn't accurate. Your mother loved you. She would never have left you. Think about what you said. You were a budding star. Wherever she went, people would have asked about you and what happened to you. It would have been impossible for her to live apart from her little girl. It didn't happen that way, Gale."

"Then what, in your opinion, did happen?"

"Your mother and Bill were murdered by hoodlums trying to steal their car. It's tragic, but it happened. Over time, you became able to deal with her loss, and until you visited your memory to see her again... You can keep your happy memory if you want, but don't ever disparage your mother. She never did anything to deserve that."

"I didn't change anything, and I remember what actually happened. You are wrong," Gale voiced loudly and slumped in her chair.

"This bit about your father, Gale. We should check it out, because it seems to fit the facts. You and he even resemble each other," Sibyl said, holding up her phone with the image still looking back.

Jeff wiped his face and took a deep breath. "Sibyl, can you take it on yourself to find out about her father? I don't think Gale can take any more stress at the moment. I'll run down the facts about her mother, one way or the other. Gale, you are going home to get some rest. Deal?"

The girls agreed, Sibyl with relish. Gale had all the fight taken out of her; rest was badly needed, and she could no longer protest or disagree. She was confused, hurt, angry, but also felt lost.

"Jeff? I agree that I need to go rest, but for the life of me, I can't seem to remember where I live. I must be very tired."

## Chapter 24

# *Hunting For Gale's Past*

Sibyl dialed the number she found on the Internet after researching John Graymoure more fully. He was currently in residence in Los Angeles but only for the winter performance season which was over in two more weeks. She could be in luck and was holding her breath that her plan would work.

"Hello, my name is Gale Randolph, and I want to speak to your conductor on a personal matter."

"Yes...he was a friend of my mother's, Josephine Randolph, the opera star. I'm sure if you tell him that, he would agree to talk to me."

"No, I can't discuss with you the reasons, only Mr. Graymoure, I'm afraid. You can tell him that it's important."

"No, I'm not looking for employment or money or anything like that. This is not a solicitation, it's personal, like I've said."

"That would be fine. I'll be expecting his call then. Thank you."

Sibyl doubted that he would call back, and was angry at herself for being so easily dismissed by his haughty secretary. She still had not determined exactly what she was going to say to the man when and if they had a conversation. If what Jeff believed was accurate, then Gale could have invented a connection to John Graymoure out of thin air. But what if it were true? It would possibly mean a joyful reunion, or, on the other hand, John Graymoure may not want to find out that he has a daughter out of wedlock. Sibyl sighed. She would have to wait and see.

It didn't take long for Jeff to find what he dreaded seeing. A page rolled up on the screen which displayed a police photograph of the murder scene, the two well-dressed victims lying on their face near the curb. The light from the cameraman's flash lit up Josephine Randolph's white satin attire in a smear of blinding light, blurred in disarray. The body beside her was hard to see clearly because of his dark dress clothing. The headlines shrieked of the tragic loss and the senseless murder of two of the city's most prominent citizens. At the foot of the article, the writer mentioned in passing that Ms. Randolph's next of kin was her daughter. Her name was omitted. One witness stated that several motorcycles were seen in the area near the time of the attack. Police had declined to comment at the time the article was filed.

"Gale changed her memory. She overwrote it with her wish to change what happened. There is no doubt." Jeff said aloud, snapping closed the lid to his computer. He sat there in the lab where he had allowed it to unfold, the place now looking different, pitiless, pompous, brutal science wrapped in its glossy white coat. He didn't know what to do, or if he should do anything but try and convince Gale that her mother never deserted her. But it was from bad to worse. She fervently believed her mother may still be alive someplace. Convincing her of known facts will once again subject her to the news that her mother was murdered, as if the information were fresh, that it had just happened. In some ways, one truth was as bad as the other, but to hold equally horrible views simultaneously, was too much for her to have to bear.

A door shut and Jeff looked up to see McLally just entering, nodding politely at Ms. Peterson on his way past her cubbyhole. His dark blue pinstriped suit contrasted with his small yellow carnation boutonnière, and his highly polished shoes flashed back the specular white light of the lab. He gave a quick wave to Jeff as he passed by and hurried into his private office, closing the door, an aura of men's perfume cascading into the lab.

*Hiding from me won't work*, Jeff thought and clenched his jaw. *He needs to know the malpractice we had just perpetrated on Gale*. He jerked to his feet and made long strides across the room, opening McLally's door without knocking. McLally was on the telephone, arguing loudly with someone on the other end. He absently waved Jeff back, his brow wrinkled with concentration on the other conversation.

"I'll sue you right back!" McLally said loudly, slamming the receiver back down with force. He stood, looking from side to side as if in a state of not knowing what to do. He pulled down his vest and turned toward Jeff, anger on his face. "Don't you recall seeing 'Private' on the door? Didn't your mother teach you to respect privacy?"

"I thought that applied only when you had female visitors," Jeff tossed back. "This is too important for formality. We have a problem."

"Yes, we do, and it has nothing to do with your paramour, for I assume that is what brings you in here unannounced. For your information, we have an issue which might bring my research to a halt before we get started. That would be an end to both of our futures, in case I have to make the point so clear to you."

"That and our poor judgement," Jeff remarked.

"Just what are you referring to?" McLally asked, placing his hands on his hips.

"Gale did just what I feared she would do. She changed her memory to suit her while under the Puszithrin, erasing the old one. Now she has a false memory of something that never happened."

"Well, my boy, is her version better or worse than the original?"

"Better, in that her mother wasn't murdered that night, worse because she thinks her mother ran off to Europe, abandoning her to foster care. Now she hates her mother."

"Just tell her the facts. Sooner or later she'll have to believe you."

"It's not that simple. She believes her memory because for her, it happened that way. The more I tell her that it's false, the more confused she becomes. We have set her up for a complete breakdown. You should know about similar diseases. Wouldn't her problem be called schizophrenia?"

"Indeed," McLally said and sat down, staring at the telephone. "I can't think of a solution to this problem. None of us knew what would happen when a person tried to do something like this. It's going to take serious study before we can act. I suggest, for now, that you attempt to avoid the subject. The girl is not schizophrenic, she just has one incorrect memory. The rest of her is undamaged."

"Not entirely true, Dr. McLally. She forgot where she has been living. At first, I thought it was connected to the medication, fatigue or preoccupation, but I could tell when I took her home, it wasn't. She had no recall of the place. It was like she had never been there."

"Ah. It could mean that she managed to overwrite other memories. Interesting. Still, we can't change that now. She will relearn that information so there is no actual harm done...so far."

"So you and I just sit back and watch?" Jeff asked.

"Of course. That's what scientists do. Remain detached, Jeff. Learn, listen and profit."

"We are talking about Gale, McLally. She isn't a lab rodent. I love her," Jeff yelled.

"And so you do. Makes little difference, does it? Since we can't change what happened to her, then we learn from the event. You do see my point?"

Jeff realized that however detached McLally was, how little he cared about Gale and her problem, he was correct. There was nothing which could be done at the moment for her.

"The bigger issue, Jeff. Care to hear about it or has your anger overwhelmed your intellect?"

"I'm listening."

"Two of my former associates in London have rushed to obtain a British patent on the drug formulations we use, leaving me out. It was a project we all worked on together, and to leave me dangling this way is revolting. It might mean that we could lose all funding for our research."

"I don't understand. This is the U.S.A. Don't we have a separate patent system here?" Jeff asked.

"True, but it becomes a legal quagmire at best. I'll have to go to London and engage a barrister to represent my interests before it's too late." He checked his watch and drummed his fingers on the desk, obviously deciding how to proceed. "Here is what we have to do," he said while standing up and retrieving his key ring. "I'll leave you with the keys to my private office and the drug cabinet so that you can continue the research we have ongoing. Ms. Peterson will take care of any appointment changes I have and refer any necessary calls to me, the others you can handle. Should take no more than six weeks. Is that satisfactory?" He pulled the keys in question from his ring and slid them across the desk.

Jeff took them and turned them over in his hand, thinking for a moment before answering. "I guess I have no choice, do I? What about Gale Randolph?"

"Yes, what about Gale Randolph? What is your question?"

"We were going to work on the problem we created for her. Have you forgotten?"

"As far as I can see, there is no solution for her situation. We accomplished a miraculous recovery for her, and then she stepped off the bridge herself, in spite of warnings from both of us. The responsibility is hers, I'm afraid."

"What if we tried to erase the false memory?"

"This time it would be more chancy than the first time. I don't think you could be sure that she would cooperate in losing a memory that she wants to keep, even if it is only an illusion. She would likely want to continue her new life while under the Puszithrin, and we would be standing there helping her do it."

"I see your point," said Jeff, thinking about Gale, her happiness when she first awakened after her dream, the smile she had when she talked about her mother. Given another chance, probably Gale would gladly continue her fantasy, even if she knew that other memories would be lost. Jeff stood, realizing that he and Gale were on their own from now on. He wondered if he should discuss his thesis with the Dean, perhaps change advisors, give up memory studies, start over.

"Well then, there is nothing more to discuss, Professor. Bon voyage and best of luck. I'll take care of things on this end." Jeff offered his hand for a shake.

"I'll be as close as the telephone, my boy. Be sure and keep me in the loop, as it were."

# Chapter 25

## *"Tell Me What I Want To Know"*

"Bob Beer Beat" the sign said above his head. Cute, he thought, no doubt the clever idea of one of those big dumb greaseballs inside. Peters shook his head and pulled the dirty door open, feeling the urge to disinfect his hands. He took off his shades once inside and looked around, still in the doorway, his blockish frame canceling the light from behind. The thumping music suddenly stopped, and all the heads turned toward him like so many chickens, looking him over, trying to determine why a well-dressed black man was daring to venture into their private world, and what he could possibly hope to achieve.

Peters slid the glasses into his jacket vest pocket and glared back at them. They were gathered in staggered small groups, mostly men, but the occasional bright red or straw blonde head of a woman was also present, creating contrast and color. All the men sported facial hair, some with long scraggly beards which were mostly kept to length by flapping in a wind created while astride a motorcycle seat. It was a sea of denim, leather and hair, supported by black squarish boots trimmed with bright metal.

"Something you want, friend?" the barkeep asked. Peters turned his attention toward the man, noting that the folds of his neck extended over his shaven head to his forehead. If he actually had a neck, that is. His face was more spherical than vertical and adorned with heavy lids and jowls, affirming an initial assessment of beer-acquired facial obesity. A muscular tattooed arm pretended to swipe the bar surface clean while they momentarily locked eyes.

Peters ignored him and defiantly moved further into the bar, his jacket hanging open to allow rapid access to his pistol, as he searched the hostile faces looking back at him. He was looking for one in particular, one that he had previously seen while on their aborted stakeout of the motorcycle club. One that had gleefully destroyed his car with sledgehammer blows while assuming that darkness would hide his identity. Peters was looking for a unique individual, not using facial features which were mostly obscured by hair, but a pattern of reflective metal studs he had seen on the man's clothing and boots, marking him to his friends but also to an observant detective looking down from the second floor.

The muttering and low-voiced threats started as a hum as the men shifted in their places, deciding collectively if they should chance a confrontation or even a sudden assault on this invader. Instead, what kept them stationary was something intangible that radiated from this well-dressed but thickset black man. He wasn't afraid. Not in the least. It was his confidence that persuaded the crowd to hesitate, to demure, to keep their place. The invader was dangerous, there could be no doubt, and what was waiting outside the door was another question entirely. Was a swat team lurking, waiting for any action to start? Would the next man through the door be holding an automatic weapon and be willing to open up with it, indiscriminately firing into the room? There had to be more than one man or else this lone wolf had a death wish. They held their place...for now, as Peters started moving among them, looking each one over from head to toe, deciding on his choice, a praying mantis wading through a colony of bees.

"You. Stand up," Peters said loudly to one. The man looked back and forth at the others, his cohorts, his kin in crime. They looked back, unsure of what was happening, and continued to stay seated. Peters didn't move or look away from his selection's face. His intent glare could not be ignored, and the threat of some alternative he had in mind hung in the thick smoky air. The man slowly, defiantly, came to his feet, rising to a height just above the top of Peters' head. Physically, they were similar, both thick with muscle and intimidatingly large. Detective Peters had the edge in training and experience and was clearly in command, his demeanor carrying the weight of inevitability, even invincibility, which held the otherwise violent and street-wise gang at bay.

"Turn around," Peters commanded, yelling his instructions into the man's face as if his hearing was impaired, or his intellect. The fellow hesitated, not wanting to comply in front of his buddies until a well-placed push from Peters spun him around. The handcuffs went on so quickly that it was hard to see it happening. As Peters started pushing the man forward toward the door, three similar men stood, squaring off as if they meant to become involved. Peters let his hand drop away from his suspect and stepped back, turning to face them. He wore a slight grin while he stood waiting for the first move. It was simply too dangerous for the gang members to protest. They, and everyone watching, knew that Peters relished a confrontation, wished for one, every fiber of him ready to strike out lethally. The men slowly sat down, clearly seeing that they had no other choice as Peters marched his man out the door.

"Where are you taking me?" he asked from the backseat. It was uncomfortable sitting on his hands, and he could clearly tell that the car was headed away from town, not toward the police station. "Hey, who are you anyway?" the man yelled, becoming more and more agitated by the silent Peters who was ignoring him. "Hey! do you even hear me?" he shrieked in near panic mode. His imagination was running away with possibilities, but one thing he knew for certain was that his fate was in the hands of the driver.

"One more scream and I'll stop and break your face," Peters said in a level tone, the truth evident by its dispassion. The car moved inexorably forward, finding, at last, a narrow winding road through the trees. When it finally came to a stop, Ray looked around hoping to see another person, a house, anything, any trace of help. They were alone, and when Peters opened the back door, Ray thought he was going to throw up.

"Out." A simple command giving no alternatives caused Ray to jump as if he had been stuck by the switchblade he carried tucked under his belt.

"Listen, man, you've made a mistake! You got the wrong guy! Please don't kill me! Please!" the whining grew louder as Ray realized his true peril. The first blow was sudden and vicious, perfectly aimed to impact the bottom edge of Ray's sternum and angled upward to forcibly evacuate his lungs in an instant. The pain was blinding, and Ray found himself temporarily unable to breathe or cry out as he fell face forward into the moist soil. He gasped for air like a fish out of water as bit by bit he was able to get enough oxygen in to diminish the sensation of dying. He spat the dirt from his mouth and rolled to one side, about to begin pleading again, when Peters' pointed shoe impacted his testicles. Never had he experienced such pain or terror. For the first time, he knew what one of his countless victims had felt as he and his fellows methodically beat them into unconsciousness. He knew what was coming next but couldn't move or protect himself, just squint his eyes and tense as Peters' kick made contact with the kidney area of his back. In some ways, this was the worst yet, the pain making him briefly lose consciousness. He awakened as Peters dragged him to his feet with one hand and slammed him against the car fender.

"I think you are ready. Do you think so?" Peters asked close to Ray's face.

"Don't kill me, man. I don't even know you," Ray whimpered.

"You beat my car into a lump, and I watched you do it. Now, I feel better about it, but if you don't answer my next questions you will find that I was trained by the army to extract information from enemy combat soldiers. I can make you tell me anything. If you don't or if you lie to me, I'll be glad to show you what I learned."

"You aren't going to kill me?" Ray asked, his lip trembling with hope.

"I haven't ruled it out. This would be a good spot, don't you agree?" Peters mocked him by trembling his own lip.

A hint of recognition came to Ray's face. This was Merchant's doing, he remembered. The stakeout car they had attacked on Merchant's orders. This was the cop, Merchant had said, who shot Chuck in the face and had chased him for miles. This cop was the reason that they had abandoned the converted filling station and scattered like flies. He felt the bile well up into his throat.

"What do you want, man?"

"Did you help gang rape a girl in Rockford two years ago? Before you answer, be sure that you tell me the truth, or you have only had a taste of the pain I can cause you."

"Two years ago? Listen, man, I was in the joint two years ago, you can check. Call your dudes, and they'll tell you. I just got out eleven months ago. It wasn't me, man." Ray felt better, now. If this was what it was about, he had nothing to worry about.

"I will, you can be sure. One more question." Peters pushed Ray's head back into the car window with a *thunk* to make his point. "Where is Merchant?" Peters' hand grabbed a big wad of Ray's greasy hair and pulled his head backward, forcing Ray to look straight up while he answered.

"Man, they know you took me. If you get Merchant, I'm done. They'll know it was me."

"You have three choices, *man*," Peters said, spitting out the last word with emphasis. "You can die right here, or they can kill you later. Or, you could take off and start over some place new. Get a job, a bath...that sort of normal stuff. Seems to me that the third alternative would be the best. What do you say?" Peters jerked Ray's head backward sharply, causing him to cry out.

"How do you know I'll tell you the truth?" Ray said, analyzing the possibility that this cop was going to kill him nevertheless.

"I'm going to handcuff you to a tree right here. If I can't find Merchant, I'll just let you rot there. In this area, animals will make a night meal out of you. If I find Merchant where you said, I'll come back and set you free, even buy you a bus ticket out of town."

"I'll tell you, I swear that I'll tell. But Merchant is terrified of you. When he hears that I was taken by a big black guy, he'll take off. He could be gone when you get there."

"Then you better hope that I'm fast enough to catch him. You're wasting our time. Talk!" Peters yelled into Ray's ear.

"OK, man. They got a little farmhouse ten miles out of town. Route Three. The Newman farm. About ten of our buddies are there with him."

"How did he come by this farm?"

"Donno, man. He just has it." The last word wasn't out of his mouth before another punch landed in his solar plexus. This time, the crack of a rib was audible. As Ray regained consciousness, he felt his face dragging against the soil and fallen leaves as he was moved by some unseen force attached to his feet. The same force pulled one of his arms straight up and a soft click welded his hand to a thick tree. His eyes searched the out of focus forest as a car started, the sound of the tires and motor receding slowly, as the voices of the forest returned.

# Chapter 26

## *What To Do About Gale*

"How is she this morning?" Jeff asked as soon as Sibyl opened the door. He pushed past her before she could answer, looking about the room wildly, searching in vain for Gale's face.

"It comes as waves. At times she seems normal, the old Gale, or I should say, the new old Gale, then, unexpectedly, she will collapse, hiding her face in her hands and weeping uncontrollably. Her fear or anger, or whatever it is, comes out of the blue. She can't function, can't talk about it and can't attend classes. And neither can I. This can't go on much longer."

"Is she still asleep?" Jeff asked, anxiously looking toward the closed bedroom door.

"I doubt it. Go on in, Jeff, see what you can do with her."

Jeff softly knocked on Gale's door, and when there was no answer, slowly pushed it open. She was still in bed, the covers draped in haphazardly crazy patterns, indicating a fitful sleep, if any. He approached her bed on tiptoes, looking for any signs of wakefulness.

"Jeff?" she asked with closed eyes. Her slender arm elevated toward him, and he took her hand with both of his. She turned toward him and opened her eyes.

"Why would they abandon me like that, Jeff? What did I ever do to deserve that?" She spoke with parched lips, her voice scratchy and dark. Jeff wanted to pick her up as if she were a little girl and rock her, soothe her troubles away, convince her of how wonderful the world was and, most of all, how much he cared for her.

"Gale, we need to have a serious talk. Come on and get up. There's coffee waiting on the table." She looked past him, seeing in her mind's eye only. He pulled her to a sitting position while looking around for a robe or gown. She turned and let her feet and legs dangle off the edge of the bed, folding limply at the waist. Jeff noted that her spine was visible along the curve of her back, and her posture indicated muscle tone loss, even early wasting, or dehydration.

"Come on, dear, stand up, and I'll help you walk," he said, wrapping her in an available sheet, one arm free. Together they made it to the breakfast table where Sibyl had already placed a fresh cup in front of her chair. Gale wearily looked up at the two of them with her eyes, her head remaining in a low, submissive position. Jeff was silent as Gale slowly consumed the hot liquid, waiting until he saw her attention returning.

"Gale, I want to tell you something, and I want you to listen carefully to me," he said. She lazily looked in his direction, then back at Sibyl who was sitting across from her, attentively watching her face. He continued, "I can tell you what actually happened that night was different than you remember. Your memory has been changed to a false narrative. What you recall so clearly did not happen. Can't you understand that?"

"But, Jeff, I remember it so well. It has to be true," she weakly retorted.

"It is not true. You invented it like a dream, and you just believe that it's true. Tell you what. You try real hard not to think about it at all. Just go on with the present as you find it. We are here for you right now, and we are real. Come back and be the happy, delightful girl you were just days ago. The one who had the world by the tail, the girl who captivated every person she met. Does it matter any longer what happened in the past? You have overcome all of that long ago. You dealt with it and even more monstrous things that you can't even recall. Just think, you and I have the rest of our lives to be happy and be together. Can life get any better than that?"

Gale sipped her coffee and looked at him with sheepish eyes, reflecting the confusing array of competing thought processes, each fighting for supremacy. She put the cup down, her face a mixture of innocence, acceptance and affection. "Yes, Jeff. I'll try. That's all I can do for now." She reached for his hand and with her other for Sibyl's. "Thanks to you both for always being there for me when I need you."

"Now can I go back to class before they kick me out of this place?" Sibyl asked.

"How about you, Gale? Are you up to returning yet?" Jeff asked.

"I didn't get much sleep. But I'll try."

"And, how about you, Jeff. You ready to give up this soap opera of ours and be a student again?" Sibyl asked.

"Me? That's a question hanging in the air for the moment. Dr. McLally has flitted off to England leaving me to my own devices. The entire project is in question...there are legal issues."

Gale perked up, searching his face in earnest. "What does that mean? Have you been kicked out of your lab?"

"Not yet. He left me his keys. I'm to continue the research without him for now. There's plenty to do, for sure."

"You mean the keys to everything? You can just do what you want?" Gale asked. Jeff felt a prod of uncertainty of where she was going with her pointed question.

"Well, I already had keys to everything but the drug cabinet and his private office. So yes, everything."

"Did he leave his harem of women friends to you also?" Sibyl teased. "Did you check his office and see if any were still in there?"

Gale raised her eyebrows and waited for his answer.

"That's the first thing on my to do list. He entrusted me to keep all his friends happy. I can't let him down."

"Just try and you'll be sorry," Sibyl retorted.

## Dean's office, 2:30 P.M.

"He's ready to see you now, Mr. Andrews," she said and held the door for him. Dean Towles was standing beside his uncluttered desk, studying a manila folder Jeff assumed contained his documents. Light from outside poured through the floor to ceiling window at Dean Towles' back, creating a silhouette of the man, the forward side hidden in dim light. He was dressed in stereotypical tweed with his vest unbuttoned, displaying an ample belly. For some obscure genetic reason, his forehead was unusually low, the hair line only perhaps two inches from his eyebrows. The persona created by his somewhat Neanderthal appearance, coupled by his typical aggressiveness, made meeting with the Dean always memorable.

"Sit down, Andrews," he said without looking up. Jeff sat in the oversized leather wing chair, perched upright instead of inappropriately lounging in it. He always thought that the chair was oversized purposely to make its occupant feel small and vulnerable. Jeff did. The dean shuffled his papers, studying each in turn and each thoroughly. Finally, he tossed the folder on his desk and sat down, swiveling into position behind his desk.

"And what brings you here, Andrews?" he asked.

"I am in the graduate program as I'm sure you know. I'm considering changing my advisor and going in a new direction."

"Why?"

"Our research has reached a possible end point due to unforeseen legal issues. I don't want to be held in limbo waiting on some court to decide my future."

"Are you aware of how much the University has invested in your project? It's in the millions. Your advisor was, and is, one of the most sought-after investigators in his field. The Board of Regents fully expects him to win a Nobel and shower this institution with well-deserved publicity and praise. You were chosen from a flock of candidates for academic merit and because you have shown promise in other ways. The news I hear from you this morning is disappointing. At the first sign of difficulty, you want to turn tail and run. I don't look favorably on you for this, Andrews. For your information, this squabble is taking place in another country. By the time the issue is settled here, you will likely be a grandfather. None of that will affect your ability to acquire a doctorate. Your request is denied. Of course, you may change institutions, if you like, or be satisfied with a masters. Your choice. Anything else?"

The tone the Dean had taken with him was painfully administered as well as final. Jeff had considered telling the Dean about the poor judgement the brilliant McLally displayed when he allowed Gale to return to her memory. He also wanted to tattle that McLally had an encounter with the Dean's vivacious daughter, likely more than once. Instead, he just sat there and heard himself say, "Thank you, Dean Towles," got up and left, quietly and humbly.

*That went particularly well,* he thought sarcastically as he trudged across campus toward his research lab. It was an impulse, a regrettable one, and he found himself hoping that word wouldn't get back to McLally about his treachery. After all, McLally had helped cure Gale of her first problem, and she had created the second all on her own, in spite of being warned by both of them. Of course, he wouldn't have actually told the Dean about his wayward daughter. Besides, the most spectacular and risky tryst of McLally's was with a married woman, the wife of one of the Regents. That story would start a small earthquake, if told.

His long legs ate up the distance quickly, and he soon found himself back at the lab. The outside door was locked, and he realized that Ms. Peterson would be gone the rest of the week, electing to take her vacation while McLally was away. The lab belonged to him and the animals alone. He went into McLally's office and sat in his chair, looking over the desk confidently and nodding to an imaginary Jeff who had come in with a small but easily solved problem. He took the key he had been entrusted with and opened the center desk drawer. In there were keys to the locked drug cabinet containing the critical research drugs which were in dispute. Jeff wondered if any additional drugs would be available in the future once their supply dwindled, considering the present argument over the patent. Suddenly remembering the time, he looked at his watch. Gale and Sibyl were already waiting for him. He hurriedly pushed the drawer closed and rushed out of the lab at a run. Jeff didn't want them walking back to the apartment without him, especially today.

From a distance he could tell that Gale's step was not bouncy, nor was she full of her usual energy. He touched his horn, coming up behind them, trying not to surprise either one. Seeing his car, they both waved and hurried back toward him. Jeff watched Gale's face as she seated herself, concerned that she was still bothered by her memories.

"And how did your day go?" he asked to the windshield, to both or either of them.

Sibyl answered instantly, "Mine was great! I met the most dreamy boy. The classes were all right, I suppose. And yours?" Gale sat there looking forward, seemingly not interested in anyone's day.

"Gale? How are you?" Jeff asked, trying to watch her and drive also.

"Jeff, I've been thinking," she started, looking at him levelly, her eyes boring into him. "My mother. I would like to ask her a question. Something that has been bothering me all day."

"Gale, please. I thought we talked this out. You must let it go and not dwell on it, don't you understand?" Jeff responded.

"It's just a question, Jeff. A very important one. You don't understand how I felt about her. You can't see my side of it." Her eyes were moist, and she looked away. Jeff could hear Sibyl sigh from the backseat.

"How did it go at work without McLally?" Sibyl asked, wanting to change the conversation.

Jeff started to answer but then looked down and started patting his pockets. His keys to the lab door were there in his left pants pocket, all right. He tried to recall something else that was nagging at him but couldn't remember what it was.

"Forget something?" Gale asked, sensing his distraction.

"No, I don't think so," he answered unconvincingly. Gale studied him for some time, silently scanning his face until he looked toward her.

"Anyone for eating out?" he asked.

"Me!" Sibyl said.

"Perhaps later. I would like to rest a bit first. Could I call you?" Gale asked.

"Sure." It was an unusual request from her, one that he hadn't heard previously, but given her insomnia, he realized that she might need some sleep.

After he dropped them off, Jeff drove around for awhile, trying to recall what was bothering him. Eventually, he returned to his apartment and settled in a chair, waiting for Gale's call. He dozed, his mind working through a patched together dream state, images and situations flickering aimlessly and without resolution one after the other. He awakened with a start, the room now in evening blackness. The time was approaching ten. Gale hadn't called, and he became concerned.

Sibyl's voice answered on the second ring. "Hi, Sibyl. Did Gale change her mind or is she still sleeping?"

"What? I thought she was with you all this time."

"No, Sibyl. She never called… Where did she go?"

"She called a cab. Said she was meeting you for a private dinner. You mean, she didn't call you?"

Jeff realized what had been nagging at him all along. He had forgotten to lock the lab on his rush out. A sick sensation came over him, and his fear of the possible consequences leapt out of the dark like a demon. Gale had likely understood that there was an issue concerning keys. He had to get back to the lab.

## Chapter 27

# *Going Home*

This close, Gale could smell the tobacco odor on Bill's clothing, that and the faint smell of dry cleaning chemicals wafting from his dress clothes. Her arm was around her mother's neck, and it impacted her, the warm sensation of skin contact, that her mother was alive and in her arm's embrace. She started to cry with the joy of it.

"My dear Gale?" Bill said tenderly. "Do your tears mean that you have some unhappiness, some misgivings about me becoming your father?" When he spoke, his words were hinting of jest, of attempting to encourage Gale to confess that she was entirely happy with the new plans. Gale shook her head against his polished tuxedo, her tears darkening the already jet black fabric.

She pushed away and looked into their smiling faces, both alive, full of future, of joy, of the promise of the good life to come. Their eyes flooded her with their love, and the moment was one that she knew she would remember for the rest of her life.

"Tell her the best part, Bill," Gale's mother asked while smiling proudly at her.

"You'll love the places we will visit. First, Lucerne for three weeks for a series of concerts I am giving, then Rome for five weeks...we'll stay in an apartment overlooking the Tiber... then off to Paris. I'm expecting you to sing there, to accompany your famous mother. You both on stage, together, will start a fire, I expect."

"But where will we *live*?" the young Gale asked, looking between them for the important answer.

"Everyplace and no place in particular. That's the best part! As long as we are together, that's where we live. We'll live in the world! Isn't it grand?" Josephine answered, her new diamond showering the room with little colored daggers as she spread her arms to demonstrate the scope of their new reality.

"And Nanny?" Gale questioned.

"Nanny is coming, too!" Bill said. Gale hoped that the poor lady had been consulted first and had agreed to this constant trek around the globe.

They raised their cocktail glasses in a toast, and afterwards, Bill bent over so that he and Gale could also touch glasses, milk tapping vodka. Gale watched her mother move when she walked across the room, one hand carried low with flexed wrist, the other daintily holding her long stem glass between two fingers, the others extended in a natural feminine gesture. Gale could see her youthful figure, full bosomed, graceful hips and small waist, and the elegant smooth control she exhibited with every movement. What a stunning package she was physically, and on top of it all was her famous soprano voice, her title of *suprema signora della lirica* often written under her name on the posters. And now it was to be Gale's turn at fame, fortune and a place in history. Her new father and her famous mother would make sure that it happened.

"Now, Gale, I'm afraid that it's your bedtime. Off you go," her mother said, her long graceful hand extended toward the door leading to the bedroom.

"But, Mother, you must promise me that neither one of you will leave here if I go to bed. You have to promise."

"Yes, dear Gale. I promised you that earlier, and I meant it. We will be right here when you awaken. Now go to sleep while Bill and I talk. In the morning, we will start our new life together just as the old sun comes up, lighting our way." She motioned that Gale should come to her, and she extended one arm to embrace her. Gale snuggled into her soft breast and felt her mother pull her closer, whispering into her ear, as she always did. "I love you, Gale. You are the finest little girl that any mother could hope to have. We were all proud of you tonight." It was the perfume, the exotic, delicate perfume, that enveloped her, pulled her memory to the many times she had her mother's neck pressed into her nose and face. This was her mother, the treasured person that she could not lose, the one and only person in her life that counted, the person who was always there for her when it mattered, and she was back again, alive, warm and real.

Gale kissed the neck pressed against her, some powder attaching to her face for a lingering remembrance after she went to bed. She would only have to hold her hand to her nose to recall her mother's touch, hear her lovely sweet voice. "I love you too, Mother. Remember your promise."

"We will be standing above your bed when you awaken, Gale. Ready and anxious for our girl to open her beautiful blue eyes and brighten our world," Bill announced from across the room.

Wiping at her face, Gale took one last look at the two of them, now sitting together on the couch, holding hands, both smiling warmly and reassuringly back at her. She felt Nanny's hands on her shoulders, guiding her toward the bedroom, the hands that gently patted her shoulder in a comforting way, the wrinkled hands that folded the sheet and covers down on the bed.

Gale closed her eyes, fearing what the night would bring, afraid that this perfect experience would evaporate, changing into something fearful, dreadful, and that somehow her mother would be gone from her life forever. She fought the sensation of coming sleep, trying to stay awake so that she could hear their voices coming from the living room, the tinkle of glasses, the musical sound of her mother's laughter, the murmur of Bill's deeper voice.

A noise awakened her, and she tried to open her eyes, the image moving just out of focus, and she struggled to understand what was above her. She turned her head, feeling the soft pillow against her ear and opened her eyes wider. The wall was flooded with streaked light separated by shadows of the partially opened blinds. The picture of the duck being fed by the little girl in blue was there, snapping into focus and recognition.

"Hey, you," the soft voice said. A fragrant hand stroked her cheek, urging her face back toward it. Gale turned, her mother's face just above hers, her long hair draping from both sides of her head as she leaned forward. Bill's smiling face was just behind her, his trimmed mustache, in its shades of brown, red and grey, bristling in the morning light.

"Hi!" Gale said, the joy of seeing them, leaping out of the bed and pulling them toward her. Her mother leaned over and kissed her forehead, her long hair caressing Gale's face, the aroma of her moist, fragrant hair jogging her again with the reality of the moment.

"Time to get up and have breakfast," she said. "You remember our trip to New York? We have to get ready and catch the train."

The train smoothly rolled away the miles, the comforting click-clack accompanying the morning like an old friend had arrived. Gale sipped her orange juice, looking out the window at the passing shades of green with an occasionally interesting building sliding silently past. Her chair was upholstered in glossy cordovan leather, the rolled seam pleasantly dug into the back of her leg, reminding her that it was there. Every so often the small table trembled slightly, sending circular ripples across the cups of coffee. Gale's mother occasionally winked at her, then resumed nuzzling into Bill's shoulder and ear. She was outrageously happy, more than Gale had ever seen, and her exuberance spilled over to the coachmen, the train conductor and the wait-staff, who all seemed to enjoy looking at her and her infectious smile. Bill was even dressed more comfortably, wearing a long sleeved shirt of muted blue with mismatching starched white collar. A vest of a rich, dark red mohair substituted for a decorative tie. He was smiling also, enjoying Gale's mother's antics and likely wishing he had asked for her hand years ago.

To be sure, Gale didn't feel left out on her side of the table, because both of them constantly consulted her on her opinions and thoughts. She advised on where they should visit, how they should dress and even helped with the choice of friends. She was part of a family, something she had never thought possible.

"Gale, I have a couple of suggestions for your next performance," Bill said,

"I thought I would sing the same ones," Gale responded, dreading the thought of learning new pieces, envisioning singing instead of playing outside in some lovely park.

"It's always good to have a repertoire, Gale," her mother suggested. "We've reserved a new tutor for you in Rome when we get there. Signor Adolphi Simone taught me at one time. A most famous conductor in his day."

"Oh, yes. Old Adolph. Yes, he will suit you fine. A feather in your cap to be instructed by him," Bill added, fondly recalling the name he knew so well.

Gale picked at her eggs, distractedly looking out the window and wondering when the giant skyscrapers of New York would become visible. She realized that this new life that she had been lucky enough to obtain would also involve some very hard work and high expectations. She sighed. That's life, you have to accept some bad with the good. Suddenly she couldn't conceive of another type of existence, the present seemed so inevitable, so much had been leading up to this moment. It had to happen this way, she reasoned. Everything in life is preordained by some force that you don't understand. You go from day to day not realizing that everything happening was destined to happen. There is no such thing as free choice, really. You do and say the things that are just waiting on the moment and are simply instructions written long ago.

"You should eat your breakfast, my sweet Gale. It's going to be a very big day for all of us." Bill smiled at her and nodded as if he knew a surprise that he was itching to tell her. She looked at her mother who was obviously thinking the same way. Another big happening was coming.

"I'll bet you two are going to get married? Is that it?" Gale guessed.

"I'll be!" he said with mock surprise, turning to Josephine and giving her a small kiss on her waiting lips. "You are correct, our little prize! Today, in fact. This evening your mother and I will wed. Guess who is going to be there beside us, at the alter with us?"

"Am I going to get a new fancy dress?" Gale asked.

"You and I will be dressed to match!" her mother said.

"Do I have to kiss the groom?"

"You will want to, I hope," Bill added with mock concern.

"I suppose, if I have to. But it will mean that I have to have a ride in a horse-drawn carriage through the park." She smiled back, enjoying the to and fro.

Bill chuckled, "I had that in mind all along. The three of us will go and have a kiss in the park in the dark."

"Then we can go to a play or a nightclub!" Gale added.

"What on earth have you been teaching this child?" Bill guffawed.

"I've been around. Can I call you Bill now?" Gale asked.

"After four, I had hoped it would be father. However, Bill is fine if that's what you like."

"I'll remember that, Bill, and give it my consideration." They all laughed loudly together, enough to attract the attention of the other diners who briefly paused eating and talking and looked their way.

Gale noticed the hollow sound of her mother's high heels clicking against the stone floor of Grand Central, the sound echoing back to them as they headed toward the main waiting room. Voices came at them from every possible source, mixing with the sounds of the trains behind them, either idling softly or motors laboring as the engines pulled their charges behind them, heading out toward some distant place. At times, a garbled message came from the loudspeakers, announcing some coming or going and the location. Gale couldn't understand the words and didn't need to since they were leaving, not arriving. Ahead, a porter rolled their luggage behind him on a small flat car. He occasionally glanced backward to be sure they were following where he led, while displaying an unusually bright and full-toothed practiced smile. They walked past the big bronze doors and under the cast lettering placed there by old Mr. Vanderbilt when the station was new.

At the curb, a big limousine was waiting, the side door open, a snappy uniformed driver standing patiently beside the door. They got in, Gale in the middle, and felt the car sagging as luggage was noisily added to the trunk. The driver returned to the wheel, and the car started, floating off without direction. He seemed to already know where they were going, and as if by magic, they eased effortlessly through traffic heading toward the cavern of big buildings.

Gale glanced behind her, hardly believing the number of people who had slowly filled the chapel. All were dressed as if for a formal dinner, the black ties and bold white shirts of the men and the glittering dresses of the women unchanging from row to row. Her new dress was scratchy and rustled when she moved. In her hands was a bouquet of mixed flowers exactly matching, except for size, the one in her mother's hand. Her beautiful mother was partially hidden behind a transparent veil, but Gale could see the beacon of her red lips gleaming through the darkness. They stood before a towering minister, dressed in black, hovering in front of them and speaking loudly with sincere and serious words which Gale hardly heard. Bill was holding Josephine's hand and looking only at her, leaving Gale to just stand there by herself, feeling left out and holding on to her flowers with both hands, trying to be patient and attempting to feel part of the ceremony.

It seemed as though some rude person was calling her name. Defying her instincts, she ignored the distraction, giving even more of her attention to the music falling from the balcony and the great organ above. The calling became louder, causing her to briefly turn and look, but all she saw was the attentive and smiling congregation looking back at her. She reminded herself to tell this person how irresponsible it was for him to call her during the wedding. But the voice came back again and was becoming harder and harder to ignore. Even the seated friends behind them started to look around, all made uncomfortable by an unruly person. Fortunately, the ceremony was nearly over, Gale realized. The minister asked for the ring which Bill had been clutching tightly in his hand. In a moment, they were going to kiss, and it would be all finished. Her new life would actually begin.

# Chapter 28

# *Awakening*

The hall clock over the door read ten o'clock as Jeff rushed under it heading on a run toward the lab. He skidded toward the corner and pulled himself around with both hands grasping at the plaster. At a distance, he could see the lights on inside the room, the meaning was clear, someone was inside. He found the door unlocked as now he clearly remembered that he didn't lock it in his hurry to leave.

She was there, just as he feared, lying face up on the gurney, nearly in the center of the room. His heart was racing as he approached her. There was a syringe and needle still in her arm, but it had no contents. Whatever she had used, she had used all of it before passing out. Her color was good, and he checked her pulse and took a look in her eyes, checking her pupil size. From all appearances, she was simply asleep, not, thank God, dead. He pulled the monitor cart over and put on the blood pressure cuff and the oximeter. After a few seconds, both showed her to have nearly normal values.

"Gale! Can you hear me?" he asked repeatedly while shaking her shoulder, but with no response. The drug cabinet door was open, and a quick inspection showed that she had used the drug

Puszithrin. The question was how much? A quick inventory showed that an entire vile had been used, and the presence of an empty one confirmed his suspicions. She had apparently used the entire bottle...all ten cubic centimeters instead of the half cc that they always used. Jeff began to sweat profusely, the combination of stress and his rush had taken a toll on him. He sat down trying to think clearly. Gale's dose was twenty times what was needed to achieve anesthesia and enable a person to direct their memories. He had no idea what a huge overdose would do to her. Due to his negligence, he had allowed Gale to do this to herself, instead of talking with her when she needed him. In his panic, he briefly considered suicide but decided that, at this moment, he was the only person in the entire United States who had any experience or knowledge about the effects of Puszithrin. Standing on impulse, he realized that he had to call McLally and get his advice as well as admit his error. The consequences be damned, he wanted out of the entire project, away from the addicting effects of McLally's Puszithrin, just as soon as he dealt with Gale, saving her, if she could be saved. After a quick mental calculation, he realized that in London the local time was four A.M. Trying to control his shaking hand, Jeff dialed the number he had been given prior to McLally's departure.

"Yes!" he answered after twelve rings. "McLally here."

"Professor, this is Jeff Andrews. I have a problem."

"Do you realize that this is the middle of the night here? What do you want, and it better be a good reason."

"Gale Randolph broke into the lab tonight, probably two hours ago. She told me earlier that she wanted to talk with her mother, and I dismissed her. From what I can tell, she has taken an entire ampule of Puszithrin."

"What! How is she? What is her condition!" McLally was fully awake now, and his mind was spinning with questions.

"I've taken her vital signs, and they are all normal. What should I do now?"

"Jeff, I've never given that much, even to a lab animal. No one could answer that question. Let's see....a normal dose of point five usually causes roughly half an hour of sleep. Given that ratio, then we could assume that she will sleep twenty times longer. Make that ten hours of sleep. If she took the drug two hours ago, then she will sleep for another eight hours, or perhaps more."

"Should I call EMS and transport her to the hospital?"

"If her vitals are good, as you say, then nothing is to be gained by doing so. You have to stay with her the entire time, however, and look for any deterioration. If you see any change, then make the call."

"Do I just stand here and look at her?" Jeff said, his voice indicating he was near panic.

"No, you pray. How did that little girl manage to break into the lab, Jeff?"

"I forgot to lock up. She just walked in. It's all my fault."

"And so it is. Any damage to Gale from this will be on your shoulders, you realize. The other thing is, if she doesn't recover, word will get out, and you and I can say goodbye to doing research there or anywhere else. It's over."

Jeff looked around and wanted to flee, to run away, to dump responsibility on someone else, a professional used to treating medical emergencies, anyone but a green grad student.

"Are you still there, Jeff? Jeff! Answer me!" the phone squawked.

"Professor, I'm really sorry about all of this. I'm not qualified to be here."

"Damn you, Jeff. You are there, and you will stay there. Do you hear me? Don't you dare abandon that woman now. Shape up, Jeff."

"Yes, sir. I won't leave."

"You better not. There is nothing more you can do until the drug wears off. Just keep an eye on her and call me if things change. I'll call you back in the morning and see how things are with her at that time."

Jeff dragged a chair close to the gurney and sat down, intent on keeping a vigilance for as long as it took. Gale gave the appearance of sleeping peacefully, her breathing regular and deep, her skin color pink and normal. He wanted to embrace her, to beg her not to harm herself, to spill out the depth of his feelings for her, to tell her that the world was waiting for her to awaken to take charge and fulfill her destiny. Jeff sniffed, his eyes clouded with his own misery. She was where she wanted to be, he knew, back with her dear mother and creating an existence which never happened but should have. If only he could make her realize that he was the one who desperately wanted to make her happy, to substitute his love for that of her lost mother. He picked up her limp hand and held it in his. It was as much contact as he had ever had with her, even though he yearned for more, ached for it, dreamed of it. The one kiss she had given him still burned hotly on his face.

Gale leaned backward on her hands, the soft grass against her flexed palms, and looked over the hill toward the river. The oval outline of the stadium obscured part of the view, but the hills of Rome arched gently on the horizon beyond the river, and the trees behind them hissed softly in the intermittent breeze.

"It's nice here, isn't it?" her mother said, causing Gale to look at her. She wore a large straw hat, decorated with tiny silk flowers, shielding most of her face, except her lips and chin which glowed in the warm sunlight. She smiled, showing her even teeth and making her glossy lips taut for a moment. Behind her was the extravagant di Macchia and the bustle of yet another wedding in progress, as the well-wishers and relatives waited in a noisy group for the bride and groom to emerge into a cascade of flowers and rice.

"I thought Bill said that we were going to be on the river," Gale stated.

"Well, there it is. For Rome, it's very close," she answered pointing to the green streak of moving water some distance away. She and her mother were both dressed fashionably in light-colored knits and cork flats. Her mother had obtained a pair of enormous sunglasses which were shaded darker at the top of the lens. Gale hadn't decided if she wanted a pair and was happy just squinting in the bright sunlight of Rome. The days were all similar and started with breakfast in a sunny corner for just the three of them. The staff were all male and exceptionally formal and polite. After Bill said his usual goodbyes and kissed both of them on the cheek, the mornings were left to enjoy. They had gone for long walks, tours, shopping and, on occasions like this one, just sat and enjoyed the day. The afternoons were spent with the egocentric and excitable elderly voice tutor, Signor Simone, the only saving grace being that he adored his former pupil, Josephine, who sat regally and mostly silent in the corner of the room, watching and listening closely to his lesson. At times, she would be called on to demonstrate a difficult singing part or to provide the proper enunciation of Italian. When she raised her voice in song, the entire world seemed to stop and listen, the power of it penetrating ancient stone, giving voice to a long-deceased composer, and always bringing tears of joy to the wrinkled face of Signor Adolphi Simone, his praise of her endless and profuse. It was during moments like this that Gale realized that her mother wasn't just a loving, doting parent but a gift to the human world, a marvel of creation with beauty and talent far above the aspirations of nearly anyone else on the planet. And she, this endpoint of evolution, was in love with Gale, forever and totally, and would move heaven and earth for her happiness. It was a humbling experience to realize that her mother expected Gale to become her replacement someday. To mature and take the place of a woman such as her was too much to expect or to hope for. Gale was bound to disappoint.

*"Perdonami per favore. Sono Ruffio. Volevi vedermi, sì?"* a youthful voice behind them called out. They both turned slightly as the young man came around to stand in front. He was slightly older than Gale and richly handsome, his dark eyes glittering under a curly cap of even darker hair. He was also dressed casually, but neatly, nearly professionally put together for effect. He bowed slightly and smiled, waiting for recognition.

*"Ah, e così si è finalmente arrivato,"* her mother said, offering her hand to the young man. He took her limp hand reverently and lightly, bowing while placing his forehead against the backs of her fingers.

"And this is Ruffio, Gale. I have been anxious to introduce you to each other, because you have so much in common. Ruffio is the protege of the impresario of the Teatro dell'Opera di Roma, Signore Callimati, an old friend. He is a most promising young singer, such as yourself, Gale. You are destined to work together in the future, it's entirely inescapable, you see. Better that you make acquaintance early."

Ruffio smiled, obviously understanding her English, and nodded toward Gale. He was very fit for a young man and carried himself with confidence. He seemed to want Gale to extend her hand but she didn't move, instead continued to survey the handsome intruder who dared interrupt their glorious day.

"Gale, can't you at least say hello? Ruffio has come across town just to see you."

"Hi."

"Hi yourself! I have heard of you, your talent crosses the Atlantic to meet with me. We will be friends, don't you think?"

"Perhaps."

"Oh, *certamente*, we will. You are very beautiful, Gale. Have you been told?"

Gale continued to look at Ruffio using the female blank expression, not giving away her thoughts or desires or even her contempt. It came by nature to her to use the single most potent device in the female armamentarium, using silence to humble an overly attentive male.

At her mother's instance, Ruffio agreed to lunch with them but insisted that he pay the tab. Josephine laughed at the young man and took off her glasses to see better this youngster attempting to act like a courting Italiano who was polished by his previous contacts with women. "Of course, you may, Ruffio!" she burbled at him, obviously impressed with his youthful effrontery. They walked together, Josephine in the middle, toward a long-established cafe with tables and chairs arranged carefully on a stone patio. Their table was chosen for its view and its large yellow umbrella which cast a favorable light on their faces, the shadows less crisp and so much more attractive. It was always interesting to watch male interaction with the glamorous soprano, even when they didn't know her name. Once they did know, at least the educated, the fawning and scraping, the smacking of lips made an embarrassing show, at least for Gale, who tried, unsuccessfully, to escape notice. She was invariably introduced as the next coming thing, and the bowing and scraping was directed at her as well.

"This is exciting, don't you think?" Ruffio said, glancing around, nodding at the antiquities nearby. "History all around us. Roman history. It's exceptional, don't you think, Gale?" He was trying any method to engage her with conversation and slowly it was working, even against her will. Ruffio was delightfully energetic with boundless enthusiasm for the most simple things. His eyes sparkled with intensity and intelligence, most of it directed at her.

"It's very nice, Ruffio," she said, the longest phrase to come from her as yet. "You shouldn't have offered, you know, to pay."

"But, you see, I have plenty of money! It's my reward for singing well! You will see."

Gale looked at her mother for explanation, getting in return a vague smile.

"Ruffio will practice with you at your lesson this afternoon. He will sing all the blank areas, the ones you pass over. Your first experience with a male accompaniment, but not the last, you can be sure."

Gale took a deep breath, trying to hide her anxiety about mixing her slowly improving voice with this...this *millantatore*. Could he be as good as her mother said?

Conductor Adolphi Simone clapped his hands, and the pianist started over. He pointed his long baton directly at Gale's face, held it there until the starting note was reached, then bobbed it just enough for her to see, meaning for her to start off with a *sotto voce*. She did, and the aria streamed effortlessly from her open mouth, filling the room with purity. She kept an eye on Simone while listening for any comments from her mother and also kept her ear on the notes emerging from the long black piano. It was a new piece for her from the old opera, Pagliacci by Leoncavallo. She was singing the part of Colombina; Ruffio was to come in as Pagliaccio, her lover. He was in the shadows of the room studying his part as she sang, waiting for the baton to fall toward him.

Gale stepped back when she was done, glancing at her mother who was noiselessly clapping her hands and beaming with pride. Ruffio stepped into the light from above which cast his face in harsh shadow, making him appear older than his years. He sang forcefully, powerfully, the veins and muscles straining from his neck. He was good, very good, and his stage presence, the way he surveyed the few people in the room and the way he used his hands, flowing, the force emanating from him, radiating the composer's will. Ruffio was indeed going to be a great star of the opera. Nothing could stop him.

When he was done, old Simone started beating the polished side of the piano with his baton in celebration, to the consternation of the pianist who looked with alarm at him. Josephine stood, a compliment like no other to a budding artist, and bowed lowly to both of them and resumed clapping loudly. Ruffio took it in stride. He had heard the praise previously, but he turned toward Gale and bowed lowly to her, raising her arm high in the air and turning her around in a small circle. Gale was blushing at the lavish attention.

"My young friends," Simone said, with heavily accented English. "The world is at your feet." He rushed to Josephine and took her by the shoulders. "Such a fine daughter, you have raised Madame. She is a brilliant star about to explode. Thank you from my heart for giving me the pleasure of watching her perform." He kissed her hand with much fanfare.

Ruffio, standing beside Gale and watching Simone occupy Gale's mother's attention, leaned into her ear, whispering, "There will be a day that you and I will marry. I will have it no other way. My entire life will be directed to that end, and I will worship you forever in my arms."

Gale pulled away from him, aghast at the premature idea and the blatant presumptiveness of Ruffio, whom she had just met this very day. She was insulted by his comment, and her lower lip protruded. She glared at him, but he smiled back sincerely. He clearly had meant what he said.

The telephone rang, and Jeff picked it up on the first ring. The time was nearing six, and the morning light was starting to come in McLally's office east-facing window.

"Yes? Dr. McLally?" he asked, hoping that it was him.

"McLally here. How is your patient? Any signs of stirring as yet?"

"Not even a flicker. As far as I can tell, her eyes aren't even moving. She appears to be paralyzed as well as unconscious. What should I do?"

"I had hoped that this would be about the time she would come out of it. Her vital signs still good?"

"Normal."

"Tried shaking her and calling her name?"

"Sure, about every half hour. No response."

"Hmmm. Well, stick with it. Hopefully not much longer."

"How much longer? What is the alternate plan?"

"Give it three more hours, then you better call in the medical people. I'll wrap up my business today...this morning...and will be on my way back across the pond by evening. That means I'll see you in the morning. During the flight, you won't be able to contact me, so you'll be on your own until I land. I'll call you before I board, if I don't hear from you first."

"What will the medical people do to her?"

"Oh, I suppose that they will give her a complete physical, labs, perhaps a CT, put in a catheter. That's all standard procedure. Have them call me, and I'll give the physician what is known about the drug she overdosed on."

"Who will pay for all that? I know she doesn't have any money."

"Why you, of course, my boy. Your mistake, your dollar."

Jeff swallowed hard. It didn't matter about the money. He didn't have it either, but somehow he would pay it and more if it would bring Gale back. The stress of sitting beside her helplessly, hour after hour was more physically demanding than exercise. His emotions were shot, his underarms reeked, and he was parched. He knew that Gale was in need of fluids also, but that was beyond his skills to provide for her.

"Should I try to give her some water?"

"Absolutely not. Do not attempt that, because you'll just drown her. Any fluids will have to be from an IV. She will need a urinary catheter once she starts fluids. Just hope that she awakens soon."

"Fine then. I'll call you before anyone else, and you can make the final decision," Jeff said, glad to pass on the responsibility.

After he hung up, he tried once more to awaken Gale using her name and pushing gently at her shoulder. She continued as before, unaware of the world.

Snow had accumulated at the higher elevations, and the train slowed to a crawl. Gale couldn't see ahead by pressing her face against the cold glass, and she worried that the train would suddenly stop, and they would have to proceed on foot.

"Stop worrying, Gale," Bill said soothingly. "They've been at this for a long time, and they know what they are doing. There's just a little snow. Once we start down the other side of the Alps, you'll see that there is nothing to prevent our going to Paris as scheduled."

"It would be all right by me if we had to divert to Switzerland for a few days. I love that crisp air up there," Josephine said. Bill acknowledged that it was true indeed by nodding his agreement.

"There are schedules, which compel us to continue, my lovely ladies, the sun and moon of my life. Besides, you both have to practice, you remember. You will be on stage in less than a week."

Gale wasn't worried. With her mother beside her, what could go wrong? She was told that the *Opéra National de Paris* would be performing in the timeless *Palais Garnier*, a huge theater and a most imposing one at that. Gale couldn't image a building as grand as they described, the genuine awe of the place obvious on their faces. They would sing individual parts and also a duet, the entire performance lasting nearly twenty long minutes. Bill would be conducting, but he would be in the orchestra pit and below where they would stand. In her mind, she could already hear the thunderous applause which was sure to come. She was more confident after the many lessons with her famous conductor mentor who had both inspired her as well as instructed her. She remembered Ruffio with fondness, and his proposal, no...his insistence...on their marriage. It made her laugh inside to think she was already engaged in a way and that both of them were destined to be world famous. Could life get any better?

The train jerked to a sudden stop, and the passengers looked around and out of the windows to find the cause. An announcement came over the speaker that there would be a short delay while the tracks were being cleared.

"This calls for an afternoon beverage, I think," Bill said, standing up and offering his hand to Josephine. "Let us adjourn to the dining car before everyone else has the same idea." They followed Bill down the narrow path between the seats toward the next car.

On the way past, Gale noticed the restrooms. "Mother, I need to stop here. Go on ahead, and I'll find you." Josephine hesitated, unwilling to let Gale out of her sight. She stood there and looked at Gale with a puzzled face for a moment, still holding on to her hand.

"She'll be fine, dear," Bill offered. "It's only in the next car. We can watch for her from our seats. She's growing up. You have to give her a little bit of freedom."

Reluctantly, Josephine allowed Gale's hand to slip from hers, keeping eye contact with her as she was being led away through the compartment door by

Bill. Gale could see remorse in her eyes, an unwillingness to let her go, even for a moment.

After she finished and exited the restroom, the train lunged forward, accompanied by a loud clank as its couplers came taut. The forward progression was jerky at first, but the train started gathering speed, going uphill with snow going by the window, piled up as high as a white glittering wall. Gale held on and pushed the compartment door open, trying to look through the small windows on the other side. She could see that the room was very crowded with some still standing. Once past the second door, the aroma of food was everywhere, along with the noise of conversation and the tinkle of metal impacting glass. She looked for her parents but couldn't seem to spot them. Her name was being called, softly at first, then more urgently. It was the same voice which had interrupted the wedding back in New York. She turned around, but the voice was coming from somewhere outside the train compartment, growing louder and louder.

Jeff saw her eyes moving under her lids, the first positive sign he had seen. "Gale! Please wake up, Gale. Can you hear me?" he repeated while shaking her gently. Thank the heavens, could it be that she is going to awaken, he thought desperately. "Gale! Wake up. I know you can hear me. Open your eyes!"

Gale was near panic trying to find her parents, looking for the blonde hair of her mother, but there were so many people pushing back and forth and indignantly looking at her as she tried to squeeze past them. Her name was being shouted by someone, someone close by. She didn't want to answer, hoping instead to find the protection of her mother. All the faces were hostile, all strange and older. She turned to head back to where they had come from, trying to make it back to her seat in case they returned. But she couldn't get oriented as to which direction she should go. The feeling came over her that she was lost, even on the wrong train. The voice was insistent, loud, and her surroundings started to become blurry.

Her eyes opened, at first just a slit of opening, then fully, her pupils constricting in the bright white light of the laboratory. She was confused and looked around aimlessly, attempting to discern where she was. Someone had control of her hand. She could feel their fingers around her wrist, restraining her arm.

"Let me go!" she said, trying to wrest control away from the confining hand.

"Gale, it's me, Jeff. Look at me, Gale."

She turned toward him, looking blankly at his face at first, then scanning his eyes and lower face rapidly with her focus. "Where is my mother? What happened to my mother?" Her face morphed to one of pain or panic, a wild creature reacting to sudden capture.

"You are safe, Gale. You were having a dream, and now you are awake."

She attempted to sit up but fell back helplessly, realizing that her body was not yet ready. In a burst of strength, she managed to twist her arm, breaking Jeff's gentle hold.

"Where am I? What's happened to my mother? I must return to my mother."

As Jeff opened his mouth to reassure her one more time, the phone rang, and he picked it up while still watching Gale closely.

"Dr. McLally?"

"Yes, Jeff. I'm about to board the plane. What's the situation there?"

"She just emerged, but she's fighting it and is confused. I'm afraid she'll hurt herself trying to get away from me."

"Disorientated, eh? No doubt expected, wouldn't we guess?" he paused, obviously thinking. "You must stay beside her, keep talking soothingly to her while the drug dissipates. If she becomes violent, you'll need to call for help, I'm afraid. Do what you can, and I'll be there in a few hours. It's a positive sign, my boy. Think of it in that way."

"I'll try, Professor."

When he hung up, he realized that Gale was looking at him calmly, studying him. "Hi, Gale. Are you feeling more awake?" She didn't answer and continued her uncomfortable stare. "Would you like some water? I noticed that your lips are dry, so you must be thirsty."

When Gale surprisingly nodded yes, he said, "You stay right there, and I'll go get a glass. Won't be but a few seconds." She looked at him while he was talking but didn't respond. He rushed toward the small drug closet where there was a small sink in the corner. Returning with a cup in his hand, he saw Gale standing in the open door to the hall, looking both ways. She had tricked him, intentionally deceived him, so that she could escape.

"Gale! Don't go out there! You aren't awake yet!"

"Where is the train? I need to find the train and get to my seat." This time, her look was hostile, even menacing. She was still lost in her false memory, he realized, not completely back to reality yet. He had to think fast.

"Please go back and lie down. Your mother is on her way. She said to stay with me, and she will meet you as soon as she can." Gale hesitated, unsure of what to do. She looked at him again but without any recognition on her face. Smiling assuringly at her, he offered her the cup with an extended arm, not wanting to seem anxious to restrain her. She accepted it with reluctance and kept her eyes on him while she drank, alert for any sudden motion from him.

"My name is Jeff. Your name is Gale, isn't that correct?" he asked, trying another tact. She handed the cup back and wiped her mouth with the back of her sleeve, childlike.

"You seem to know my name. You've been calling me. It's your fault that I got lost."

"Can you tell me how old you are, Gale?"

"It's none of your business," she said defensively, then appeared to reconsider. Perhaps it would help find her mother. "I'm ten. You know that."

No, he didn't know that, but it explained her behavior. He decided to go along with her, to discover what she had been doing under the anesthesia. "Where were you going on the train, Gale?"

"To Paris,"

"Oh! Just you and your mother?"

"And Bill. He's my father."

"What were you going to do in Paris? Was it just a vacation?"

"No...I'm not sure I should tell you anything until my mother is here."

"I know her. She's a famous opera singer just like you, isn't that right?"

"I'm not famous...yet. We are going to sing at the Paris Opera next Saturday."

"Wow! You must be very, very good to do that."

"That's what they tell me. Adolphi Simone thinks so also."

"Who is Adolphi Simone?"

Gale looked at him with disgust. He clearly was ignorant of the singing world. She wondered if he was tricking her. "He's the world famous conductor and my private tutor when we were in Rome. Are you sure you know my mother?"

Jeff realized that Gale had created an entire alternate life for herself while under. The memory she had created was her reality, a complete and complex one that would be impossible to deny. Refuting any of her recall would lead to mistrust and withdrawal. He had to earn her trust until McLally returned.

"Gale, do you remember me at all?"

She studied him again, not quickly answering. He had a sensation that she did remember but in a dim way, her memory of him not reconciling with her present existence. "I really don't....but, sort of. Have you been to our apartment?"

"Yes, Gale. Many times. Do you remember Sibyl? She was your best friend."

"Sibyl? Yes, I remember. She has hair like Mom's."

"Yes. Long beautiful blonde hair. She is pretty, just like your mother, don't you think?"

Gale looked lost in thought. Something wasn't right. Sibyl's face was familiar but she recalled Sibyl as a woman, more her mother's age than hers. How they could have been friends was confusing.

"Would you like to have Sibyl visit you while you wait on your mother?" Jeff asked, rapidly formulating a plan. Gale shrugged, still not sure of what to do or whom to trust. She wanted to find the train and resume her trip. This was all a distraction.

Jeff made the call, still trying to keep calm, just like things were ordinary, hoping to not arouse any strong emotion in Gale.

"Hi, Sibyl," he said calmly when she answered.

"Jeff!. You bastard. You could have called me before now. Where is she. Did you find her?"

"I'm with her now. She's awake, but she's waiting on her mother. Listen carefully, Sibyl. You recall that Gale is ten years old right now and that she and her parents were on a train. She's expecting her mother to arrive at any time. Could you come to the lab and give me a hand?"

"I'll be right there. That bad?"

"Yes. That's the way it is. She remembers you but might be confused when she sees you. Take it slowly."

"Count on it."

"Can you call my mother and tell her where I am?" Gale asked.

"I don't think there is a telephone where she is. Don't worry now, your friend Sibyl will be here in a few minutes. Can I get you some food or water?"

"Yes, I'm hungry. We were on our way to the dining car. Could we go there?"

"Tell you what. When Sibyl gets here, we could all go together. Would you like that?"

"Yes," she said and hung her head with childish displeasure. She seemed to notice herself for the first time and felt her breasts with her hands, realizing her size and her womanly features with surprise. She looked at Jeff with alarm, now aware that her memory didn't jibe with her body or her surroundings. Twisting about, she noticed the big white machine occupying the middle of the floor. She put her hand to her face, trying to recall what it meant, how it was connected to her and what she was doing in this place. Looking up at Jeff, she locked eyes with him, and he could feel the Gale that knew him flickering back and forth with the child, her eyes propelling her conflicting emotions toward him. He wanted to hold her and whisper in her ear how utterly glad he was that she was nearly back again.

Another personality emerged from her, this one petulant, wanting to strike out at him for frustrating and interrupting her perfect life. "You told me that you love me," she recalled, but not with affection.

"I said that, and yes, I do love you."

"Well, you should know that Ruffio loves me also and is going to marry me when we grow up." She was taunting him, trying to hurt him. It was in her eyes, a ferocious little cat clawing at his face in the only way she knew.

"If Ruffio loves you, that's grand," he answered calmly, not taking the bait.

"Ruffio is a singer like me. We are going to be famous. Married and famous."

Another swipe, this one did sting a bit. "I'm just ordinary, Gale. Not a singer like you or Ruffio, never destined to be famous or rich like either one of you. But I still love you and always will."

The hate in her eyes dimmed a little bit, but neither was there love or real recognition. There was a rustle at the door indicating that help had arrived. Sibyl came in slowly, beaming a big smile at Gale and giving her a little wave with her fingertips. Gale watched her come forward but without any return sign that would indicate welcome.

"Hi, girl! Wow, you are looking grand for this early. You must have had a long sleep which you desperately needed." Sibyl glanced at Jeff for support, but he shrugged. She would have to invent her own approach. Sibyl was always forward, ready to jump rather than consider, and on occasion, it was the right approach. She put her arm around Gale and kissed her cheek.

"Well, aren't you glad to see your old friend? Where have you been?"

"Well, we went to New York for their wedding, then to Switzerland, then to Rome, then we were headed to Paris. Have I told you about Ruffio?" she said, looking at Sibyl with her big ten-year-old conspirator eyes.

"Ruffio? I love that name. Is he your new boyfriend?" Gale asked her, but looking at Jeff with a smile, knowing that he would be irritated.

"He's really smart...good-looking, also. Ruffio is going to marry me."

"I'll bet you met Ruffio in Rome."

"We sang together. It was grand. Even my mother clapped." She stopped her train of conversation and took another long look at Sibyl, putting her in a different light. Suddenly she threw her arms around Sibyl, pulling her tight. "What's happened to me? I don't understand what's happened. Do you know my mother?"

"Gale, do you see that fellow over there looking at us?" Sibyl asked softly, pointing directly at Jeff. Gale nodded, wiping her tears with the back of her hand.

"He loves you. I love you. You are safe with us and right where you should be right now. We are very happy that you woke up from your long sleep. I see that you are confused right now, so we need to go really slow, and you will start to remember. Can you do that?"

Gale nodded that she could, and looked at Jeff with her little girl eyes, a mixture of fright and wondering.

"Gale mentioned that she was hungry. Do you think we can take her out for breakfast until her mother arrives?" Jeff suggested.

"Sure! I'd love that, wouldn't you, Gale!" Sibyl said excitedly. "She can tell us everything that happened to her. I especially want to hear everything about Ruffio."

# Chapter 28

# Chapter 29

# *Awaiting the Professor*

Gale swiped her hand across the somehow familiar checked table cloth, tickling a memory just out of reach. The place, its odors, the noise from the street and the overhead embossed metal tiles were familiar. She had been here previously. She looked at her two companions and recalled that they had been here with her. Their faces were known to her, and it gave her comfort to have them close, but how was that possible? She wondered if her mother could explain things when she arrived.

"Would you all like to start with coffee?" the waitress asked and started writing it down, knowing that they would.

"I'm not allowed to drink coffee," Gale said.

"That's right! You are too young to drink coffee," Sibyl remembered. The waitress raised her eyebrows and shrugged.

"Two coffees and one orange juice. Will that be okay, Gale?" Jeff asked. She shrugged, expecting chocolate milk but not wanting to ask for it.

"Tell us about Switzerland, Gale. I've always wanted to go," Sibyl asked.

"We were in a big hotel with a patio looking at a huge lake. Lots of mountains with snow at the top. There was always music, violin music."

"Do you remember the name of the city?" Jeff asked, hoping that her memory wasn't that detailed.

"Lucerne. Sir William gave three concerts while we were there. Mother and I went to every one of them and sat on the first row."

"The detail you remember is amazing," Sibyl said. "I'll bet you even remember the dress you wore at each concert."

"Of course I do! We purchased a new one for each. I still have them in my trunk." With that comment she paused, thinking about where her life had gone, her belongings, their plans, and her adoring mother. Gale's eyes became moist, and her lower lip trembled. That world she loved and which loved her was now some other place, perhaps lost and gone. Over. She nearly fell into the table, the agony hitting her, the intensity of her loss, trembling with tears which gushed from her eyes.

"Gale, dear Gale," Jeff said, lightly caressing her neck. Her pain was his pain, even more since he bore the guilt, the omission, the sin of incompetence.

"What are *you* going to do, Jeff," Sibyl demanded. Her look told him that she also knew that Jeff was responsible, and because of that fact, it was up to him to solve Gale's problems.

"I am waiting for Dr. McLally to return before making any plans. Gale's situation is unique. There is no precedent, no predictable outcome, for any of it." Without saying it, he also knew that Gale would be quickly diagnosed as having schizophrenia. With her level of delusion, commitment would be the first choice of any psychiatrist called in to see her. She would likely never be allowed out again, since she could not be cured of something she didn't have. Gale was normal, she had just overwritten her memory, a great deal of it, and built a vast false history in its place. There had to be a solution.

Gale pushed away her plate, little interested because of her advancing grief. She sat there and looked around aimlessly, lost, abandoned. All her hopes were gone, along with her mother and her new father. She had no idea of where she was or how she got here.

"Gale, do you want to see our apartment, perhaps take a little rest?" Sibyl suggested.

Gale shrugged. Her face was blank, the tears dried and replaced by a vacantness. Jeff nodded that he thought that was an excellent idea. Dr. McLally wouldn't arrive for another five hours or so. He wished that he could sedate her, but the thought of pushing anything else on her was frightening. She had enough happen to her. They got up to leave, Gale in the middle, and they held on to each other on the way to Jeff's car.

"Do you remember our old couch?" Sibyl asked, surveying the old wreck. It wouldn't survive to another owner when they were done with it. Gale walked around from room to room, looking at each item in turn. When she reached her bedroom, she found the little painting of the small girl in blue and stopped.

"That was mine, wasn't it? How did it get here?" she asked.

"You put it there yourself, don't you remember?"

Gale thought for a moment and did remember hanging it. It was something, the only thing, she had left from childhood, and she always treasured it. It brought back a flood of memories of her old room, the way the light came in across the park in the evenings, the yellow-tinged mellow light, the sounds of horses and carriages, an occasional honking auto horn. She touched it tenderly, remembering the day they bought it at a small antique store. It was a long time ago. She was so small at the time that she couldn't help hang it. A movement caught her eye, and she turned to see herself in a full-length mirror attached to the closet door. She was an adult, not a child. Her dress was not crinoline and silk but cotton and plain. Her bosom was full, her waist small, and her hair had darkened from its yellow blonde into a sultry cinnamon. Her image captivated her, and she touched her face to be sure she was looking at herself. She remembered the train and her mother's last long look into her eyes; it was not this morning but a long time ago. Where had the years gone? What was in-between? She sat on the bed, exhausted by confusion and doubt.

"Jeff, you'd better come in here," Sibyl called. Jeff came quickly, looking back and forth at them. "She saw herself in the mirror," she explained. Jeff sat on the bed beside Gale, his shoulder touching hers.

"Gale, you are seeing the truth, and there is an explanation, a very easy one, but it's going to be hard for you to accept."

"Hi, Jeff," she said. It was a gong being struck, a bolt of lightning.

"Hi, Gale." He slid off of the bed and kneeled in front of her. "You are going to remember more and more over time. We will be here for you, always."

"When is my mother coming back?" she asked.

"You need to rest first. Remember that you have to take an afternoon nap? This is a good time for it, and this is your bed, so lie down for now, and we'll see her later." Gale leaned back and drew up her legs in the protective curl of childhood. They covered her and gently closed the door.

"You are going to get caught in that lie about her mother coming back, you know," Sibyl said.

"I'm just buying time, Sibyl. Just waiting for Dr. McLally."

"And what if the philandering genius has no ideas?"

"He'd better."

"You know that she's worse off now than before you guys touched her. At least then, she knew who she was and dealt with her issues better than this. Now she thinks she's ten but has the body of a woman. It's nuts."

"It's a case of unforeseen complications. This is the story of a person who had a happy childhood that was abruptly taken away from her, and the rest of her life was miserable. No wonder she wanted to go back to it. Anyone would. The world she invented was so much better than the real one. No one knew that it was possible to overwrite memory like she has done. How could we prevent something that we couldn't predict?"

"I knew she would do exactly what she did, and if you are honest, you would admit that you did also."

"I did. I did, and I warned her not to change things. You heard me. Enough of this blame game. I take full responsibility for all of it, and I'd do anything to change her back to the way she was after we erased her bad memory."

"You wanted to get your hands on her, and you were afraid that if you didn't give in, she would dump you. Isn't that the real truth?"

"Yes. Now shoot me, and get it over with. I'm guilty."

Jeff's phone rang, and he looked at Sibyl with hope that the caller was Dr. McLally and that he would have an answer.

# Chapter 30

# *Merchant*

"Look here, Johnson," Peters said holding up a trash can. "There is a lot of hair in here. Someone has cut off his beard and some of his long hair, and I'll bet I know who it is."

"He's terrified of you. Now that he's changed his appearance, he'll be even harder to find," Johnson said.

"Run the DNA. It's him, and this will prove that he is the man I've been looking for."

"No, Peters. We'll run the test, but it will only prove that *someone* is the person you are looking for. There were nearly a dozen of them around this house. How do you assume that Merchant was the one who shaved?"

"Honestly, Johnson, you are making this way too hard. You know I'm right," Peters said.

"You can be known to overreact also. Locking that greaseball to a tree in the middle of the woods was on the far side. What if he had died out there? We would have to take you in for it."

"He didn't die or suffer any harm did he?"

"If you call about a hundred thousand mosquito bites harmless. Glad it wasn't me."

"What did your boys do with him?" Peters asked.

"Well, since there were no formal charges against him…"

"You mean you let him go? That's the joker who pounded my car. You saw him do it."

"You never filed a charge. It was your car," Johnson retorted.

"I'm glad I don't work for this department. You people are too much into details and correct by the book procedure. Need I remind you that by using initiative, I likely saved the lives of the farmer and his wife? I'll bet they will thank me, even if you won't. Pity that we missed that bunch. I should have come out here alone and not called you."

"And you would have shot, say, ten or so of them all by yourself?" Johnson sneered.

"That's for sure." The way Peters said it, it was no brag or joke. Johnson kept quiet this time.

"Well, what's next, Inspector?" Johnson asked.

"How about stopping every motorcycle in the area. We know he's riding one."

"New York does stop and frisk. Not here, I'm afraid. Besides, there are too many of them, and they are too hard to catch."

"Run that DNA, and let me know, will you?" Peters asked.


Merchant felt naked without his beard, and he frankly missed the long hair that used to fall over his shoulders during a ride. This just wasn't the same. He gunned the bike harder, trying to remember where that little slug lived, the one who was always trying to be one of the boys, the little pretender biker.

He had to get away from the gang until that black bastard left town again. When he heard that the cop blatantly and singlehandedly invaded a gang bar and took one of his men out without anyone trying to stop him, he was screaming angry. At least at the other guys. Privately, he wondered if he would have had the balls to draw down on this particular cop. This one wanted to kill and would do so for any reason. This cop was different. You couldn't hide behind the law with a killer on the loose, carrying a badge.

He remembered, sort of, where Gunnar lived, and he slowed down, looking for the dilapidated pretend chopper he rode. A crummy Japanese copy of a chopper. He spotted it parked under a light, as if someone would actually want to steal that piece of trash. Merchant pulled alongside, shut his bike off, and stood looking around, wondering which of those hovel low-renters Gunnar inhabited.

"That you, Merchant?" a voice nearby called out. The shape came out of the shadows and under the blue street light, looking Merchant over before coming too close.

"Yeah, Gunnar. Came to visit."

"No kidding!" Gunnar said excitedly. "I've always wanted…. Say, I've just three six packs in there. Should I go get some more?"

"No, man. That's just fine. Are you going to invite me in or what?"

"Of course, Merchant. …Aren't you missing something? I mean you look different without your beard. I almost didn't recognize you." Gunnar said the frightening word 'almost.' Merchant realized that just changing his hairstyle wouldn't be enough. He had to go all the way. The black cop was relentless and ruthless. Merchant would have to metamorph or die. He had dressed the same way for so long that he didn't own any clothing other than a couple of pairs of jeans and assorted leather and denim jackets. Nothing to hide in, especially if they were looking for colors.

"Say, Gunnar, do you want to be a real pal?"

Gunnar nodded enthusiastically to his hero. Anything, including murder, anything to be considered a brother.

"Then you need to get me some threads, you know, real clothes. Tonight."

"Gee, man, I don't know much about that," Gunnar said. Pity that Merchant was so much bigger than him, plus he was very short of dough.

"Here, take this," Merchant said, thrusting a wad into Gunnar's hand. "I'll write down my sizes. You can go, while I take a break and down some suds."

Gunnar was slow, but he caught on quickly. "On the lam?" he asked in a whisper.

"Yeah, something like that. Don't tell anybody. Got that?"

"Sure, Merchant. I got it." Gunnar took the cash and gave Merchant his keys, looking like the cat who just swallowed Cleveland. To think Merchant was depending on him. Now, for sure, he would be allowed in. He had it made.

"Hey, Gunnar," Merchant called as he walked away. A metallic object was flying toward Gunnar, and he stuck up his hand to catch it. "Take my bike. Crack it up, and you'll answer for it."

Peters turned down yet another seedy street, lit principally by cheap neon, marked by rows of angled motorcycles, all leaning in the same direction. He drove slowly, looking for the distinctive extended chrome forks and the extravagant chrome motors so favored by the gangs. He didn't want to crash any of the bars, which would just alert Merchant by putting him on notice that he was being sought. Surprise would be better, Peters knew. He wanted to watch them leave. The first hardcore biker who was clean shaven would be in for a surprise. He pulled into a dark corner and settled in for a long wait. The bars would all be closed by three. After that, he could leave and get some rest.

He had laughed at Johnson when the DNA came back just as he knew it would. Positive match. Merchant was part of the rape gang who had attacked Gale Randolph and likely many others. He was going down, and Peters preferred an excuse to perform the execution himself. Save the trouble. He had obtained *carte blanche* to stay in this town until the criminal was caught. There was a collective guilt about the Randolph girl in her hometown. Her world famous mother was murdered some years ago right on a city street, and the perps were never caught. The town then allowed the orphaned Gale Randolph to be abducted from a city street and raped for four days and, afterward, abandoned for dead. *They...we...owe her*, Peters swore silently. Shooting

Merchant wouldn't be enough, there had to be some other way for vengeance to be satisfying.

Gunnar was riding a real bike this time. A rev produced the most delicious crackling thunder from the straight pipes on the right side. He craned his neck trying to watch for a blue flame out the back but was tentative because of the inherent instability of the long fork. He decided to take a turn down Rampart Street, the local nest of hangouts. Someone, anyone, might see him go by, hanging from his hands on the high bars, and it would spark envy and wonder.

He made the turn with his right foot down, still unaccustomed to the pathetically long turning radius of this machine. He went by slowly, revving every few seconds, causing small groups to notice. Some even removed their sunglasses to see him better. This was the life, Gunnar knew, to actually *be* somebody.

One person did notice, and sat up in his seat, squinting at the passing awkward motorcycle as it thundered by. The rider was sitting on the bike like a beginner, Peters recognized. He was wobbling a bit too much for it to be his. He started his car and eased out into the street about a block behind the motorcycle. There was a package draped across the rear fender. A soft package. Clothing perhaps. The rider was dressed in the usual fare, jeans, boots and denim, but there were no colors on the back of his vest. Something was amiss. After leaving Rampart street, the motorcycle accelerated briskly but was easily followed because the rider for some reason dared not break the speed laws. Clearly, the bike had been loaned, borrowed or stolen, and Peters doubted the stolen theory. He had a feeling in his gut that this was his lead to Merchant. It fit. Merchant was hiding, and he had given his bike to an unknown, a wannabe who was not in the sights of the law. Peters was certain that this motorcycle was never going to get too far from Merchant's grasp, and he determined to follow it to its source.

# Chapter 30

# Chapter 31

# *"Want To See Your Mother?"*

Jeff had the receiver at his ear by the first ring. "Hello?"

"McLally here. I'm back in town. What's up with our patient?"

"She thinks she's ten years old. Her roommate and I can't seem to dislodge her memory. She's forgotten so much of her life that she's not the same person at all."

"What's she doing right now?"

"She's been asleep for three or four hours."

"Get her up and bring her to the lab. I'll be there by the time you arrive."

McLally was waiting when the three of them came in. Gale remembered the lab and initially refused to enter. They patiently explained that her mother would be there soon, and if she wanted to see her... McLally was seated behind his desk watching the little parade come toward him. Gale stopped short when she saw him, clearly recognizing him but not wanting to get any closer. He stood and came to her slowly, smiling and friendly, stopping well before he got within arm's length.

"Well, Gale! You look fine and rested! Won't you come in so we can talk a bit?" He backed away and extended his arm to the chairs in front of his desk.

"It's all right, Gale. We'll be right beside you," Jeff said close to her ear and put his hand softly on her back urging her forward. The three sat opposite McLally, with Gale in the center.

"I just got back from England, London really. Ever been there, Gale?"

"My new father is from London," she answered.

"Well, it's a small world. What's his name?"

"Sir William Greyson."

"Wow! The famous conductor. So he married your mother?"

"Yes, and adopted me."

"Where were you before you woke up in there?" McLally indicated the lab room with a flick of his thumb.

"On a train."

"Where were you going?"

"To Paris. We just left Rome. We were in the mountains."

"Oh, yes. I have used that train myself. Did you see a lot of snow?"

"Yes, they stopped the train to clear it."

"Do you remember ever being there before?"

"No. It was my first time in Rome."

"Interesting." He looked at Jeff wanting to tell him something but hesitated. Gale was looking at his face, trying to analyze whether he was friend or foe. He decided to chance it. "Jeff, do you know a key moment in her memory of this entire event? Let me specify...early, very early, in this series?"

Jeff didn't have to consider very long. He had heard the story after she emerged the first time and remembered when she had started inventing a life. "I would say, when she sang before a large audience. The night things changed for her."

McLally got the picture. Jeff had to be referring to the night her mother was killed, actually before she was killed, a part of Gale's memory constructed of remembered fact. He cleared his throat and retrieved a large sheet of paper and spread it out on his desk. With a marker, he started drawing circles, one after another, each one linked to the previous one. He went around the entire perimeter of the paper and then tossed the pen aside.

"Memory can be linked. One memory follows another like a chain. You start by remembering one thing which leads to another like a map of the highway system. In the real world, all the separate links are connected in a nearly continuous stream but are accessed by recall of physical events. For instance, down here," he pointed to a random link and tapped his finger on the spot. "I can recall that event because a car horn sounded, or Aunt Thelma called at that moment, or nearly anything. The memory of a sensory stimulus of any kind, you see, is the entry point. If you have a memory chain which had no actual sensory inputs, then the link can only be accessed from the start of the chain. Break the chain anyplace and the entire chain is lost. Another way to look at it is that normal memory is dense, layered and accessible from many emotional and physical links. A dream memory, a false one, is thin, superficial and has only one entry point. Break one link and it is gone. Think of a stout steel chain holding a boat to a pier. If you cut it any place, the boat drifts away never to be seen again. Am I making this clear?" He looked at Jeff, the only one he had to convince.

"Which would leave a large vacant spot where the boat had been moored."

"True enough, but you can always park another boat there."

"Am I losing my brain cells listening to this crazy stuff? I don't get what you are talking about," Sibyl said, looking back and forth at them.

"I am talking about changing a memory. It's what our research is all about, Miss. Just pay attention and don't comment," McLally said sharply.

"Are you talking about me?" Gale asked in a very small voice, afraid to speak up. She looked at Sibyl, then Jeff, for support.

"Gale," McLally asked. "What do you want? Is there anything that we can do for you?"

"I want to go back to my mother."

"You heard Jeff just now talking about the night you sang. Do you remember that time?"

"Yes. That was the night Bill asked Mother to marry him. I was there."

"Would you like to visit that place again, to actually sing on stage that very night with everyone watching, including your mother?"

"Yes."

"I can arrange that for you. Would you like to go there right now?" he asked.

Sibyl shifted in her chair, wanting to scream at them, to refuse the proposal that would once again put Gale at risk, this time the risks should be obvious. She looked at Jeff, but he shook his head *no*. He also wanted to treat Gale like a laboratory animal. More and more, would they ever learn?

"Do I have a say in this?" Sibyl asked.

"No." They both responded at the same time.

"Jeff, could I have a moment with you?" McLally asked. He motioned with his hand at Sibyl, indicating that she should stop talking about it. They went into the lab and closed the office door behind them.

"We should try an intervention, Jeff, erase the false memory she has built," McLally said.

"How are you going to get cooperation from her? She is going to return to the exact moment she wants to, no matter what you suggest."

"That's the idea. She will return to it. Remember that her memory is linked from its start to wherever it was interrupted. The only way in is from the beginning of the chain. I planted the suggestion that she recall her performance. I would assume that she sang for a few minutes, at least. She has to start somewhere near that spot to get in."

"Why can't she simply return to when she separated from her mother before the drug wore off?" Jeff asked.

"I'm sure she will, if given enough time. We'll administer the isotope at the same moment as the Puszithrin. She'll have a little over thirteen minutes to find the spot and restart her memory again. It's the only way I can think of. Our best chance."

"I'm responsible for her present condition, but I'm afraid to be party to any more errors. It seems that we just don't have enough information yet on how the memory process works. It's all guesswork."

"What happens to her if we don't do something, if we just stand back and watch?" McLally asked.

"She's never going to function like she is. The memory she created is too large, too clear and perfect for her to ignore. Clinically, she'd be diagnosed as insane."

"She acts like a ten year old, because she believes she is. Erase that corrupt memory and she'll be a normal gal who can't remember much about her past. From what you told me, most of it was horrid after her mother died."

McLally was right, Jeff reasoned. Something had to be done before Gale could get away from them and back into the world. It was a desperate measure and full of unknowns but the best hope.

"Tell me one more time how you get her back to one specific memory?" Jeff asked.

McLally winked. "I have a plan. Watch me."

They returned to the office, finding Gale leaning into Sibyl's shoulder and looking at them with fright and alarm as they approached.

"Gale? Want to see your mother again?" McLally asked. She nodded without leaving the protection of Sibyl's shoulder. With encouragement, they helped her into the lab and got her on the gurney. Jeff and McLally busied themselves getting the equipment running and the cart prepared as Sibyl remained with Gale, holding her hand and whispering in her ear.

After the IV was started, McLally leaned close to Gale and affectionately stroked her forehead. "Do you remember what you sang that night?" he asked.

Gale paused in thought, remembering that night. It was a long time ago, but it was the most important night of her life and had never been repeated. It was the night she made her mother proud of her.

"I remember."

"How did it go? Can you sing just a little bit for me?"

"There's no music," she protested.

"Well, just the words then. Can you recall the words? Even the start would be nice."

Gale pinched her eyebrows, trying hard to remember. What were the words? It's been so long, she thought.

# Chapter 31

# Chapter 32

## *Mother, Sweet Mother*

Gale remembered the feeling, the sensation of wind pouring smoothly over her face and wings as she glided over the world. She had no competitor, no enemy, and no friend. She was alone in the air and master of this world of lights. Far below they twinkled, each one precious, but all of them together representing her entire life, every moment of her life. All she had to do was to choose. But what was the song she was hearing? Where did it come from? She looked around trying to find the source as the song grew louder, boring into her mind, repeating itself over and over. She couldn't escape it, couldn't tune it out. The song became an orchestra. Forty-five instruments were playing the same tune in front of her, she could nearly feel the vibrations on her face from them. And the lights shining up at her face from below and from above, darkening the room except where she stood, the heat of the lights penetrating her hair and warming her ears. She looked into the distance and saw heads of people, rows and rows of people, and all the heads were looking at her, waiting for her. She glanced over her shoulder at her mother who was just behind the fold of the dark red curtain, standing there instead of on the stage where she belonged. Her mother was smiling, her eyes moist and flickering in the reflected light from the stage spots. Out of the corner of her eye, Gale could see the conductor, his baton would tell her when to begin, pointing to her when he was ready. Sir William smiled over his shoulder at her and nodded. It was about to start, she knew, and she took a deep breath and tilted her head back as the words flowed from her, a steady stream of words, of sounds, of music, beautiful music. The song was her, it floated from her and toward the audience, hypnotizing, stunning them, capturing them all. She had no sense of self, no feet, no body, only a voice, a pure sweet girl's voice representing all of human suffering, love, devotion, all coming from a small girl in a satin dress bathed in bright light and worshiped by thousands whose spirits soared with her into the night.

The song ended, thunder erupting frighteningly, coming at her in waves where clapping coincided, merging together as a single clap, then dispersing into thousands of individual hands slapping back and forth endlessly. She bowed lowly, as she had been instructed, and the clapping grew in volume, now accompanied by shouts. She bowed again as Sir William's baton fell in her direction, indicating that another was expected. The roar was never ending, unlike she had ever heard from the other side of the stage, when her mother was standing where she now stood. She was relieved that it was over, elated by the joy from offstage, but now without thinking, skipping toward her mother with her arm extended, pulling her onstage with her as the audience came to their feet, the clapping resuming even louder than before, as both bowed toward the audience together for the first time.

"We'll take you home as soon as Bill finishes," Josephine said and hugged Gale to her chest. "I'm so proud, Gale. You were perfect, better than even I anticipated." The door opened a crack after a soft knock, and the conductor's head appeared slowly.

"Come in, Bill. We're waiting for you," Josephine said. Bill pushed the door open fully.

"My fair young Gale Randolph!" he remarked, his hand in the air like he was still standing in front of the orchestra. "You are being celebrated tonight! What an achievement for us all, and to think that you are only a mite, a fledgling, not yet a woman, and still you have the world in your grasp. I bow to you." And he did, lowly and sincerely.

Gale's mother helped her off with her stiff gown and removed her bright shoes. She slipped on a cotton shift and tied her comfortable canvas shoes for her, smiling at her and chatting about tonight's performance. Gale was tired, even limp. For the first time ever, she understood her mother better. Josephine Randolph had been through the same thing a thousand times. It was a way of life for her, yet she understood that her precocious young star would be spent, the fight gone for now. Tomorrow was the time to discuss tonight, where every detail could be examined, every favorable comment would be repeated. Now was time to rest for young Gale.

Time to return to being a little girl instead of a celebrity.

Sir William Greyson knocked at the door with the tip of his walking stick. He wore a magnificent black cape with crimson lining which was gloriously exposed when he moved his arm. He stood away from the door beside Gale and her mother, politely waiting for Mrs. Becker to open it for them.

"Well, don't the three of you look handsome! Indeed!" she exclaimed, clapping her hands together. "And how did our young singer do tonight? Did she bring down the house?" Nanny Becker was always the same happy person, always willing to give another her respect and well-wishes.

The digital clock was steadily counting down, the numerals changing in a blur, measuring minutes, seconds and milliseconds. At exactly four minutes from automatic firing, they pushed Gale's gurney into the circular opening of the big machine and a deep clanking sound preceded a series of electric servo motors adjusting as the machine set up parameters based on Gale's data file. A panel of green LEDs simultaneously turned on. The machine had taken charge and firing was scheduled at the end of the count-down of thirteen minutes, seven seconds, thirty-one milliseconds from the time of administration of Ted-Zeththrinoid. Jeff studied Gale's face intently trying to discern where her mind had gone. He thought that McLally's trick of inducing her to conduct a subconscious memory search was an ingenious innovation and, if it worked, most impressive. Her face was placid, without lines or even a hint of emotion making it impossible to decipher by observation alone which memory she was recalling.

Standing beside the unconscious Gale, Jeff had an epiphany, the reality of his own nature became more clear than ever. He cared, deeply cared. Jeff absolutely could never perform a procedure on a subject which entailed risk or injury. If he was to remain a scientist, it would have to be a theoretical one, not one who used test subjects, either animal or human.

The time relentlessly dwindled toward automatic discharge of the focused microwave beams. Jeff felt his pulse and anxiety rising and fought the urge to run away so that he couldn't contribute to any more injury to this woman whom he loved so completely. It was too late to leave, being only seconds before whichever neuron activated in her brain would be targeted by the beam.

McLally was calm, methodical, and displayed no concern about the outcome. Like a surgeon, he was able to separate himself from his patient emotionally and proceed according to a logical scientific pattern. Any outcome was interesting, not good, not bad, just data to be used to further or change an existing hypothesis. He went about the task of Gale's memory erasure with his typical thoroughness toward detail, and also his typical dispassion.

Gale was happy. As a result of her pleading, her mother and Sir William would stay with her instead of leaving her alone. She turned toward her mother and reached for her hand, feeling her soft touch, her warmth, and looked into her loving face. It was true. Her mother would do anything for her, all she had to do is to ask.

Nanny Becker backed away from the opening, her large arm inviting them inside while Gale's mother's hand was on her neck, gently guiding her forward. A stunning, blinding white light flashed, blotting out the apartment in an instant, then as quickly reverting to dark, velvet black, where no light, no shadow or image was visible, the edge of space, of nothingness, not even sound. Gale found herself standing on the edge of the change, the future gone, the past behind, her mother's hand still warm against her neck. She no longer understood what was going to happen, only what had happened. She felt herself rising, floating, alone, her wings carrying her aloft, the air supporting her weight as she glided far above the surface looking down, lights glittering below as far as she could see, but also noting a shroud, a black cloud, hovering close to the surface over a vast area, blocking the light from her vision. The amorphous form had indistinct margins, and was thin in spots where small dots of light escaped while dense and black in others. She pulled her wings in, plummeting toward the center of the cloud, attempting to see through it as it swept by beneath her. She strained to penetrate, to make out any detail or to get a suggestion of what was beneath the darkness but without success. Whatever had taken place was not to be reversed, her memories were lost, covered by an impenetrable mist which blocked out any access, any recall.

"Gale, can you open your eyes?" McLally asked. Her eyelids fluttered, her subconscious uncertain if it wanted to stop searching for her lost memories. "Gale?" he persisted.

Her eyes opened, finding McLally's, holding them firmly and clearly in focus as her awakening brain searched for the meaning of this person floating above her. Then, she remembered. He had asked her to sing the song from that night on the stage, the song that she had practiced for months and that had so moved her audience. In her mind, the orchestra was playing again, the baton hovering, waiting for her to start once more. Her voice rose, echoing from the hard tile, resonating her melodious words and penetrating the souls of the three gathered around her gurney. *"Caro nome che il mio cor festi primo palpitar, le delizie dell'amor."* The purity and sincerity of her voice, its power, the words of Verdi once more come alive again, holding them spellbound. None of them had ever been this close to a singer of her virtuosity, her words seeming to come from an angelic source, an immortal, beyond human ability to create or understand. In their minds, Gale was transformed from a helpless, frightened, little girl into a force of nature, a unique being of magic. She sat up and swung her legs off the edge of the gurney before continuing her aria, *"Mi dêi sempre rammentar! Col pensiero il mio desir a te ognora volerà,e pur l' ultimo sospir."* She stopped and looked at each of them, one at a time, her eyes clear and unafraid, her face transformed into something noble and timeless.

"What am I doing here?" she asked calmly.

## Chapter 33

# *Transformation*

After spending the rest of the morning and afternoon with her, Jeff and Sibyl agreed on one thing. Gale took in information but gave out little. She was a sponge and absorbed the world as fast as it came at her. After only a short time, it was difficult to decide what she had learned compared to what she recalled. Within moments of her awaking, she knew their names, and soon after walking into her apartment, she seemed to understand everything about it. She looked at them with her clear comprehending eyes, which looked through them as if they were cellophane. Gale showed no fear, but neither did she display joy, friendship, gratitude or any particular warmth. She was a computer downloading data, gobs of it, any amount of it. She was interested in her schedule and studied it briefly before casting it aside, memorized.

Previously, each time Jeff had managed to tell Gale that he loved her, it had taken a lot of courage. He was only giving way to his passion for her, his yearning to be close, and his most fundamental desire to share the rest of his life with her. That was before she was rid of her false memory. The new Gale who had emerged didn't have a past that she could remember and no hang-ups about it. She had no recall of her rape or her many foster parents or her poverty. It was as if she had escaped nearly every formative thing that had made her Gale Randolph since her mother's death. This Gale had just walked away from a celebrated stage appearance which was still fresh in her mind. Nothing else mattered to her other than music. Jeff gathered that she was uninterested in how she had gotten where she is or who had helped her. Only the future was interesting, and she was rapidly forming ideas about it.

"Gale?" Jeff finally asked. "Do you remember where we first met?" It was a casual remark but designed to determine her ability to recall her recent past.

She looked at him blankly, the only indication that she even heard him was a slightly upraised eyebrow on the right side.

"And me, Gale? Do you remember me?" Sibyl repeated.

"You are Sibyl. We share this apartment."

"True. For two years. Do you remember that?"

Again, the raised eyebrow. Gale suddenly looked disinterested in their conversations and went to her room, softly shutting the door behind her.

Sibyl raised her hands in a helpless gesture. "Does she even hear us?" she wondered to Jeff.

"If she does, she's totally uninterested in the subject. We simply are here, part of the scenery. By the way, did you ever contact the man she said was her father?"

"I'm glad you reminded me. He called back the same day, and after I told him who I was, that is, who my mother was, he was very interested. He was aware that Josephine Randolph was murdered. After all, it was international news, and he had heard about Gale's debut performance that same day. According to him, he wept when he read the news. I came right out and told him that my mother said he was my father."

"Wait a minute," Jeff stopped her. "You told him that your name was Gale Randolph?"

"It seemed more…personal that way. It was a great move, because he was too polite to reject me out of hand and then asked about my birthdate. The best part is that he wanted a DNA sample."

"What kind of sample?"

"I sent him Gale's hairbrush and her tooth brush. That'll do it. He hasn't called back yet, but I thought I'd give him a week before I called again."

"So it was…is…possible after all. I wonder how Gale got his name out of an invented memory?" Jeff mused.

"What do you make of her now that you and genius have 'fixed' her? Has she become what you thought?" Sibyl mocked.

"Not exactly. At least she's not ten any longer. I don't know what lies ahead. Besides, I can't even tell what she's thinking."

"She's like a robot to me. Learns fast, learns everything in fact, but there is nothing inside. She's empty. I think you two guys have ruined her, if you want my opinion."

"The blank memory spot we created has been absorbing everything in sight. I wonder if it will ever fill up," Jeff said.

### *Voice lesson with Monsieur Villetaurse*

"Your presence here today is surprising, Miss Randolph; after all, you have missed the last three sessions. I had nearly given up seeing you once more. Does this mean that you will mend your ways and actually attempt to graduate?" Villetaurse huffily said as she came in.

"I am here to learn. Is that not enough?" Gale replied. She looked poised to leave, and her face implied that there was to be no apology.

"Yes. Then, do come in, and let's get started. Have you worked on Puccini's, *Turandot*?"

"No."

Villetaurse looked disgusted and shook his head. "How do you expect to accomplish anything if you never make an effort? Singing is hard work, and you have to labor to improve."

"I can sing it," Gale assured him. Her placid face, her steadiness, was unsettling. Either she didn't care what he thought, or for some strange reason, actually thought she could perform a difficult aria without practice.

"We'll see about that," he said and threw a tattered score on the piano music stand. He sat down and, with a contemptuous last look at her, started playing. At the first sound of her voice, Villetaurse looked up from his keyboard, almost by reflex. This was not the voice he remembered her having. That voice was timid, unexpressive and delivered with her head often lowered. This voice was commanding, tonally perfect, and delivered with sincerity and a head that postured the vocal canal for maximum effect. He was mesmerized by the beauty of what he was hearing. It was if an experienced and celebrated artist had come in her place. Gale was no mere student. She didn't even belong at this institution nor with him, a mediocre has been. He played with feeling, wishing for the piece to never end, to loop and continue for the rest of time. She finished to applause from Villetaurse, his face awash with pride and awe.

"My dear Miss Randolph," he stuttered. "How....why..." He didn't know where to begin, but something radical had happened to this most obscure student. She had become a blooming orchid of rare and intoxicating talent. He stood before her, nearly wanting to bow or fall to his knees, then he noticed something else. She was ravishingly beautiful. It was the way she carried herself, the confidence she radiated, the expectation of approval from lowly persons such as himself. Gale Randolph had been reborn or had been inhabited by the ghost of a prima donna. She looked away from the lust in his heart, turning her profile to him which made the effect she had produced magnified many times.

Villetaurse tried to control himself, rapidly considering how to best use and display such talent. After all, as her primary voice coach, he was in for a great deal of the credit for her abilities. "May I call you Gale?" Villetaurse nearly pleaded. His student ignored him as if he was struck dumb, or more likely, reduced to insignificance. "Very well then, Miss Randolph, you must, you simply must, sing for the public and show your considerable talent. And as soon as possible. Are there any pieces that you have worked up and are ready to perform?"

"I will perform with an orchestra only, Maestro. The question is: which are the pieces that *they* have ready?"

It struck Villetaurse that a second assumption would be in order. Gale Randolph had been liberated in some way, her native talent unleashed, and the resultant energy would burn as brightly as a star. The thought struck him that her background was somehow connected to the stage, then he did remember. Gale was the daughter of the world renowned prima donna, Josephine Randolph. Of course! Her daughter had inherited this God-given talent, and for some reason, it was now exploding. *Louer les cieux!*

# Chapter 34

## *Predator*

The motorcycles were side by side but, by necessity, staggered, with the long fork of the expensive chopper out front. Merchant rode the smaller one and felt humiliated on it. His bare face and short hair, and the fact that he was astride a beginner motorcycle, made him hope that he wasn't spotted by any of his gang. They would have a good laugh at his expense. Merchant wanted to kick out at the other bike beside him, to teach him who is the superior but couldn't, because the other motorcycle actually belonged to him. It was in the happy control of the little germ, the unwashed insect, the pretender, Gunnar. When this was over, Merchant swore, he would even the score with Gunnar. They rode together for a reason, at the insistence of Gunnar who wanted Merchant to see the location he had spotted. Merchant would have never agreed to go in broad daylight, but he needed an outing. Two weeks in the can would have been better than two weeks in the dirty smelly apartment rented by the day by Gunnar. The place wasn't fit for a pig. Two weeks absent of women were also taking a toll on Merchant, the pressure building. He assumed that the black cop had left town by now but wanted to take no chances before he attempted to return to the gang. He had listened to Gunnar go on and on about this place and how unguarded it was, how easily an invasion could be done, and how absolutely luscious were the babes inside. College girls. Cute and unsoiled. It was tempting, and the more he thought about it, the more it became an obsession. At least he could take a drive-by look and determine if Gunnar had any common sense.

Gunnar pointed, and they slowed to a crawl while Merchant sized the place up. He was told that the target was the upstairs apartment which had a back entrance. Sure enough, this time Gunnar was right. There was a big rear parking lot backed up to a tree line and a large fence on the opposite side. The building was older and needed paint and repair. It just hung there as it obviously had for years, the tenement owner raking in the dough and doing nothing in return for his tenants. If they didn't like it...well, they could go someplace else and pay more. The story about two women fit. Merchant could see floral drapes across the windows. They rode slowly around the block. No unwelcome surprises would be the first thing to consider. Other structures around the entire block were similar, likely filled by student occupants. Merchant knew that university students were poor tenants, noisy, messy and prone to standing outside in loud groups all hours of the night. The outcry of two women would hardly go noticed. Indeed, Gunnar was on to something. It might be a good spot to do a little forced womanizing. After one more pass-by, they picked up speed and disappeared down the street.

A nondescript midnight blue Ford sedan eased away from the curb on the opposite side of the street and headed in the same direction as the motorcycles. He knew where they had come from and where they were going. Summing all the facts, he also knew who were riding the bikes, exactly who. What he didn't know is why they were casing the apartment, the very one occupied by Gale Randolph and her roommate. It might be what he was waiting for all this time, and the thought made him smile.

# Chapter 35

# *Fireball*

"And how is Gale?" McLally asked from his leather chair. He had his feet uncaringly placed on the polished wood desk, his arms behind his head. Jeff pulled the metal chair closer and sat down on the other side.

"She's had what I would call a strange reaction," Jeff summarized.

"How so?"

"She's clearly no longer a child in a woman's body. But what she is...well, it's hard to describe. The only attachment she has, her only commitment, is music. Her singing. From what Sibyl said, her professors have been startled at the change. Word about her is all over campus."

"I see. And how is the boyfriend/girlfriend thing going?"

"She knows my name...that's about the extent of it."

"And you had hoped to be closer. That sort of business, eh?"

"After the first treatment when we removed her fear of touching, for a short time, it was wonderful. I could tell by just looking at her that she and I were going to become close, even intimate. All of that is gone. She won't even engage in a conversation with me."

"A question, Jeff. Do you think, or can you tell if, she is aware of all the things you have done and are currently doing for her?"

"I just don't know what she recalls, but I can say with certainty that she no longer cares, even if she remembers."

"It's sad for you, my boy, but I have a point of view that you may not have considered. She has no past after that night her mother was murdered. She overwrote it, and we eliminated it. She went from a childhood star to her present state with no interruptions. From a child to a woman but without all the emotional events which shape a child. She has not experienced any emotional milestones in years and that has allowed her to concentrate on the only thing she knows...her singing. To win her again, you have to start over, bit by bit. You have to create the emotions of a woman, to awaken what is for sure in her."

"I would give anything to do just that, but she has not the slightest care about me, no interest at all. How do I go about it?"

"Have you any musical abilities?"

"None."

"Well, you might have no chance of success then. In my view, all you can do is to be there for her when and if she needs you. Never protest or feel sorry for yourself. Give, give, give. Someday she will notice you."

"Or not."

"I've been thinking about her case nearly constantly, and for sure she is an interesting study.

With her, we might just be able to tell if theories about memory storage and retrieval are accurate or are in need of revision. She seems to have no memory of the past several years. On the surface of it, I am convinced that most of her memory is still intact, though. It's the retrieval mechanism which has been either damaged or altered. There are many routes to a city, many choices of roads or rails, but the destination ends up in the same place. My bet is that, given the right trigger, she will recall nearly everything that has ever happened to her...someday. She might even recall that you mean something to her after all. Be patient, Jeff."

"But...doesn't that negate the very foundation of our research? Isn't the operative theory that we can change a neuron enough to eliminate its synaptic connections?"

"Of course. And we saw it work on you and on her, or don't you recall?"

"Yes...but..."

"We did change something, but it might have only been an entry point, even a major entry point, or in some examples, the only entry point. There may be others, though, which will return a person to a memory. Her false memory, however, had only one entry point. That one is gone forever. Do you understand?"

"I think so. A hard theory to test. How will we know which version is accurate?" Jeff asked.

"When a memory returns unexpectedly, we will know."

# Chapter 34

Peters drove around the block again, this time very slowly, looking into every corner for the two motorcycles which had been parked side by side in the same location for three weeks. They were gone. He gritted his teeth, an unuttered curse on his lips. This was unexpected. Bad timing. They could be gone for good or just riding around again, there was no way to tell. He pulled to the curb trying to think it out. There was the trip they took to Gale Randolph's apartment. Why? He never understood how there could be a link, yet he had observed for himself their interest in the place. It could not have been a coincidence. Automatically, he reached for his key and started moving. Gale's apartment would be the first place he would check. The risk to her was too high not to.

Gunnar was not particularly good at stealth. In fact, he was not good at anything, Merchant thought, as they quietly ascended the staircase. It creaked with their weight, and Merchant used his hand against Gunnar's chest to keep him from going too fast. If the girls were in there, they had to enter suddenly and without warning for their plan to work. Merchant still had not decided whether he should kick in the door or simply use Gunnar's stupidly simple idea of pretending to deliver a pizza. Surely, an unexpected delivery would incite them to call the cops before opening the door. Still…there was a chance that the girls would answer or even open the door for them. They reached the top of the landing and looked down the narrow hall. Nothing else was stirring, not even the sounds of cooking or music. As far as Merchant could tell, no one was in the entire building. Better that way, he mused. He nodded that Gunnar could knock and moved away from the peephole so as to not be seen.

After three raps on the door, it was apparent that no one was home...yet. Merchant thought of a better way. Be inside when the girls arrived home, where surprise would be complete. He took out a big knife and went to work on the jam. After probing, his blade found the right place, and the door swung open. Standing there and listening, Merchant knew that his plan was going to work. All they had to do was wait.


Gale was standing alone when Jeff arrived. She started walking toward his car as if nothing had changed.

"What happened to Sibyl? Isn't she coming also?" he asked.

"No. She had a date. He'll take her home." She got in the front seat and sat down, obviously finished with her limited conversation. Jeff turned his head toward her, burning with questions, nearly anything to engage her in conversation.

"How was your day?" he asked. "Anything exciting happen?"

"I sang before the music school faculty this morning. They had to be sure I was ready for a concert before it could be scheduled."

"And...what happened? Were they impressed?"

"Of course."

"Isn't it just a miracle, Gale? I mean the way you can sing now. It's amazing to everyone."

"No, there's no miracle. I could always sing well. My mother taught me." She was looking out the forward windshield and not at him. It was all matter-of-fact with her. There was no thrill of being so appreciated. She expected it.

"How about letting me take you out for dinner before you go home? You'll be alone there until Sibyl returns."

"No. I have to learn my lines. Just take me back, please." Jeff sighed and started his car. Talking to her was painful. He couldn't get through, not even in the smallest way. It wasn't that she had rejected him for someone else. She didn't care. Jeff was unimportant, just a tool, a pet that you never petted but who was always there for you. McLally's advice came back to him, that he had to keep at it if he wanted to succeed with her.

When they arrived at the apartment, Jeff could see that the apartment lights weren't on, and he decided to see Gale all the way to the door this time. He followed her up the stairs, and they paused in front of the door as she searched for her keys. As the key went to place, he noticed something odd and quickly grasped her wrist.

"Stop! I see some damage that I've never seen before," he whispered, pointing to the gouges the knife had made. Gale looked at him blankly, not really understanding the import of a few scratches. Jeff tried the door, but it was still locked. He hesitated, not sure that the marks had not been there unnoticed until now. He gently pushed Gale aside and turned the key himself, cracking the door as he looked and listened. The apartment was dead silent and dark. He flipped on the lights and looked around.

After they entered, he stood in the center of the room wondering if he had actually seen signs of forced entry or just invented them. Gale was looking blankly at him, probably wondering if he was ever going to leave.

"Well, then, I'll go now and see you..." he stopped in mid-sentence. Gale's face had changed. There was something in her eyes that he hadn't seen in some time. She was afraid.

"What is it, Gale?"

"He's here." Her eyes rolled around expecting to see something returning from her memory, as her purse slipped from her arm and fell to the floor. Jeff was about to act when he heard a noise from close by. A cough or grunt from the area of the bedrooms. Someone was inside. He grabbed Gale's wrist and pulled her toward the entryway, just as the bedroom door slammed against the wall behind them. They fled together down the staircase with the noise of heavy boots pounding the floor, coming after them. Jeff stiff-armed the exterior door, and they burst into the small parking lot, the sounds of two men close behind. Jeff spun around to face them, holding Gale behind him.

"Well now, isn't he brave?" Merchant mocked. "Going to protect the little woman all by yourself?"

Gunnar grinned from behind. It was perfect, just the type of action he had always dreamed of. Together, they would beat this college boy senseless and then have the girl to themselves.

A car slid to a screeching halt in the street, small puffs of smoke curling away from all four tires. Merchant tried to see who it was, who was stupid enough to interrupt his fun, but the car was dark, darker yet inside, dark enough that no driver was even visible. Something radiated from the car, alarming Merchant. There was a presence inside, something frightening, primitive, violent. Merchant knew who it was even though he couldn't see the black skin or yellow eyes. It was the cop, the entity he most feared meeting again.

"Run for it," he warned Gunnar, pushing him aside, while sprinting for the motorcycles partially hidden in the trees. Gunnar stood there trying to understand what made the fearless Merchant flee, when the situation at last dawned on him, and he turned to run, just as the long-forked motorcycle started moving toward the street. Gunnar had been left to his own slower bike and to his own devices for flight.

The blue car had not moved, remaining awkwardly stopped in the middle of the street, turned slightly to one side. The only way past for Merchant was a small opening in front of the car, and he was on his way toward it, the motorcycle barking a loud harsh thunder as it struggled for speed. Just as it banked, turning sharply away from the car, a tongue of flame erupted from the car window. At first it seemed as the shot had missed, but in an instant the street was lit by the explosion of the motorcycle fuel tank, the fireball centered just under the hapless rider, quickly encasing him in a huge cage of flames which ignited his clothing and his body above his boots. The motorcycle seemed to hesitate in midair as flames shot skyward, silhouetting the helplessly flailing stick figure inside as the fuel-rich fire consumed him. The bike wobbled at first, then struck the curb on the far side of the street, the rider and machine separating into two burning masses, coming to rest twenty feet apart. Gunnar obviously saw what had happened to Merchant, and terrified of meeting the same fate, he tore toward the street with his throttle at maximum. Gunnar's motorcycle leapt the curb and for a short distance was airborne, which prevented the machine from making the necessary turn onto the street. His motorcycle continued diagonally across the street, impacting the corner of a building with terrific force, nearly decapitating its rider.

As Gale and Jeff watched the burning mass across the street, the car door opened, and Peters slowly got out and walked over to the charred corpse and bent down for a moment. Without a word, he got back into his car and slowly pulled away. From far away, sirens became audible and slowly increased in volume.

Gale was trembling, and she allowed Jeff to nestle her in his arms, while pressing her face into his chest.

"It's never over," she mumbled.

"What do you mean? Both of them are dead. They can never hurt you again," Jeff said.

"The attack years ago. I remember it."

"How could you? We erased that memory. It was gone."

"It was the smell. The same smell that was on me for days. I knew he was waiting for me in the apartment as soon as we opened the door."

Jeff just held on, his mind repeating what McLally had postulated. Gale will be able to recall everything over time, just in a different way. He noticed that she was pressing against him very tightly, more of an embrace than a reaction to fear. He kissed her forehead, and she responded by looking up at him. It was a different look than he had seen since her last treatment, full of emotion, and not quite so much confidence.

"Thank you, Jeff, for protecting me. You are always there for me, aren't you?"

"I try to be, because I care for you. But you already know that."

"Yes, I do know. Things aren't the same, Jeff. I have started in a direction which will lead me away from here. It is something that was meant to be, a life my mother would have wanted for me."

"You mean your singing career and that I won't be a part of it, don't you."

"You don't belong to that world, but I do. It will mean travel, nearly constantly, and crowds and pretentious people and, of course, endless music. Stay here and do your research. You are very smart and have a destiny also, just a different one than I do."

She pulled his head down toward her and kissed him with passion. They separated very slowly and reluctantly, and only because the police cars had arrived in force, lighting up the area with sirens and blue flashing lights, the lights flickering on their faces making memories which would be lifelong.

# Chapter 36

# *Prima Donna*

The overhead lights flickered back and forth, the signal that the evening performance was about to begin and commanding that the audience should take their seats. Jeff twisted in his seat and looked around. It was going to be a packed house, the first one he had ever seen. Usually, student performances were sparsely attended and only by friends of the performer. Not this time. Word had spread that a remarkable singer would be the guest of honor tonight, and not only the faculty but the Board of Regents and distinguished alumni were all assembled to hear her. Most of the older crowd were dressed in evening wear and sat together, talking amongst themselves.

The orchestra was ready, and only the occasional tuning notes could be heard as the conductor took his position and sternly looked over the musicians beneath him. The crowd fell into a hush broken by an occasional muffled cough.

Gale would perform solo tonight, Jeff read from the program's listings, and she was slated to sing four famous arias from different well-known operas. He wiped his sweaty hand on his trousers and swallowed hard, as nervous for her as if he had to sing himself. They had been given the best seats, at

Gale's request, because no one at the university would deny her anything she wanted.

Sibyl punched him with her elbow and pointed with her little finger to someone in the first balcony, the one which seemed to overhang the stage. Jeff looked where she pointed and saw an older man sitting alone, dressed in a black tuxedo. As he watched, the conductor turned toward the balcony and gave a low bow and a wave. The man smiled back.

"Who is he?" Jeff asked.

"That's Gale's father. I thought he would be here tonight, and he is!"

"She hasn't seen him yet?"

"No. I've got that planned for later. Unless they mess my plans up at the party."

"What party?" Jeff whispered. Sibyl ignored him, her eyes were on the conductor who had his baton in the air. The room fell into a deep silence, waiting breathlessly just as the conductor was waiting. A beautiful woman walked onto the stage headed toward the center, taking long confident strides. She was dressed in a pure white gown which extended to the floor but with deep cutaways in front and in back. Behind her waist was a large satin bow of slightly contrasting white. The single point of color was a small rose pinned above her right breast, which was just slightly redder than her hair which flowed freely behind her. A swell of applause started and built to greater and greater heights as she took her place and gave a small bow to the conductor. As he brought his baton down sharply, Gale let her hands drop by her sides and tilted her head back, her eyes looking above her, possibly seeing her mother looking down at her, smiling, the tears flickering in her eyes, reflecting the bright lights from below.

She sang, the orchestra played and time passed with each listener enchanted, enthralled and hypnotized. Every time she paused, they seemed to lean forward, driven to applaud but hesitating as she started again. The performance could have gone on for hours, and it was what the audience desired, pleading in their hearts for her to sing more and more and more. Her voice was bringing tears, joy, delight and a sense that tonight would become a legend. A night when an angel came to earth to entertain the entire human race, a night and a performance never to be repeated, a night that every person present became a privileged part of history. Each time she stopped, the audience jumped to their feet, applauding in waves which seemed to flow around the room, making patterns of their own. And each time, the stern conductor had to face the audience and wave his baton in their direction as if a magic spell was being cast, compelling them to sit so that the music could resume. And it was a magic spell that was cast. Jeff felt his own tears washing down his face, and when he pulled out his handkerchief to wipe them, it was snatched by Sibyl for her own uses. When they were applauding, he was aware of Sibyl's shoulder against his, and each time he looked at her, she was looking back at him.

Gale was a wild bird that they had nursed back to health and then taken outside to set it free. She was soaring above them now, looking down at them occasionally, but her attention really on the far horizon. When she started that journey toward the limits of her vision, she would be gone from their lives forever, the separation permanent and necessary. The wild bird would return to its flock where it belonged, leaving the ground-based humans looking up and marveling at the wonder of flight.

The applause continued past her third return to the stage and her third bow. This time she remained standing and looked back at them with a smile. She would do an encore, and this time without the orchestra, an *a cappella* performance without any distraction. The purity of her voice unadorned, unaided, every syllable, every breath, going to the hearts of those watching. Jeff glanced up at Gale's father and saw that he was wiping his eyes also.

She sang *Vissi d'arte* from Puccini's <u>Tosca</u>, and it poured effortlessly out of her as if her birth and life had all led to this singular moment on stage, her words and music becoming imbedded in the brains of her listeners which would now compare every following singer unfavorably to her. When the moment ended and she smiled again that perfect smile showing her perfect teeth, the audience delayed coming to their feet, not wanting to spoil the moment, not wanting to break this perfection or have it disappear as it must. Jeff saw her clearly in that instant. Gale had become her mother, the life she had led Gale would now lead as if it were preordained. He, McLally, and Sibyl had only been there to fulfill her destiny, to be with her until she sprouted her wings and could take flight. And at this moment she had taken flight. Jeff had lost her forever. She was never his and would never have been his. It was always just a dream, a false memory he constructed to make him believe that it could happen. He was an earthling, plodding from place to place, unnoticed, unclaimed, just another human copy pretending to actually be alive.

Jeff and Sibyl remained standing as the audience slowly made the shuffling trip toward the exits. They felt limp, exhausted, empty. There was no more to do or to say. Gale was complete and now owned by the world at large. She would leave a very big hole in their lives.

"Going to the party?" Sibyl asked. "You and I were invited, you know."

"I've never been to a post-production party. I didn't know that was done at a university."

"It isn't. Just this time. Everyone wants to meet the star in person, stand for a second or two in the bright light of her power. We have to go, you realize. She's expecting us to be there."

"Of course, my dear Sibyl. We'll go and smile and praise her, then we'll go someplace quiet and cry in our beer."

"Is that an invite?" she asked coyly.

"You and I have been together the whole time. I wouldn't dream of parting with you, too."

"My thought exactly, Jeff." She smiled up at him as she took his arm for the first time.

The room was densely packed with people, all of whom were wearing expensive clothing...except for Jeff and Sibyl. They felt like crawling around the edge, hiding under a napkin. The noise and laughter were most dense against the wall where Gale was obviously holding court. Using polite pushing and shoving, Jeff led the way as they passed between people holding cocktails and talking loudly to another person just like them.

Jeff met her eyes briefly and knew that she saw him. She was standing against the wall and alongside the conductor, Maestro Vittoria, a short well-groomed man who was smiling broadly at her every utterance. On the other side of her was Maestro John Graymoure. He was looking at Gale intently but not with awe like everyone else. His look would be best described as longing. She was wearing the locket, the one that had belonged to her mother, the same one retrieved that night by Peters from the smoking body of Merchant. Peters had it cleaned before leaving it in an envelope with a note to Gale that her case, and the one of her mother, was finally closed, the remaining perpetrators killed resisting arrest.

"Oh shit!" Sibyl hissed. "I knew my plan would get sabotaged. And I had it all worked out for later. I never told Gale about him. It was to be a surprise. Now what do I do?"

"Looking at him, it might have already happened. You won't get a private word with her now, there are too many people who are trying to do the same thing.

You might as well hang back and watch," Jeff observed.

They made the rest of the way to the front of the group by being rude but apologizing for it on the way past. Gale smiled at them, looking from Jeff's eyes to Sibyl's and back again. No words were necessary. They all understood the affection shared mutually between them. Their friendship was for life, even though the past was now coming to an end. John Graymoure seemed to be gathering his nerve to speak to her. What he had to say was hard to voice in a situation like this, but he was now functioning on compulsion and emotion, leaving reason behind.

"I knew your mother, Gale," he said lowly to her. She turned and looked him in the eye, her gaze rapidly switching between his pupils. He had captured her attention.

"My mother? How did you know her?" she asked.

"I was in love with her. Still am."

Gale turned fully toward him, ignoring other comments directed to her, focusing all her intelligence on him.

"Who are you?" she asked.

"I'm your father. My name is John Graymoure."

She didn't react. It was somehow what she expected from him. She felt a connection earlier the first time she saw his eyes. It was as if she could read his mind, two bells ringing the same note at the same time.

"We have a lot to talk about," he said. "You look just like she did the last time I saw her. I've never forgotten."

"I always wondered who you were."

"And where I was. I never knew until you called me recently. I ran the DNA you sent. We're a match. There is no doubt."

"I never called you," Gale said, then realized what had happened and looked toward Sibyl. Sibyl shrugged and smiled back.

"Your mother had her career. I was in the way, I think. She never told me that she was having a baby, or I would have been there for you."

"I forgive you. She never told me about you either."

"But...how did that girl know to contact me?" The both looked at Sibyl at the same time, both wondering the same thing.

"Hello, Maestro," Jeff said. "I'm a friend of Gale's. I'm Jeff." He offered his hand, and it was taken.

"Hi, Maestro," Sibyl said. "I'm Sibyl, but you can call me Gale. We spoke previously."

"Hi Jeff, Sibyl. Say, what was the reason you contacted me?" John Graymoure asked.

"Gale told me your name. She doesn't remember, because we erased her brain, or something like that."

"Actually, it's very complicated, Maestro," Jeff spoke up.

"It doesn't matter now. It turned out to be the best thing that's ever happened to me." He turned back to Gale who had been silently studying him. "Your performance was the best I have heard since your mother's. In fact, you sound just like her. Truly, it's like she is still here and standing right before me."

"She is, of course. I am part her and part you. I remember everything about her, and now I'll get to know you as well."

"I happen to be in demand as a conductor. If I have to, I'll beg, but you must let me put you on the stage. You are ready for it, and I can make it happen. It would be my fondest wish to introduce you to the public."

"You don't have to beg. I'm willing," Gale said. She took his hand in hers and shook it. John Graymoure slowly pulled her toward him and pressed her against his chest while affectionately kissing the top of her head.

"Isn't there someplace that we have to be, Jeff," Sibyl asked. She patted him on his back, out of view of Gale and her father.

"Yes, there is. A beer is waiting for us in some little private place, a place where we can talk."

"Or something," she said.

## Chapter 37

# *Epilogue*

"**B**obby, for the last time, eat your breakfast. You have to leave for school in ten minutes!" she said, more loudly this time. Bobby looked down at his plate and poked at the eggs. He hated eggs. "Well, at least eat your toast. You have to have some food to last until lunch." Bobby was obviously going to school hungry. He looked back at his mother with a bit of devilry, knowing that time would save him from his food, and she could do nothing about it.

"Jeff! Are you going to hide behind your paper or act like a father and make your boy eat?" Sibyl said. The paper rattled a bit, but Bobby's father wasn't about to take part on the losing side. They all knew that Bobby would get his way in the end.

"Are you coming home for lunch?" she asked, pulling down the paper so that she could see his face. He smiled at the sight of her, the wisps of blonde hair falling across her forehead in that delightfully endearing unkempt look of hers. She was so much more beautiful in her natural state as compared to the look she sought when put together for their infrequent outings.

"I don't know. McLally might ask me to do his lecture today. I never am sure where he will end up. Someone has to teach. It's what they pay us for."

"Seems to me that since you are a full, tenured professor just like him, he wouldn't be able to pull that stuff any more. Have you any rights at all?" She was angry about the constant inconvenience of Jeff's relationship with the head of the department.

Jeff shrugged. It was the way it was. A small price to pay for the near-celebrity fame their joint research had brought. It was at times like these that his memory returned to their first case. He dared not think of her willingly, but she came back at unexpected moments, her beautiful face waiting to be kissed, her age unchanging with time, and his passion for her still undiminished. Without full control of his emotions, he felt his face flush, the memory of Gale in his arms seen a bit too clearly.

Sibyl saw it also. In her heart, she always knew that Jeff's love for Gale was undiminished. He also loved her, she knew, but she had given up trying to erase Gale from his memories. It was enough that she had him body and soul, had his child, owned his future. He could have the occasional thought well up about his first love. It wouldn't change anything, anything at all.

She pushed the paper lower until he looked at her, his face still tinged with pink. "Did you read about Gale Randolph yet?"

"Whatever do you mean?"

"She's in there. Page three, as I recall." She let the paper go as he flipped the pages.

"Ahh. You are right. I would have missed this." There was a pause as he rapidly and hungrily scanned the lines. "My god! She's getting married. I thought it would never happen. To someone named Ruffio. He must be a singer, the way the paper raves about him. Ever heard of him?"

"I looked him up long ago. Gale told us about him after changing her memory. I wanted to see if she had made him up or if he was a real person. He was an up and coming young singer at that time, and real for sure. Today, he is the only tenor said to replace the great Pavarotti. He seems to have no last name or perhaps first name. I saw his picture in a magazine only last week. Ruffio is ravingly handsome in that Italian way. You know, the dark curly hair, the bronze skin and penetrating eyes."

"Stop right there. I don't want to hear any more about Ruffio." Jeff couldn't help having his heart sink a little with the thought of this suave Italian possessing Gale. It was something that he couldn't give up, his Gale. He finished the article and took a big sigh. "Well, young man!" he said to Bobby who was waiting patiently for his parents to notice him again. "Go and brush your teeth. We are leaving in three minutes."

Sibyl was looking at him, wondering what he was thinking, wondering if the news of Gale's wedding would be the final break in the link. He stood and adjusted his tie and took a last sip of coffee. He went around the table and took Sibyl's face in his hands and kissed her on the lips. "I love you. Especially in the mornings." He slung his suit jacket over his shoulder, pushing young Bobby ahead. As they got in the car, he thought to himself about how to convince McLally that he desperately needed another session in their machine.


**The End**

# A Note of Appreciation

The worst and the best writers seek one thing above all others. A reader who not only reads their book, a work of astounding personal effort, but who shares his/her experiences with the world. We want to know what you think about our work. Truly we do. Of course, we want you to like it, and us, and will be so grateful if you take the time to give us even the smallest amount of praise. I really entreat you to do so.

If you have constructive criticism you want us to hear, please, out with it! Writing is such an isolating experience. I begin to live in my books and come to nearly feel that my characters are real. When someone criticizes one of them, I feel their pain. And some of my own.

But if you enjoyed this novel, I beg you on scuffed knee to give a positive review for me. I assure you that is the best way to see more of my work in the future.

Thanks again for reading this far.

*Alexander Francis*